MURDER PROPERLY DONE

BOOK Twelve

of the

SECRET BUTTERFLY SERIES™

A NOVEL BY

Rosemary Lightfoot Ness-Bitner

A BRIEF PREFACE TO THE INSANITY VOLUME OF THE SECRET BUTTERFLY SERIES™

Insanity. It's a big word, a sort of shocking word. It's a word that describes something that no one really understands. It's a condition of the human mind. Excepting causation caused by physical injury, we can't really know what causes it. Does it come about instantly; like by receiving an unexpected shock? Does it come about slowly; like through prolonged exposure to an intolerable situation for a human's brain processes to cope with or rationalize away? I'm not an expert in psychiatry or psychology. I've never taken course in those subjects. So, I assure you, I am only expressing my thoughts through personal observations, experiences, and my limited readings.

I titled the middle three book volume of the SECRET BUT-TERFLY SERIES™ the 'INSANITY VOLUME.' I chose to call the books that because they revolve, primarily, around my character, David. I have lived with this character in my head for more years than I would care to admit. And maybe before? Yes, maybe I was living with the influences of David's character, or from characters like him in my childhood, until, I met a real live persona with his traits.

I chose insanity as the title for this three-volume section for at least three reasons. I think they help a reader recognize the traits of a personality who engages in behaviors beyond *control freak* behavior; getting into intentional destructive, even intentionally self-destructive behavior. Also, they help one see the effects such a personality has upon those who are in its orbit. Here, I'm trying to reveal different characters' coping mechanisms; trying to help readers see the futility of trying to cope with a David character; helping readers question why people do not simply leave a David character's orbit. Finally, I try to help readers recognize the steps of progressively deteriorating disorder in our David character's mind; how his behavior descends from that of a seemingly innocuous prankster to a malevolent murderous genius; who becomes consumed by his rage state; who is monstrous, hideous, depraved, all humanity hating; and who, ultimately, becomes a calculating agent of unimaginable death and destruction plots. Readers may find themselves wondering how can love survive a persona as large as David's? Can a love borne out of evil survive the evil that birthed it? Once that evil turns on that love?

The INSANITY VOLUME of THE SECRET BUTTERFLY SERIES is intended to be a reveal process, something like peeling layers from an onion. But I prefer to reflect upon my work more as a series of Venn diagrams. Stating with David's first reveal to Bob that he is a male Jew, I took that big circle of all male Jews and intersected it with a circle of all people who are insane, thus getting a slivered slice intersection of male Jews who are insane. This selection of population starting point in no way reflects antisemitic thought. But I chose it as my starting point because our David character's foundational outlook on life is defined by his *Us Against Them* religious biased mindset. He could as easily have been a Christian or Muslim zealot; but I chose to make him a Jew because of the Hebrew tribes' ancient sacrifice practices, which

I contrast with David's innovative method in MURDER PROP-ERLY DONE. And I needed murder theme consistency to give my characters' relationships a horrific commonality about which they could all orbit.

I then took that slivered slice of insane religious males and con-sidered it to be a new population circle, which I then intersected with another population of all those persons who are delusional, like our David, who believes he has frequent discussions with Don, or Adonai, his God; close friend and best buddy, barnyard playmate. Then, I needed to reduce that subset further to intersect with the set of the world's ridiculous, obnoxious pranksters, like our David character who devised his impish paper clip trick so he could fondle Barbara's breasts; thus, getting us to a new, even smaller population.

This smaller population I then intersected by a population which had macabre tendencies, like our David character who murders pigeons, deer, and people with equal detachment and who has an unhealthy fascination with the processes of death and decomposition. But this, now much smaller subset popula-tion, does not even begin to describe David's character. I needed to take the macabre, prankster, deranged, delusionally insane male religion obsessed subset and create one that peeled away a much deeper, frightening layer. I needed to intersect my now tiny subset with the subset of those who are malevolently evil toward society as a whole, or towards a society which is not theirs or not understood by them. These people would be willing to engage in mass murder or genocide. This grouping would include such infa-mous characters as Caligula, Nero, Genghis Kann, Hitler, Tojo, Mussolini, and US Brevet General George Armstrong Custer. I thought I was scratching the surface.

But I had a much further way to go to reach the final reveal which defined David. In LOVE AND MADNESS and

BUTTERFLY LOVE readers will discover that David is the product of the absence of love. With his bizarre involvement with Rublina, David seeks to recapture the lost love of his childhood; but that scheme reveals David's deepest need. Unfortunately, for David, it abruptly hits a dead end. And as much as David denies to himself that he needs love, he finally reveals love's absence effect to Bob.

But by then, Bob has lost patience with David. Bob, with Barbara's help, comes to understand that David uses the Firm as his vehicle to attack civilization and shred society. The Firm's two top executives have a fur fight which sets legal precedents. Barbara sees opportunity and chooses sides. The old rabbi's chair, which survived the Tzar's pogroms; the ghost of Marvin, a picture of a handsome red fox, the billions of dollars' worth of precious gems which bought some Jews' survival from the Shoah, a wily antelope, a vicious Lobo, drunken grave diggers, and superstitious elk hunters are all useful props to our saga.

The props usher readers to the climactic confrontation which David must have with his arch enemy, Susan. Pitifully, he attempts to disguise his need for love from Susan. As I developed the reveals for David's pathetic helplessness, I was reminded of his childhood character who tore wings from butterflies and houseflies; and who tore legs from helpless ants. Had he always empathized with those hapless insects? Did adult David finally reveal that he saw himself as one of those crippled creatures? Did his feeble attempts at male love reveal his crippled emotional state? Perhaps? But I did not wish to disparage the sexual preferences of anyone, regardless of how those preferences came about. Remember this is fictional David's character we are revealing.

Susan hears David's pitiful pleas for mercy. But Susan has lost all empathy for David and she will not be bribed. She never was a compassionate sort of woman; loving, ravenously sexy, avaricious, yes; but never compassionate. After her years with Marvin and her whoring she has become heartless, embittered, and cold. After all, she saw her own mother as a misguided, religious sock puppet nitwit; and her father as a useless has been. And she thought nothing of the harm her liaison with Marvin caused her daughter, Marty. Finally, she decides she must be David's baby sitter one last time. And she says goodnight to him.

As readers come to know David, surely, they will feel some measure of empathy for him. I ask you to keep this in mind as you read this volume: Is your empathy for David justified? I mean, as you come to know him; his childhood and the way his parents did and didn't raise him; the choices they made for him and the choices he made for himself, just ask yourself these questions: Whose fault is David? I mean, what makes a man think he talks with God? What makes a man enter rage states where he believes all who question his judgement should automatically be labeled enemies whom he must destroy? Did religion do that to him? Goodness! Can religion be that dangerous to society?

And what could possibly cause a man to believe the ultimate in human enlightenment is to achieve a complete absence of feeling and empathy for others? What could cause him to believe that enlightenment's nirvana is to become as pure and holy in character and focus minded as a food seeking insect? What causes a man to believe that a certain black sheep has a special, empathetic relationship with him, which includes bestial, conjugal relations? What drives a man to believe in his heart of hearts that he and his sheep are the only two normal personas in the world?

And what gave rise to David's fascination with morbidity? Why does he believe his ideal protégé is a fetus, swimming in a jar filled with formaldehyde? Does the fetus represent the triumph of death over life? Why does David leave dead animals to decay and be devoured by insect swarms, rather than burn or bury their corpses? How, David, readers wonder? How did you become the way you are?

When David has his unplanned rendezvous with his baby sitter, Susan, ask yourself these questions: Which character gets the best of the other? Which one finally became freed from misery? And will the insanity that brought those two to that bluff above the river, ever end?

I did not write this three-book volume to attack religion and booster communism. Both seem dangerous social drivers to me. Perhaps the US constitution is the best solution for social sanity because it lives and breathes and continually drives power away from concentration in one segment of government or one person.

Good luck to all who contemplate these questions. I have no answers, only questions.

Rosemary

This twelfth novel in Rosemary's
THE SECRET BUTTERFLY SERIES
is dedicated to Lovers and Loving.

Hello, dear listeners. This is Minna Morinette, your narrator. In LOVE AND LOVERS, David put Marty in chains. Why such shocking behavior? Is he a closet psychopath? Will his ingenious crime methods be discovered? What gears and wheels turn in the mind of this deviant sociopath? Maybe we'll learn how someone can commit heinous crimes while believing he's perfectly normal. David's comments about how the world works reveal his vicarious reality warp that has no beginning or end.

While Marty was visiting David, Barbara was revealing a few secrets to Bob. He now understands that someone set him up to be the fall guy for misappropriated funds and possibly much more; but whom? Diligent researcher Barbara also uncovered the truth about Marty's prostitution activities outside the office. She removed the scales from Bob's eyes. He now realizes his love when first sighting Barbara was true love all along. Barbara never doubted her conviction in her love. But Bob did. And Barbara now understands why. And she forgave him. The two lovers have reunited but they are in a very delicate position. Barbara suspects foul play on a murderous scale; but fearing for Bob's safety, she holds back key information.

We'll soon dive into a deep rabbit hole, dear readers, and listeners. We'll trip horror triggers that will make you gasp and scream 'STOP!' But, to understand how David's plunge from sociopathy into psychopathy takes our characters' lives along for the ride, we must flutter through this storm. It's a huge one. We cannot fly around it. We'll see depraved insanity at its basest level, as David's mind derails and all pretenses at normalcy are abandoned. Fear not! We can brave this storm together; I know we can. And it will be worth it. We'll learn a lot about psycho behavior. Our skies will beautifully brighten afterwards; I promise. We've encountered other storms as we've fluttered through our series. Those were warm ups. This will be our most challenging.

Be brave, precious butterflies. Stay close together. The swifts and barn swallows will not get you. We will soon pass through the eye of evil. Our trip into David's world will leave you questioning all things human. When the sun comes out again, David will try to run Bob's mind through his brain washer. Will Bob ever be capable of warmth and love again? Will Barbara's love finally quell Bob's passion lust for porn star Marty?

Let's not forget: Marty originally feared Barbara for a reason. Will Bob discover that secretive Barbara is the most seductive minx of all? Won't Bob be surprised to learn her ways; how irresistible she is? Will the smoldering embers that Bob always carried for her suddenly burst into raging flames? Will Bob finally have the life he wanted? Can he follow where his soul wants to go? Fear not, dear readers. I'm Minna Morinette. And I'm a very brave butterfly. I'll lead us through this horrible storm into sunshine and blue skies. Come flutter with me as I narrate: MURDER PROPERLY DONE, the twelfth book of THE SECRET BUTTERFLY SERIES.

SECRET BUTTERFLY SERIES ™ CHARACTERS INTRODUCED IN "MURDER PROPERLY DONE"
(MAJOR CHARACTERS ARE BOLDFACED)

Readers reference guide to where a character is introduced. (CHARACTER, DESCRIPTION OF CHARACTER, AND CHAPTER WHERE CHARACTER IS MENTIONED)

GUTA, PILA AND SCRAPS, BODY DISPOSAL EXPERTS, DAVID'S PIGS, MURDER PROPERLY DONE (MPD) CH3

TANG'S SPIRIT, THE MONARCH BUTTERFLY OF GOODNESS, MPD, CH2

DON, DAVID'S NICKNAME FOR HIS PERSONAL FRIEND, ADONAI, GOD OF THE HEBREWS, (MPD), CH3

DEATH, DARK SPIRIT SOUL, MARTY'S AFTERLIFE LOVER, MPD, CH2

MARTY'S APPARITION, FIRST OF SEVERAL APPEARANCES, MPD, CH4

CHAPTER ONE

Murder is born of love, and love attains the greatest intensity in murder (Octave Mirbeau: Garden of Tortures)
Murder, like talent, seems occasionally to run in families (George Henry Lewes: The physiology of Common Life)

GLORIOUS BUTTERFLY

David held an ether-soaked handkerchief over Marty's nose and mouth. She struggled briefly while he held her arms. She was jostled out of her memories of past orgies and her dreams of dominating the Firm into the shocking reality of her present dilemma. Her mind raced wildly with thoughts of a woman crazed:

'What's David doing? Where's my bunny?'

She struggled and gasped for breath. The air she breathed into her lungs was intoxicatingly cool. She suddenly became dizzy and fell into unconsciousness. David had timed his attack perfectly. After Marty exhaled, she breathed the ether in. In fifteen seconds, she succumbed.

When Marty finally awoke, she had a mild headache. She realized she was sitting naked on a hay bale. Her hands were bound behind her; her ankles were chained together. Her mouth was covered with duct tape. Her mind was groggy. Events leading up to her predicament seemed to be a blurred fog. She realized she could not trust her memory. She shook her head, thinking that might dispel her surreal happenstance:

'This must be some kind of joke. But I don't like it. David is way out of line!'

Marty squirmed and groaned to free herself. But her struggles were no use. She looked up. As she focused, she saw David. He stood three feet away with a smirk on his face, and out of her kick range. She shook her head up and down; then twisted her neck and moved it back and forth, resenting her predicament; and silently demanding with her body language that David free her at once. He stared intently at her, like a man transfixed and with a trace of amusement, seeing her struggle. His face wore a faraway, detached look, like he was focused on something that was a mile through her and held his interest. After a while, Marty stopped struggling. It was no use. She was only exhausting herself. And if this was another one of David's games, she thought it best to conserve her strength for whatever was coming next. She settled into glaring at him, her eyes demanding an explanation. But her outrage registered no effect on him. He just stared. Her motions; grunts; eye talk; breathing variations; all resulted in nothing. He just stared.

Then her instincts told her this was not some game. She felt a sudden fear-based chill. Droplets of perspiration trickled down between her shoulder blades. Beadlets of sweat prickled her forehead. Thoughts raced through her mind, telling her that her relationship with David had changed. His ambush was not a mere prank. Her situation was serious. She sensed how vulnerable she was. Here, in a barn, in an open field, a mile from any neighbor, on a dead-end road which had no traffic, she was chained, bound, and gagged, seated naked on a hay bale. And who was here with her? Yes, he was David. He was a man she did business with; nefarious business; murders. A man she had witnessed being cruel to animals and vicious and heartless in his dealings with others. But she always assumed she was different from those creatures he murdered and maimed. She believed she was exempt from those he screwed in business. Why was she exempt? She questioned herself for the first time. Well, she told herself, because she went along with all of it; went along with all the evil he did.

But now, suddenly, she wasn't so sure of herself. Her false confidence in her relationship exited the faux stage she had lived on for all these years. Suddenly she realized she might not be different from all the others. She might not be special at all. In fact, she might be viewed by David as a threat to him because she knew so much. She could place him with her when she murdered. She could reveal his prostitution and drug empire, and his connection to the drug cartel, and his money laundering. An inner panic took hold of her. Her thoughts cried out:

'Miss Iniquity, where are you? I'm sorry I didn't consult you last night. I'm sorry I only listened to Miss Promiscuity. I'm sorry I got impulsive and came here without thinking. Please tell me what to do now.'

Miss Iniquity was silent.

'Please. Say something!'

More silence.

'Miss Promiscuity, you got me into this mess. Tell me what to do.'

'You can't very well be promiscuous while you are all chained up like this, now, can you? Miss Promiscuity gave Marty's imagination a vacant look and shrugged her shoulders. *'Girl, I'm as confused as you are. I don't know what to do. Maybe this is David's idea of BDSM foreplay? Maybe David will soon tell us what this is all about? Then, we'll both know.'*

Marty stopped her struggles and stared at David. She was his helpless captive. He simply stood before her, expressionless. His eyes stared through her, like she didn't exist. Marty became impatient. Thinking this could be one of David's mental games, she broke her stare; her eyes glancing to the side. Her diamond and her pearl necklaces hung from nails on the side of the barn.

'You bastard,' she thought. 'Is this about taking back my pearls and reneging on my diamond choker? What kind of jerk does that?'

David read her mind. Finally, he spoke:

"Marty, I have the utmost respect for you. You are an extraordinary woman. Most women are silly creatures. They are selfish, vain, incredibly boring, pathetic beings who go through life focused on ridiculous trivialities and obsessed with petty jealousies. They are insufferable company for men of ambition and purpose. They do not even comprehend that their only purpose for living is to please men and breed. They concern themselves with who, among their circle of nitwit women, lunches with whom; who attends whose parties, and who says what to whom. They are maddening, boring, despicable, narrow-minded beings that men have been cursed to suffer.

"But you are different. You correctly identified your life's purpose. You understood that a woman's purpose is to please men. And you've made the most of it. You are like your mother. You both figured you could make considerable fortunes by shamelessly plying your best asset. You both mastered the techniques of feminine guile to get men to do your bidding. You, even more than your despicable mother, learned how to conquer men by using your fabulous cunt as your greatest asset. I salute your genius,"

David grinned as he raised his hand, holding an imaginary glass stem as a mock toast, as if honoring her immoral accomplishments. "I harnessed your genius for the good of the firm. You can appreciate that."

Marty's eyes narrowed. Fierce anger flared her thoughts at David:

'Don't patronize me, you asshole. How dare you pay me complements while you have me in chains? When I get out of this, I'll slap you silly.'

"But there's something you should know," continued David. "You have a tiny scar on your right little finger. You had a nub of flesh there when you were a child, don't you remember?"

Marty remained silent. She lifted her chin defiantly. David held a pocket knife blade point against her nostril, threatening to cut her if she refused to answer.

"*Well, didn't you have it removed?*"

She nodded with calculating sangfroid, suddenly afraid of David; but instinctively determined not to let David notice her fear. The longer David's game continued, the less it seemed like a game. Her mind struggled to find reason:

'*I don't know where this is going but I don't like it. This is not funny. What is he going to do?*'

Marty made a muffled protest. The fierceness in her eyes disappeared. She sensed that communication through her eyes was the only way she could possibly influence David. Bertie had trained her in the many ways to use her eyes. Now they pleaded for her freedom.

"*I noticed your nub. I saw it when you were a little girl,*" continued David.

Marty's eyes had not been persuasive. Her earlier struggles, her eye-based communications, had no effect on David. Apparently, nothing would deter him from his agenda.

"*You were at Dad's house in Rondel Hills, bouncing a soccer ball. Remember?*"

Marty shook her head nonchalantly. By pretending David's actions were inconsequential she hoped to throw David off his track. Hopefully, he'd stop his scary game and unchain her. But her stomach felt queasy. She didn't like where this game was going.

"*Well, that's okay Marty,*" David chuckled. He didn't fall for her deflection. "*I remember. That's all that matters. I knew someone else who had that same nub on his right hand's little finger. He had his nub surgically removed, too. Do you know who he was?*"

Again, Marty shook her head.

"*He was my father, Marty. MY FATHER!*" David screamed as if releasing a deep hurt. "*I saw his nub when I was a boy. One year he sent me to summer camp. When I came home, his nub was gone.*

"*You and I have the same father! You didn't know that, did you?*"

Marty shook her head violently. This revelation suddenly frightened her. Her fear spiraled out of her control. Her eyes widened. They betrayed her. David noted her fear.

"*You WERE NEVER Joseph Maloney's daughter. You're Marvin Sustack's daughter. You and I are half-brother and half-sister.*" David paused to let Marty absorb his shocking truth. Obviously, David nursed a deep hurt.

Marty lowered her head and leveled her gaze at David. Perhaps, she hoped, her mind could draw his into hers. Perhaps they could talk this out? Perhaps she could ease his pain? But her hopes of talking faded when evil glee appeared in David's eyes.

"*It's okay, Marty. I don't hold it against you that you're beautiful and I'm not. Our mothers were different. They determined what we looked like, not Dad. Dad was handsome. Your mother is beautiful. You're beautiful. My mother was ugly; so am I.*"

David stared at Marty before he continued. Her eyes flared; glared back:

'*So, that's what this is about; sibling rivalry. How was I supposed to know?*'

Both pairs of eyes were intense. Marty now understood the truth: there was no chance for a meeting of minds. Contempt and hatred flared between them.

"*But, you see, we have a serious problem. We're brother and sister so we're not supposed to fuck together, but, vicariously, we did. We broke a mitzvah. And you broke another mitzvah when you fucked Muscle Boy. You broke the one that forbids a betrothed to fuck someone other than their betrothed. You shouldn't even fuck your betrothed until after you're married by a rabbi. I see you're shaking your head to everything I'm saying.*

Is that because you're not a Jew? You don't think these rules apply to you, do you?"

Marty shook her head. She hoped he could read her thoughts:

'You jerk. Abraham and Sara broke that mitzvah before they even started the Hebrew religion; way before there even was a Torah. Don't you understand anything? Besides, at this point, what difference does it make? We didn't do it, David. You stupid man! You've never had your penis inside me! We did not fuck! Now, snap out of this!'

David ignored her head shake. He didn't want to hear what she was trying to say. Her thoughts were not needed. He wasn't in the mood for arguments or logic. His mind would not be dissuaded from its singular track.

"Ordinarily, that distinction would make a difference. Since your mother is a gentile, that makes you a gentile. Jewish law shouldn't apply to you. But you're not ordinary, Marty. Why aren't you ordinary, Marty?"

Marty shook her head curiously, slowly. Sadness settled over her thoughts. She realized that David was possessed by his unique belief system; one she didn't understand. There was no changing his mind.

'Why has my life come to this?' she wondered.

David supplied answers to her unspoken why:

"Because Dad treated your mother like she was his wife in the office. In MY COMPANY. That's why, Marty. Susan wasn't an ordinary Shiksa. She was Dad's office wife! By Susan being Dad's office wife, you became the daughter of a woman who sought to become a Jew. But Dad didn't marry Susan. She could not join the tribe through marriage.

"I don't expect you to understand everything I'm saying, but Dad desired to have Susan as his wife! But for Mother being in Dad's way, he would have married Susan. Do you think they would have had a Jewish wedding, Marty? I mean, if Dad had my mother out of the way, do you believe he would have married Susan in a Jewish wedding? Well, do you?"

Marty shrugged her shoulders. Her eyes pleaded with David to stop this. But David's years of hurts would not be silenced. He needed to unburden himself. He couldn't stop.

"Dad loved Susan and you more than he loved Mother and me. Dad pushed us aside to be with Susan and you whenever he could. You probably don't remember that, do you? All those times while I was sent to Yeshiva; all those times when I got sent to doctors and camps; and moved out of my home to live with rabbis, I do remember, Marty. I got SCREWED, Marty.

"Dad was with Susan all those times; fucking her. Dad loved your mother so much he tied me to that whoring bitch through his will until the day she dies. Can you see why I think of Susan as Dad's wife? Can you see how that makes you a Jewess from my perspective, even though no rabbi would ever agree with me?"

"Susan, Mother, and Dad, all hurt me, Marty. They ALL SCREWED ME!" David shouted. *"You and I need to correct that. That brings us to why we're here, and why you're chained up."*

Marty shook her head vigorously. She sensed madness had possession of David.

"According to our ancient tribal rules of five thousand years ago, when someone comes into contact with a corpse, we must perform a Red Heifer sacrifice. That's a heifer with not a single hair on it that is not red. Sometimes people used to cheat the temple priests a little. If a heifer happened to have some white hairs, they'd just pull out the white hairs, figuring the priests wouldn't notice. But our circumstance is a little different. In our circumstance, I figure, although you're not an actual corpse, you have a dead soul. That's kind of like the same as being dead, Marty. Maybe it's even worse than being dead. I'm not sure; but I think it is. You see, you're hopeless Marty.

You're committed to whoring. I'm sure about that. I just watched you fuck for diamonds. I observed you while you betrayed your future husband. Your behavior was highly unethical. That's how I know your soul died and became a corpse.

"I don't think any rabbi will agree with me about what we must do to cleanse your soul, Marty. So, I can't guarantee you that my idea will work for the two of us. But I think it will. I think I know more than a lot of rabbis know anyway; so even though I'm a little confused about this, I'm convinced we must do something.

"So, I'm going to hold off from giving you the diamond choker neckless, Marty. It was my mother's. I saw her wear it one night while Dad had sex with her. Maybe the neckless helped Dad think Mother was beautiful. I don't know. Maybe she wore it so she could pretend she was beautiful for Dad. She probably wore it to take Dad's mind off how disgusting she looked. You women have complicated personalities, Marty.

"Some days I wonder if I'm going crazy, Marty. Do you think I'm crazy?"

Marty shook her head no, hoping that would endear her to David. He nodded slightly while staring at her. Then he paced back and forth in front of her.

"Sometimes I think God made a mistake when he made me, Marty. Sometimes I think he intended for me to be an insect. But his instructions got mixed up somehow and I became a human instead. Do you know why I think that way?"

Marty shook her head. Obviously, David's mind was tortured. Her eyes tried to express sympathy.

"Well, you should know. We might become closer if you knew. When I think I'm an insect, not a human, I feel okay with myself. I feel okay being alone and unwanted and unloved. Then, Mother's and Dad's rejections don't hurt me. Then, I feel it's okay to have no feelings about other people. I feel it's good not to have emotional

feelings. Then, other peoples' emotions have no effect on me. I don't care if they feel love or hate, or anything at all. People are just inconveniently there, that's all. And I feel it's a good thing to get rid of people; to kill them because they are competition for me; for food, for life, for existence. So, I tend to think of all people as my enemies, like insects think most living things are their enemies. Can you understand that?"

Marty's eyes widened. She shook her head vigorously, trying to communicate to David that he was not thinking rationally.

"But I am stuck with being a human. I know that, Marty. So, I try to be true to my insect self while staying inside the mind and body of a human. Never mind shaking your head anymore. I just needed to tell you that. I don't understand why I feel I must do the things I do, but I try to do what's right by God and the way God made me, Okay?

"Maybe our purification ceremony will help me figure things out, Marty. I want you to appreciate that I'll be trying to do the right thing here. I'm not sure I'm thinking straight about this. I know I should go to my rabbi and ask him what's the right thing to do. But I can't tell him how I feel about myself. I can't just leave you here while I go find him. Do you understand that?"

Marty shook her head; then nodded it. She flipped her messaging from being sympathetic to his quandary to encouraging him to do the right thing. Her eyes urged David to go find a rabbi.

"No, I can't chance it, Marty. While I'm gone talking to my rabbi, you might not stay put. Besides, my rabbi would probably tell me to let you go and forget about what we did. I'm not sure I can trust my rabbi to make the right decision about this, Marty. So, I'll have to make things up as I go along. I'll try going from memory here.

"I heard about this when I was a little kid in religious school. So don't get upset with me if our ceremony seems weird. Just trust me that I'm trying to do my best. My memory could be off a bit. I slept a

lot in religious school. I didn't even want to be there. But Dad made me go, anyway."

Marty looked at David and rolled her eyes. She thought:

'He's lost his mind. David's sick. First, he gets his jollies learning about my innermost feelings; then, he watches me fuck Muscle Boy. Now he's saying everything I did for the company, which he PAID me to do, was immoral. He's telling me he's an insect want-to-be. What next? Will he spank me? I haven't felt this confused and abandoned since Mother sent me to boarding school. I wish Bob would come and put a stop to this craziness. Where could he be on a nice weekend like this? I wish I hadn't told him to stay away.

'MEN! They surprise you when you don't want to be surprised. But when you need them around, they're off doing something else. Damn it! This isn't fun anymore. I can't think straight. Just wait until David takes this tape off my mouth. I'm going to give that crazy bastard a piece of my mind. After all I've done for U G G A, how dare him treat me this way? He got loyalty from me—bottoms-up loyalty. I've fucked my ass off for U G G A. Where's David's loyalty to me? Nobody should treat their best employee this way. Why is he doing this? When can I get my necklaces? Where's my floppy-eared rabbit?

'Why won't someone shut the pigs up? They're so damn noisy. I wish David would feed them so they'd shut up. Where did he go? David, I can't see you. You can't just walk away and leave me sitting here like this. I can't think with those pigs grunting like crazy, and I can't speak.

'DAVID! Come back here. What are you doing? Where are you?'

.Narrator: Pronunciation guide: CHATAT sounds like: Ka Tat;
QORBANAT sounds like: Core Baa Nay.

CHAPTER TWO

I am convinced that there is such a thing as living again, that the living spring from the dead, and that the souls of the dead are in existence (Socrates)

I am very sure that my spirit will live on in a different place, as it has lived many times before (Tina Turner)

Live so that thou mayest desire to live again, that is thy duty, for in any case thou wilt live again (Freidrich Nietzsche)

CHATAT AND QORBANAT

Marty's situation was precarious. A day that began with promise, fun and games had suddenly turned weird and scary. The hot summer afternoon sun beat down hard and merciless. The daffodils and Iris were wilted, finished; but not the roses. The roses defied the heat and hung on to life. Prairie grasses withered and shriveled, saving the scarce moisture they held in their roots. Cattle lay quietly under shade trees, watching nothing in particular; waiting for the cooler late afternoon to chase away the heat. The air was still. The cloying humidity promised thunderstorms. No breeze or sound interrupted the stillness except the occasional cry of a magpie or the shrill 'Tuh-Weeee' of a male red-winged blackbird. One stood sentinel watch on his cattail at the edge of the barnyard's ponds.

Marty had arrived casually dressed in tightly fitting blue shorts, sans underwear, accentuating her barely disguised anatomy. She'd given David her obligatory hug for his magnanimous generosity. She had accepted his pearl necklace as his offer of good faith. She was refreshed from a good night's sleep, telling herself she was about to have one of her best days ever. She believed she would achieve one of her long-sought goals this day. She had convinced herself she would finally seduce David. Her self confidence would draw him out of his shyness.

She felt confident that David had good intentions. Just the two of them, alone in the barn. Yes! Her assumption was perfectly logical. This was her perfect time to be forward and shameless. Naturally, innocently, she would express her gratitude for her reinstatement and gifts; and then she would defeat David's reluctance to make love. He'd see how wonderfully loving she was. He'd fall in love with her! Of course, he would! This day she would be the most irresistible whore ever. He would surely succumb to her charms.

He had told her she was being reinstated with a raise in pay, a diamond necklace, and a floppy-eared rabbit. Best of all, she felt David would not object to her reuniting with Bob. On the drive over to David's, she thanked her lucky stars. She wondered what other company would set her up like this: with an office, a title, and a staff. Who else would give her a front for her growing erotic film empire, pay her a handsome salary, assist her with her murders, and indulge her orgy fests? Where else could she ensconce herself in a corporate culture that paid her fabulously well to fuck her brains out?

What other company would build its business model on the ravishing sexual appetite of a nymphomaniac? David didn't conceal her whoring in some corporate closet. He did the opposite. He subjugated the other employees to her. They kowtowed and catered to her every demand and whim. They made her appoint-ments; took her messages, ran her Premium Service at no cost to her; picked up her laundry; cleaned her home, maintained her property, its lawn, and her car; and buried all her costs in corpo-rate expenses, hidden from auditors and the prying eyes of tax authorities.

David's companies paid all her health and medical expenses as well. She never worried about forgetting the pill. If she needed to have her womb vacuumed and cleaned, David covered those costs, too. If a Premium Member got out of line and her service couldn't handle him, she merely told David and waited a week or two. The man would disappear. David had his ways and his means. Troublemakers were murdered cleanly. Their bodies were dis-posed of in some mysterious, discreetly well-planned way. Marty never troubled herself about the gristly details of these murders. She took comfort enough knowing that her sources of irritation could never be traced back to her. David was wonderful to her. He was detail thorough, vigilant, and always protective.

Thinking of her wonderful arrangement made her moist. Could she thank him enough? Would he even let her? She hoped so. Her instincts told her that this day he would. On her drive over to David's she imagined making love with him. This would be the day, the *that* day; the day when, finally, David would allow her to flood deeply into his life. Intimacy, glorious, wonderful, forget the world and everything and everyone else except *it*; lovely, precious, immorally sacred and secret; marvelously, scrumptiously naughty; forbidden, all the more wonderful to treasure *it*, intimacy; beauti-ful, place it upon an altar and worship 'IT,' *intimacy*.

In her drive over to David's, her mind had already imagined the twenty ways she would fuck him this, her wonderful, memo-rable *that* day. Her confidence soared. Already, before she reached his driveway, she imagined feeling his cock inside her. Fabulous!

She imagined it was ejaculating his semen into her when she turned off the car's motor. She opened the door and got out of her car. *Hello David, I'm here!*" Her shout announced that she was more than ready.

She had ignored David's policy reversal about office romance. She overlooked his temper tantrum when he first learned of her engagement. She blocked those negative signals and the cautions of Miss Iniquity from her thoughts. She convinced herself she was doubly blessed. Lucky in business; lucky in love!

But matters took an unexpected turn. Now, she listened carefully when David instructed her to be still. He said he wanted her to fully comprehend the events which were about to transpire. Before today she had no idea that she and David shared the same bloodline. Only now could she imagine her half-brother's innermost thoughts; that their common blood made her a potential rival for deceased Marvin's assets, should she ever discover her parentage. She now realized she could contest Marvin's will and David's inheritance. But it was too late for that! She finally appreciated David's position. Horrors! He had to get rid of her!

Suddenly, for the first time, she saw the world through David's eyes. She was twenty-six years old. Her allure would soon fade. She'd carried the firm's sales on her back, literally, for the past few years. But her results had plateaued. There were limitations on her seduction time. She was maxed out. She also planned to marry David's most highly prized salesman.

David saw the marriage as a threat to sales. Marriage to Bob could result in the two of them striking off on their own; and, with her voracious libido, there was no telling what turmoil David's sales leader might encounter. Sales could suffer. Surely, David's paranoid mind traveled these same paths. What others? She could not fathom; but she intuited that they were likely legion.

Marty shuddered. *Am I just a pawn in some game?*' Fear's chills raced through her blood. Her instincts told her David was in a dark place. She'd seen his distant stare before. He sometimes lapsed into some other world but then he always returned to normal. David had bizarre behaviors, but she'd never seen him act this strangely.

'How long must I wait until David comes back to his senses?'

David had known all along that he was taking risks with Marty. Her whoring could bring the authorities and regulators down on the firm; she might witlessly divulge their murders; she might discover her true parentage and challenge his inheritance. He had quietly accepted these risks without complaining or intervening. He'd conferred with Dolly, his imaginary secret confidant. He was certain his black sheep advised him to tightly control the company and events. But Marty presented an ever-present obstacle to his control. She had carte blanche authority at the Firm. She came and went as she pleased, traveled, and dined whenever and wherever she pleased; cavorted, and seduced whichever salesmen she wished. And all her expenses were born by the Firm.

How could he control Marty? Surely, Dolly knew how. He'd spent hours discussing his dilemma with the black sheep. He convinced himself the sheep advised him to commit a heinous act to control Marty; but only after he found the authority to justify it. For that authority, David delved deeply into his historic roots. He searched his ancient Torah scrolls. There, he discovered a long forgotten, obsolete, no longer practiced mitzvah. He spoke with Dolly about it. She assured him the mitzvah applied to his present situation. Marty's soul was dead. Psychologically speaking, he had defiled her dead soul by pretending to make love with her, before he substituted Muscle to take his place. Now, armed with his ancient mitzvah, David believed he discovered the perfect solution. But he thought Dolly also had cautioned him that he needed to perform the ritual properly. He believed he needed to make a kosher sacrifice to God.

David returned to the barn and stood before Marty. This time he held a large hunting knife. His eyes stared their weird stare as if they looked right through Marty, without seeing her. But David did see something; something that existed long ago and far away.

He imagined he was in a distant place, reliving events of five thousand years ago. His mind was not in today's world; and he was disconnected from his barn. Wherever that faraway place was, he couldn't know. Evidence of sacrifices performed five millenniums ago had long disappeared. But what they did then was real to David's here and now. He desperately wanted to participate in what would have happened then. He intended to recreate it in the here and now. He approached close to Marty and stared intently at her with demonic eyes. His gaze was no longer far away. Now, it was a present, malicious stare. He imagined Marty had joined him, in his faraway fantasy from long ago.

David's mind often traveled to that faraway place of simpler, clearly defined, right and wrong times. His mind was there now, living its simple agricultural life with his ancestral tribe. He abstracted away from reality this way, when he felt conflicted or shunned. His mind joined his body to his *them tribe* in times like these. He lived among *them* again. Every one of *them* understood and accepted him. They all agreed with him. They knew what he needed to do. Their acceptance gave him strength.

He found freedom in his imaginary world. Here was refuge from Marvin's pressures; failing to meet Father's standards. He liked it here. He could daydream and fantasize. No one here cared if he was dishonest or if he harbored tribal hatreds. They harbored them, too. He could think evil thoughts here. No one cared about the things he imagined. They had similar imaginings. Here, David could be paranoid like them. He could imagine the entire world was his enemy. They did, too. He was like them; one with them.

As David grew older, his mind retreated more often to his imaginary world; and it stayed there longer. He discovered exhilaration in his illusions. Here, *he* was in command. Here, *he* ruled over everything and everyone. Here, in his twisted mental reality, *he* was master and king of his imaginary world. Everyone obeyed his every wish and whim. He was the high priest of his fantasy kingdom. He did whatever he pleased. No one objected to his decisions, nor dared to interfere with his actions. There were no regulators; no parental checks; no social or peer pressures; and no inner voices of reason or decency to interrupt him or cause him to vacillate. There was only *David, master* of everything and every-one; and, of course, Dolly, his trusted sheep in whom he confided. She approved of everything he decided; everything he did.

David believed Dolly was one with him; her mind being somehow connected to his. In David's delusional mind, Dolly's mere presence was his green light signal to act upon his fanta-sies and commit all manner of insane deeds. She was here with him now, loyally standing by; watching. Obviously, she approved! Her presence emboldened him. He was free to correct things and make them right by Adonai, his god.

Dolly permitted David to torture others. He believed she loved his illusory reality. In his convoluted upside-down world, David believed heinous deeds were sometimes necessary to make things magically good and holy. With Dolly as his trusted advisor and reliable prophet, David became convinced that there were special favors that only he could offer to God. And, David believed that, sometimes, outrageously heinous deeds were more acceptable than good deeds, because God was not a good boy himself; at least not always.

God had a dark side that very few people understood. But David believed that he understood it. He and God were soul mates; buddies, boys who played together and related to each other on a first name basis. David even called God by his nickname, Don, which was his shorthand name for Adonai, God's biblical creation name. David was convinced that Don loved destruction more than he loved creation. Don caused disasters of flood and fire. And David also loved watching people die in floods and fires. So, naturally, David believed that, surely, Don thought about people in the same ways that he did. David believed Don, like himself, licked his chops when he witnessed murders and mayhem; otherwise, why else would Don allow those things?

Goodness and kindness were traits which David disdained. Good people disgusted him. He reasoned anybody could please God by being good; but only a select few, like himself, could earn Don's praises by being a chosen evil one. Dastardly deeds, like pulling wings off butterflies and legs off ants, honored Don; or so thought David. They showed his buddy, Don, that he, too, could cause pain and suffering.

David's imaginary world was securely anchored to madness. When his eyes stared far away into his fantasy place, he could will his mind to follow. Once there, his thoughts bathed in his dark world of convoluted psychological comforts. This private psychotic escape was David's solace. Reality could not intrude.

He now looked at Marty as if he were seeing her for the first time. She sat before him, bound, and gagged, completely at his mercy. He had done all the talking. She grunted and made squeamish struggling noises. But those sounds didn't count. They didn't tell him anything. That's how he wanted things. He didn't care what she had to say. He ignored her. This was going to be *his* special ritual to be performed *his* way in *his* private nut hatch world. Marty would be their special penitence offering to Don. He and Marty would perform this ritual in the company of David's imaginary tribal friends. He believed their sacrifice would honor Don.

Her role in God's mitzvah was to compliantly accept God's will. David was excited. He could include Marty in his fantasy! He and Marty would perform the first ritual ever of its kind; never previously performed in human history. David had convinced himself that he was the only man on Earth who could impress Don in this special way. He would show Don that he, alone, would perform history's most magnificent sacrificial offering.

'You know she might not agree to this. If she's unwilling, it might not be pleasing to Don.'

David heard that. Had Don spoke to him? It was his sane mind struggling to be heard. But David was too far into insanity to pay heed. Stopping the ritual now, after all his preparations, was out of the question. He explained to Don:

'She'll understand the significance of playing her part in something historic and wonderful. She only needs a little time. I know she's acting strangely, but I can't let that stop me. It's not up to her to decide what we need to do. I'm in charge here; not her.'

David's insane mind resented the intrusion by his rational thought. It noticed Marty struggling violently, resisting her bondage as if she feared his madness. But David knew, in his insanity-based world, that he was not mad. He was obeying his calling to honor Don, by sacrificing to Don. The entirety of the situation was normal; perfect. He oversaw an imaginary world that was ordered the way he knew it needed to be ordered. He was being Don's close friend; honoring Don by showing Don that he obeyed him. David struggled with his understanding about his own role in the ceremony. But, because he held novice status, he believed his buddy Don would forgive minor errors, if he made them. Faith fortified his confidence:

'Since me and Don are buddies, I can do no wrong. Whatever I decide about Marty must be right.' David rubbed his hands together, relishing his duty.

Today he would pay an extra special tribute to his buddy, Don. He would not be a willful, sadistic murderer with a penchant for terror. On other days, David could be a ruthless, cold-blooded killer. But not today. This day would be different. Today he would purify himself of all his misdeeds.

Marty was David's ideal choice for his historic ritual. He had captured her, like he captured helpless butterflies when he was a child. But Marty was not pure like those butterflies. She was a naughty girl. She enjoyed adultery and gave no indication of ever changing her ways. She'd told him that she intended to continue with her adulteries while married to Bob. Clearly, she was an impure being; unfit to be sacrificed. He struggled with that fact. Somehow, he needed to remove her moral blemish; make her pure for sacrifice. But, how?

If only he could find some way to make Marty pure, surely his good friend Don would take his effort into consideration and bless his offering. David thought it best not to tell a rabbi about his plan. They always got skittish about controversial decisions. Besides, he was tired of people telling him what he could or could not do. He decided that Marty needed to suffer to become pure. That was unfortunate, but he accepted it as unavoidable fact. He needed to do what needed to be done.

It helped that David never developed feelings for others' sufferings, be they insect or human. All life was the same to him. Humans were no different than ants. He reminded himself that he was a living, junior version, of Don. Therefore, whatever he decided for any life form had to be justifiable. Besides, Don would likely approve of his ritual since he would be performing it to honor Don. David decided that one minor detail should not prevent a cleansing offering from going forward:

'Dolly agrees! Don will approve. It's a brilliant plan. I must proceed.'

"Marty," David spoke in a low confidential tone. His mind stayed in its imaginary, faraway place while his eyes stared through her. *"When someone defiles God, they must atone. I know we don't*

like to atone, but we should." He looked away; then stared up at the blue sky above the open barn door, as if asking a higher power if there was any other way than this way. He returned his gaze to meet Marty's eyes.

"*We must do this. There's no other way. God tells us it's the right thing to do. The serious way to atone is through sacrifice. You can't just pay money, like defiling God is like running a red light. It's not as simple as a traffic ticket. You can fix a traffic ticket. And it's not like paying taxes, because we cheat on paying taxes. No Marty, defiling God is serious. And the only way to pay is through sacrifice. My religion stopped doing sacrifice practices thousands of years ago when the Romans destroyed our temple in Jerusalem. Those filthy bastards murdered over nine hundred million Jews. Dirty fucks! That was a lot of us. Filthy pricks! Maybe the destruction was three thousand years ago. I can't remember. I slept a lot in religious school.*

"*It doesn't matter that I can't remember anything. All that matters is that I know what I'm doing. I told you I didn't pay close attention in religious school. They couldn't flunk me. I kind of remember that the sacrifices which we did in the good old days are forbidden now; but that doesn't make the practice any less valid, especially since I'm serious about atoning. I'm sure I'm right because God is on my side. The rabbis are wrong. They are wrong about lots of things, Marty. They tried telling me to love Mother and Father. Can you believe that? My parents pushed me away! Who loves people that push you away? The rabbis were asking too much. They were ridiculous!*

"*But I'm always right, Marty. I like to sacrifice. That way I stay good with God. I even made my own altar in my basement. I worship God there, in my own way, whenever I want. I don't need to be around other people. I can even worship naked if I feel like it, like Joe Biden swims naked and shows his dick to the female secret service agents. My altar is first class, too. I hid it behind a bookcase.*

A secret button opens the access wall. It's modern. It's even got gas-fired burners and a vent hood. I even grill hot dogs on it when I'm not using it to sacrifice. Don't tell any rabbis that I do that.

"I'm a traditional guy, Marty. I can't feel purified unless I sacrifice. There's no sacrifice on Shul altars anymore. The rabbis stopped that thousands of years ago. I can't remember exactly when. Don't expect me to remember everything. I already told you that I slept through religious school. But just because everyone else stopped sacrificing that didn't stop me from sacrificing. That's why I built my altar. I'm a lot like Abraham, I like getting close to God, too; so, I built my own personal altar. It's like the one described in the Torah; only mine is much better. It's the best altar ever made. It uses natural gas. I think Don, that's God's nickname, likes me a lot because I've got a high-class altar.

"I built my house and altar facing east, toward Jerusalem, where the ancient priests sacrificed before our temple was destroyed by Romans, those dirty, filthy cocksuckers! They'll get what's coming to them in the end. You'll see. I'm not certain the Romans fucked up everything. It might have been those fucking bastard Nazis or Stalin. Doesn't matter. They couldn't get rid of us, or Don. Asshole pricks. We beat them. We took some hits at the Alamo and Pearl Harbor, but we still beat them.

"Today, we'll offer our sacrifice together, like a loving brother and loving sister should. It will purify both of us. It's called Chatat, or sin offering. You get absolved of sins by participating. Don is going to love us for doing this."

Marty was dumbfounded. She only half heard what he said. Her thoughts blocked David's gibberish voice:

'Is David mad? I thought he said he was going to absolve me of my sins, but how, and why? He pays me to sin. The more I sin, the more money I make. How can he absolve anything? He's not a rabbi or a priest. Why am I bound up this way?'

Then she focused her mind, listening intently to her half-brother:

"Marty, this offering is a little weird. It atones for contact with a dead person. I'm not clear about it. Maybe it absolves people who commit necrophilia, or maybe all you need to do is touch a dead person. I'm no expert on five-thousand-year-old rituals. But as I explained, your soul is already dead. You are morally lifeless. That's worse than being dead. But, don't worry Marty. You're in good hands. I'm like the government. I'm here to help you. Ha, ha.

"Don't get me wrong, Marty. You're wonderful. I love that you have no morals. That's excellent, Marty; perfect. Your conduct is totally aligned with our corporate culture. I've always admired your immorality. I'm very proud of your murders and your seductions. You did a masterful job when you murdered Bertie and George. I was pleased beyond words with you that day. Your whoring's and murders were key to growing the Firm. You've done a superlative job.

"But Don didn't like it. And he didn't like me for encouraging your whoring, either. I knew you loved whoring before you joined the Firm. I didn't think it was wrong to encourage you to do more of what you loved doing anyway. I also thought our murders helped our mental health. And, we got rid of many annoying people.

"So, I gave our situation a lot of thought. We have a special case of sin here. We've sinned so much that we need to do a red heifer offering. That's a really, big deal, Marty. It's huge! We're going to atone like our ancestors did.

"It must be a red heifer offering because I staged so many of your past events. I was wrong to do that. But I did not create a new wrong by helping you. You see, I already knew you had lost your soul. I watched you lose it years ago. You were a whore before you even started working with the Firm. So, I paid for a lot of your whoring because I wanted to make sure you didn't have any stresses on you.

I wanted you to concentrate on your seductions and orgies because I knew you loved whoring so much. So, I sort of entrapped you. And I must atone for that.

"We'll make a Qorbanot offering. It's extra rare and extra special. It's how we tell Don we're very sorry we messed around with dead people. I knew you were morally dead when I messed with you, by proxy, with Muscle Man. So, we're commanded to do this. Don will be thrilled to see this! We'll be the first to perform this ritual in at least two thousand years, maybe even five thousand years! I hope you're as proud to do this as I am.

"It won't be perfect like the ones performed by priests thousands of years ago. My altar doesn't even have a blood gutter gouged into it. But I've got hay bales. They'll have to do. They might even be better. I don't think they baled hay five thousand years ago. If they did, they might have used them. I don't think Don will be upset with us for using hay bales. I hope not. I don't want to make him angry. I don't have offering incense either. We'll have to pretend that everything smells fine. I don't have a razor-sharp obsidian knife, either. I'll use my trusty hunting knife. It's all I've got. It's a little jagged but it's pretty sharp. It should work okay. We'll see."

Marty's eyes bulged outward. She shook her head and made noises as if she was saying no. David ignored her and continued:

"Unfortunately, this brings us to the hard part. I don't have an actual red heifer to use for our offering, and our faith stopped using priests thousands of years ago. So, I'll have to substitute you for our heifer and substitute myself for our priest. We'll improvise, Marty. Substitutions weren't permitted in ancient times; so, forgive me, this won't be exact. But, trust me, I'll do my best. Stop shaking your head and squirming, Marty. I'm your big brother. You need to listen to me. I know what's best for us."

Marty's head shakes became more violent. David shook his finger, admonishing her for her struggles:

"I told you to relax. Now pay attention, Marty. You need to understand how important it is to do this properly. Your hair isn't red. It's dark brown, with that little streak of red which seems to come out of a cowlick. The mitzvah says a proper red heifer sacrifice uses a heifer that has only red hair. I'm not going to remove all your dark hair and just leave that little patch of red. I figured out a more sensible way. Since you are not a real heifer in the first place and since you only have a little patch of red hair, we're going to reinterpret that mitzvah by reading it from left to right, like the way gentiles read books, instead of our way of reading from right to left. Pretty clever, huh? It'll be okay, Marty. It should work."

Marty twisted and contorted her body in a vain effort to escape. Her efforts were futile. David shook his head, expressing his disappointment in her. He then continued explaining his plans for the sacrifice:

"Since you're not a hoofed animal and I'm not a priest from thousands of years ago, Don might not grade our effort an A Plus; but if I concentrate, I'm sure I'll get it done. Don will see that we've made a good effort. Maybe he'll at least give us a B. We'll apply the Torah instructions backwards to make our service fit what we need to do. I'm going to first remove your red cowlick plug. At least, that will make your hair uniform; perfect without any irregular hair blemish. You'll be our dark-haired human version of a red heifer. And you'll be without blemish. You won't have that red hair streak because you're not actually a heifer in the first place.

"The more I read the Torah about this, the more I realized that the key to the sacrifice was to remove all signs of blemish; so, I don't think it matters too much that you have dark brown hair instead of red hair. I know all this hair stuff must sound confusing to you, Marty. But don't worry about it. Just trust me, I'll get it done. Don will be pleased with us. This will be the first time Don has seen a

sacrifice like this in maybe five thousand years; maybe longer. He'll probably be thrilled out of his mind!"

Marty screamed at the top of her lungs. Unfortunately, the duct tape covering her mouth prevented her words from escaping. David smiled his wan smile at her. His eyes became a shade darker now; impersonal, like a shark's eyes that were focused on its prey. With his self-assurance that he would please God, David pulled on the rope that ran through the pulley block which he had attached to the rafter of the barn. Soon, Marty hung upside down above the hay bales. She was horrified. She squirmed and struggled and screamed her muffled shouts in feverish earnest; but her efforts were useless. Only David saw her; only David heard her. David grabbed her hair, stopping her gyrations. She was helpless to resist him. What would an unthinkable atrocity to normal people, demented David believed was his solemn duty. He was committed to carrying it out:

"Marty, maybe you'd like to say something about our sacrifice? I guess that's okay since you're a big part of it." David peeled the tape away from her mouth.

Persuasion was Marty's last and only hope:

"David, please listen to me. You're not in your right mind. You don't need to do this. We don't need to do this."

Despite her urge to scream for help she suppressed it, knowing that screaming wouldn't do her any good. They were too far away from the next home or from anyone who might hear her screams. No one could come in time to save her, anyway. Marty tried reasoning. It seemed to be her best chance.

David looked at her funny. She had insulted him. No one had ever told him he wasn't in his right mind before. He stared at her and considered what she said:

"No, Marty, I'm in my right mind. I'm sure of it. Don talked about it in the Torah. He explained how to do it."

"But, I'm not a heifer, David. I'm your sister! And I love you, like a sister loves a brother. I'll even love you as a lover. I'll commit incest if you like; you know, like Abraham and Sara committed incest." She raised her voice, hoping that would help.

"That doesn't matter. To atone is what matters. The whole idea of atoning is to become pure; and that means we must sacrifice. Don't try to confuse me, Marty. I'm doing the best I can."

"David, please. Take a moment. Just think about what you're doing."

"Don't insult me. I have thought about it. Stop trying to confuse me! I know we're doing the right thing. I don't want to hear any more. I'm taping your mouth shut again. You need to contemplate your sins and appreciate our sacrifice." David taped Marty's mouth again.

He held her hair to keep her from spinning on her chains. He used his dull knife and carved out a circle of skin scalp, removing her streak of red hair. He examined the scalp plug carefully, as a surgeon might assess a surgical incision. He closely inspected her head. When he was satisfied that he'd removed all her red hair, David tossed the small plug of red hair on the floor behind the hay bale. Then, he sneered at Marty.

"Now, don't you feel better, knowing that we have begun our ritual? And knowing that you are purified to be sacrificed?"

Marty held her head up. Her eyes pleaded through her terror for David to stop. Her blood trickled from her hairline and streamed over her face and cheek.

David nodded to her eyes. He empathized with her feeling of terror. But he enjoyed it too. He felt he had a religious duty to tell her that their sacrifice was proceeding as commanded by his understanding of his Torah.

"Now you are without blemish, Marty. You are perfect in the eyes of God. It's safe for us to proceed."

Marty directed a furious stare at him. But David was non-plussed. He watched her blood dripping onto the hay bale beneath her, satisfied that there was enough hay to soak up her blood. He smiled an understanding smile to her. He knew by the angry flames in her eyes that she understood she was being murdered. David studied her breast. Her heart was racing. He noted that as a good sign. Her rapid heart beat would help her bleed out quickly. She was getting into the spirit of their sacrifice. He felt smug. He had her completely trapped. Like a sacrificial animal, she could not escape the horror he had planned. He knew he should have sympathy for her, as a sacrificial animal surrendering its life; but he couldn't bring himself to have that feeling. Instead, his psychopathy unleashed his most heartless macabre nature. He was torturing her like he'd tortured countless insects as a child. He enjoyed watching her terrified eyes while he continued explaining his extraordinary ritual:

"Marty, by participating in our ritual, your body will be freed from sin. Don will accept our sacrifice. When he comes and rolls up the earth, he'll release our spirits to join him for rebirth on Jerusalem's Temple Mount. Your purified spirit will reenter another body, somewhere in the universe. I should be saying a prayer about now, but I don't know what words to say, because I hardly ever go to temple. Rather than making up some prayer that might be unacceptable to Don, let's just get on with it."

Marty shook her head. Her eyes begged for mercy. David chuckled at her torment.

"I can't guarantee the outcome, Marty. Your spirit might never know eternal peace. It might go deep into the earth and reside with those spirits who seek sin and debauchery. That's for those people who embrace evil ways. Your vagina—or your cunt, as I prefer to call it—might never again know the pleasures of penises and tongues. But it will live forever in the debauched minds that follow your path.

"Whenever a Monarch butterfly opens and closes its wings while it flies or draws sustenance from a flower, people who see it will know that your spirit lives within that butterfly. Their minds will enter your immoral world. They'll imagine their tongues and penises are inside you. They'll embrace your beauty and your free spirit. I can't know where your spirit will go. But I must proceed as my voices instruct me. Your voices dictated your behaviors. My voices are also telling me what I must do.

"Oh, Marty, I almost forgot to tell you something. A murder properly done must include carefully planned provisions for the deceased's estate. I want you to know that I've taken care of that. My attorneys investigated the wills that George and Bertie filed with Probate Court. They told you the truth. The must have really loved you. They bequeathed to you their extensive real estate holdings, including all their residences and ranches; and, Marty, they left you their two hundred-million-dollar stock portfolios as well.

"Apparently, they loved you as if you were their own daughter. Too bad you won't live to enjoy your inheritance. But, here's the good news! As your blood half- brother and your only living relative, besides your mother, I will patiently wait until Susan passes, which will be soon. When it's time, I'll arrange for her to have an accident.

"At the appropriate time, as your only surviving lawful heir, I'll claim your inheritance from George and Bertie's court appointed trustee. Isn't that wonderful, Marty? All that wealth is just waiting for me to declare my rights to it! I thought you would enjoy knowing that your inherited wealth will become your loving brother's. Consider their murders your personal gift to me. Heh, heh, hah, hah! You should know by now, Marty, that my murders are always enjoyable and profitable!" David's sinister laugh resonated through the barn and reechoed off its walls.

David noticed Marty's visceral shock. She suddenly realized David had a monetary motive for her murder as well as his desire to silence her from ever talking about their murders. She was furious over her loss of inheritance. She struggled violently to free herself. Her shock impulse pleased him.

David reminisced. He was once again witnessing a phase of victims' torture which he had observed as a child, while he pulled appendages from insects. Taking Marty's considerable wealth was causing her severe psychological pain:

'Perhaps an insect having its legs removed suffers a similar agony?'

He wondered about that for a moment. He smiled and chuckled, enjoyed his macabre thought while watching Marty writhe in her agonizing horror:

'Humans really aren't all that different from insects. How about that?'

After Marty spent her fury, David explained the procedural aspects of her murder.

"Our sacrifice is elegant, Marty. I'm going to slit your jugular first. It's supposed to be humane and painless. You should barely feel it. Don't worry; your blood won't make a mess. It will drain onto the hay bales. I will give you a little push after I cut your throat. You'll feel a swinging sensation; you'll become dizzy as you bleed out. Swinging will spread your blood around into the hay. The animals will eat your blood-soaked hay. Dizziness will also make your death more peaceful. I'm being a good, thoughtful person, Marty. I don't want you to feel pain. Can you appreciate the irony of swinging upside down while you are bleeding out? You've always been a swinger!"

David let out a loud guffaw. He bent down to look into Marty's terrified, upside-down eyes.

"Then," he continued, *"I'll eviscerate your corpse. I'll remove your gut pile. The gut pile is not part of the sacrifice. I'll feed that to the pigs. If you were a real red heifer of thousands of years ago,*

I would remove your tenderloins from next to your spine and place them on the altar fires for the priests. But since we don't have priests anymore and since you're not a real red heifer, I'll just throw your tenderloins onto the gut pile for the pigs. They will be the tastiest part of you. The pigs will enjoy a good meal. They will appreciate you. You might appreciate this humor, Marty. I extended the words Gut and Pile to make the names for the pigs: Guta and Pileo."

David laughed out loud in maddening, self-absorbed hysteria. Then he discerned Marty's barely audible plea through her taped mouth. She prayed for David to have cardiac arrest or be struck by lightning. He removed the tape from her mouth, oddly thinking that he would enjoy her torment more if he heard her voicing her horrors.

David shook his head and resumed his narration:

"You need to be a good sport about this, Marty. Listen while I tell you what will happen to your body. Guta and Pileo are my biggest pigs. I call the small runt: Scraps. He gets whatever Guta and Pileo leave him. After eviscerating your corpse, I'll render your flesh into oversized buckets; then I'll take those parts to the altar in the house. I'll put you to good use, Marty. I'll roast your flesh while I pray for our atonement to God. Your flesh, including your glorious vagina, will be chopped into small portions, and fed to my dogs and the pigs. I'll grind your bones into fine powder and small chips with my wood chipper. They'll become fertilizer for the roses.

"My roses will thrive on your bones, Marty. Just think how exciting that is! Bob once told me he loved a girl named Rosie. He said you resembled Rosie. Appreciate the irony, Marty! When Bob sees my roses reaching for the sun, he'll appreciate their beauty. Do you think he'll relate them to you, somehow?"

Marty's eyes glared: *'Bastard!'* she spit out the word. She was not amused. Now she shrieked in horror. *'Ohhh! What! Ahhh! Noooo! 'I feel you cutting around my stomach, David. What are you doing? No! No! No! You are taking my baby from me. Please don't do that, David.* Marty screamed furiously. '*No! Ahhh! Stop! Ahhh! Ahhh! Whaaa! Yeow! @%**' Screeching; screaming. 'I want my baby! I want to love it and nurture it and raise it. I want to be a good mother to it.*'

David ignored the message Marty was sending him through her eyes. '*I'm taking your baby from you, Marty. I need to have a protégé I can trust. And I will raise your baby in my own image to become a leader, just like me! You're just a whore anyway, Marty. You wouldn't be a good mother to your baby. So, I'll relieve you of that responsibility now. Feel that cutting? That's my knife. I've got your fetus surrounded now. I'm going to cut its umbilical cord now and tear it out of your womb. Don't worry about it, Marty. It will have a good home with me. I'm putting it into this formaldehyde filled jar, now. See?* And David ripped Marty's fetus from her womb and placed it into his huge formaldehyde jar.

Marty sobbed with muffled screams now. '*Oooh; Oooh, No David. No. Oh no. What have you done to me! What have you done to my baby?*' She knew all was lost.

"*Just so you know, Marty, after you die, I'll smash your teeth with a hammer. I'll scatter your tooth fragments in the guinea hens' pen. They'll put the fragments into their crops to grind grain and insects. The fragments will eventually wear away to nothing and pass through the hens.*

"*I'll keep our sacrifice a secret, Marty. I promise. I've processed many, many bodies. I'm good at eliminating evidence. I've even planned how I'll dispose of your car. It's not likely that anyone will think you came here to repent and join me in a sacrificial ritual, but just in case someone does, they won't find any proof. You can rest easy about your clothes and the hay. The goats will devour your clothing and your shoes. The sheep will eat the hay. Your necklaces will go back to my safe deposit box where they came from. They were gifts that our dad gave to my mother, so they belong to my side of our family. I'm sure you'll agree that is only proper.*

"Finally, Marty, I sincerely want to thank you for your exceptional service to the Firm. You helped build the company. You never complained about your duties. You did everything I asked of you, and more. No firm ever had a more dedicated, loyal employee. Your efforts are deeply appreciated.

"Don't obsess over dying. What we're doing doesn't matter. Our lives and our wealth will glorify God and Israel. That is all that matters. Everyone's' souls and assets go to the same place in the end. Nothing else matters, except Israel. What we are doing today is good and noble."

David laughed while he delivered his mock compliments. He affixed her chin lift to the chains around her feet. Then he pulled down on the rope that controlled the pully lift. Suddenly, Marty was hanging upside down over the hay bales. Then, in a blindingly swift slicing movement, David severed Marty's jugular artery.

Marty rapidly became delirious from her rapid blood loss. She succumbed to her hopeless situation and resigned herself to her fate. She no longer heard David's laughter. A new, ringing sound entered her ears. She heard her mind's voices. They guided her past behaviors. Could they help her now?

'Do not bemoan your fate, Marty,' said Miss Promiscuity: *'Your spirit will join with ours. You gave many young girls their confidence. A Monarch tattoo will be the badge of shameless pleasure seekers, like yourself. They'll seduce many men, steal countless husbands. Your free spirit will guide millions of souls. Your immoral teachings will inspire nations.'*

'Yes,' chimed Miss Iniquity: *'Your spirit will dance and romp with us spirit sisters, in the minds of many femmes. We'll instruct them in temptation's ways. We'll nibble their nipples with tickles of pleasure. We'll fill their titillated twats with adoring, consensual,*

pleasure-pleasing cocks, and loving tongues. Your protégées will experience nirvanas of endless orgasms.

'Our egos will bask in their seductions' glory. We'll revel in their unleashed social havoc. Your spirit will see behaviors you couldn't imagine. Lovers will betray betrotheds. Mates will murder mates for their freedom to dance with us. You'll see! Death only begins your merriment. Your body was but one we succored with our pleasures' nourishments. We instructed you. Your debauchery is ecumenical, and eternal. U, the great universal spirit, loves you; loves all promiscuous women. U welcomes all who wish to join us. U lives in our human DNA. We helped you express it. We are U's eternal spirits. Trust your spirit with us. Let your body die. Come away with us. We love you.'

Marty waved her hand. She tried to shoo away her imaginary friends. Her mind was spinning:

'I don't want your life of sin anymore, not even in death. I've lived it. I am wretched because of it. I am possessed by lusts that I cannot control. Go away. Tell U I want a different next life. I want a better me. I want life with Bob. I want to be married and have children. I want to know the joys of raising them in the ways of the Christians. I am so sorry for the sinful, ungodly lives that I have led in my past. I want the opposite of all that immorality in my future. I want to be Bob's wife. I want our souls joined as one. Do that for me. Leave my mind now. Be gone, all of you.'

David again removed the tape from her mouth. She struggled to force incoherent thoughts to her mouth. Her thoughts dimmed. Delirium came with her brain's blood loss.

"*Bob, know I love you with my whole heart. I hold you in my arms. I know love now.*"

Her thoughts short-circuited. She stared, vacantly, at David with dimming eyesight.

"*David, your face looks pale and far away. What's that bloody thing you are holding? It has a penis! I see it. Where did you get it? Oh, I feel so empty and my insides burn. Did you put an onion and garlic inside me, David? What burns me like this? Maybe I should start life over. Yes! I'll do that. I'll be better at math. I'll remember my multiplication tables. David, has your face become the moon? Are you full of green cheese? Are you hollow inside? Has something eaten away all the cheese inside you? What will happen when my roses die? Will the canes grow wild? Will ivy and weeds choke them? What will my squirrels eat when there are no rosebuds?*

"Why must I die, David? There's so much to do! Where's my floppy-eared rabbit, David? You promised me a bunny! I want to hug my bunny. How can I save fifteen percent on my car insurance? How can I do anything in this condition? Something smells! Where is that smell coming from? I'm very tired. Where is My Pillow, the one that gives me the best night's sleep in the world? I need it. I need sleep. I'm thirsty. Life and death. What's the difference? Maria, Trudy is away for a long weekend. Come stay in my room. Bring your dildos and vibrators. We'll sixty-nine and play vagina kiss-kiss. We'll doggie and scissors. Nothing else matters.

"David, don't get my blood on my blue shorts. I look so good and fuckable in those shorts, don't I? David, please put that bloody little white thing into a bag. Its penis is too small for me. I don't like looking at it. Put something over it. I don't want to see it. I want these men on this wheel. They are coming around to make love with me. Oh, what is happening now? The entire sky has flown into my tummy! There are thousands of things from the sky going into my tummy. They are eating me. I'm not a milkweed leaf. These things hurt me and tickle me. Like onions and garlic. Are they onions and garlic, David? What have you put in me that makes me feel so empty? Jesus, I need to pee. Why can't I pee? Something is not right, David. David! My ears are ringing. Stop that. I can't think. What have you done?

"My Daddy is a better man than you, David. I'm going to tell him about this. I feel very tired now. I want to go home. I want a warm bubble bath. Bob will sponge my back and rub my feet. He knows how to relax me. He'll hug me and make me feel better. How can I watch the Super Bowl while everything is upside down? Tell Bob to hold the television upside down. I want to watch the halftime show. I don't like blackboards and their chalk dust. They screech when my fingernails scratch them.

"Let's stop, Let's not play your games anymore. David. Let's go to the zoo and look at animals. I like animals. Where is my rabbit, David? Let's play my music. Why is that black sheep standing there? It is upside down. What is wrong with that animal? It's crazy. Is it stupid? Why is it standing upside down, David? Why is it staring at me? I think I'd like to try to read a book. Yeah, I'm going to do that."

Marty's weakened heart pumped her blood's final dribbles onto the hay bales. Her last delirium thoughts were of her and Bob. They took her back in time; returned her soul to lying in a pup tent with Bob, in Virginia's Shenandoah Park, looking at the stars again; talking of marriage. She prayed silently:

'Dear Jesus, God, somehow, let me meet Bob again. Please, U, give me a monogamous life. Forgive me, God, for all the marriages I destroyed; for all the children's lives I ruined. Forgive my murders, especially Bertie and George. Let me see them again. Let us all be best friends again. I'm sorry for everyone I've hurt; very sorry. Please forgive me and accept me into your kingdom, dear Jesus.'

Wavering shapes appeared in Marty's mind. She imagined running through a forest. Daylight was fading. She imagined lurching past huge trees, veering left; then right, avoiding them. She feared a presence that she couldn't see. Then it appeared, boldly; proudly, right in front of her. It stood beside a massive tree, blocking her way. She couldn't get around it. It demanded her attention. It was a gigantic penis! It dripped creamy white semen. Obviously, it wanted her. It demanded to be inserted into her vagina. It yearned for her. It strained and gleamed in the moonlight. It refused to leave her or stand aside; or wilt or wither. It stayed hard and erect as a steel pole. Its enduring strength and persistence frightened her. It demanded her; only her. It spoke:

'No other woman will do. It's you; only you I want. I must have you.'

It told her that no other woman pleased it. It craved sex with her. It refused to relent or leave her until she guided it inside her and gave it what it needed: her. She searched for something. But the penis stepped in front of her, blocking her way. It had hands! They reached out and held her close. They held her tightly in place against the penis; preventing her from leaving. A limbic brain wave swept her; made her surrender to the penis. She couldn't deny it any longer; didn't want to; wouldn't. She suddenly appreciated its need; wrapped her arms around it; began kissing its head; licking it; loving it. Then she slid it inside her. She tried to feel it inside her; yearned to feel it; but it gave her no feelings.

'Something is very wrong! It's so big and beautiful. I should feel it. Why can't I feel it?'

Azure blue skies and the sun's bright yellow orb were fading to evening glow with night's approaching dusk. Marty's circadian senses produced a dim awareness that her life was also passing into darkness. The sun had already transited beyond the Rockies' high peaks. The peaks glowed beneath the sky's orange fire-streaks now. The sky colors were deep purple hues with reddish streaks at their edges. Daylight was ending, concluding David's micro-fury; moving westward. Daylight had seen enough. It readied to depart. Conflagration's colors raged anger across the heavens, protesting David's dastardly deed. They held back the night watch; clinging to their turf, as night stars appeared.

Marty's senses dimmed. Her eyes saw blurred gray shapes and lengthening fuzzy shadows in the departing light. Gravity drained her remaining blood from her head. The imaginary penis faded. She saw nothingness. She wondered:

'Did that little bloody thing and its tiny penis also disappear into the darkness?'

Dizziness became her companion. It ushered her toward eternal blackness. Thoughts and voices rushed madly out of hidden mental doors, trying to spark dying memory cells that no longer retained them.

People, thoughts, and voices blended together in a rapidly changing kaleidoscope. Gray images of Maria, Donny and Billy, Teacher, the Four J's, Darren, Carl, Bob, Marshawn, Josh, Dominick, Charles, Sam, Rita, George, and Bertie appeared and disappeared again and again. They embraced her; held her; kissed, loved her; then faded away. The voices of Promiscuity, Shameless, and Iniquity collided and blended with the blurred images of people. People and voices blurred. She could no longer distinguish one voice or one person from the others. The gray shapes gradually became darker and became part of the background. A frightful blackness loomed. Waiting.

A green-black image of David appeared. It resisted the blackness; refused to join the other figures that had returned to the dark. The David image dripped with blood. Strips of human flesh clung to it. Lice, roaches, silverfish, and ants crawled over it. They rose from a slimy putrid stench fog; then fell away from David and back into their slime pool.

Marty's body gave a convulsive shudder. It wanted the wretched image to retreat back into the black void from which it had come. But it would not leave. She tried to run from it. But it laughed a morbid laugh at her and refused to let her pass.

Marty's weakened hands pushed out against the chains that held her. She struggled to shove David away from her. But David was no longer there. He had gone, leaving her hanging in her chains. In his place there next appeared a long corridor with pastels and dancing swirls of softly colored ribbons and sparkles that were laced all through the corridor's ceiling, floor, and walls. At the end of it a soft white light appeared. Instinct told her to run toward the light. She knew it was a special light. She knew it would end her confused dreams and her pain. She knew it would save her from David; help her escape him; take her away from her memories and voices; spirit her away from the frightening forest and its enormous penis that demanded sex with her.

She imagined her arms opening. Relief! It was near! A profound happiness overwhelmed her. She cried. Tears blurred her faded darkening vision. Then! Suddenly! A dim shadow emerged from the light. It grew larger and came closer. A man appeared! He looked familiar. He dressed plainly. Casual pants and a simple white shirt. She blinked, trying to recognize this man. He became larger; closer. He was not a lover. He did not want anything from her. He only wanted to be with her; to help her; to make sure she was safe. The man outstretched his arms. He got down on his knees. He was crying. He waited for her to run into his arms. Marty saw him for the first time since he went away. *'Father!' Oh Father! It's me, Marty!'*

She saw the opened arms of her father's spirit. He'd waited many years for her. Now he called her to come to him. He motioned her to come; to cross over that thin barrier that separates mortal life from spirit life. Her dimming mind understood what Father wanted. She had his love again. She wanted his love more than she had ever wanted anything. She raced through the tunnel into his arms. There, clutching him, she discovered peace again. Her lips mouthed: *'Father.'* Three more times. Tears flowed down her cheeks. Safe in her father's arms, her fading thoughts turned to her mother; and her failure to forgive. Near death, Marty sobbed. She mouthed words from her trembling, near lifeless lips:

"Father, what is happening to me?" Marty whispered to her father's soul.

"Your soul is joining my soul." He answered. *"We are about to journey together into new lives. Cling to me, dearest daughter. Do not be afraid. The Spirit is preparing for our returns to life. Your soul will enter new bodies of Connie, Sheila, Cecilia, Linda, JoAnne, Sandra, Patty, and others. You will know my soul again. My soul will join your soul and stay with it. Life will go on for you as it does for everyone: forever, endlessly, without the constraints of time. In the life eternal, which the Spirit gives us all, there is no end of life. Trust. Be not afraid. You are in the Spirit now. You will visit Death. You will leave your body with Death; but your soul will leave Death, and you will experience an explosion of new lives."*

"Everyone, Father? Even David?"

"Yes, even David. No soul lingers forever in Death. All souls get new lives. I know that's a difficult thing to understand, because David is a disgusting, fucked up, weirded out, asshole, vomit bag; but new lives for all is the will of the Spirit. Everyone gets endless chances to do better in their new lives, which become rejoined with their souls. It is what it is. That's the bottom line. That's how it is. At the end of the day, we are where we are. Your mother's soul awaits her death on Earth. She is still there." Joseph's soul pointed to Susan's soul, standing apart and looking forlorn. *"Please, Marty, forgive. Your mother seeks forgiveness."*

Marty's soul turned to her mother's soul. Her eyes teared:

"I do forgive you Mother. I was so terribly wrong to judge your life. I was wrong to hate you. I know that you and Marvin had the hots for each other. I know what that feels like. It's okay, Mom. I understand that you did the best you could. I love you Mother. Please forgive me."

Marty voiced her words from her heart; and her mother's soul heard them.

David, thinking Marty was now dead, freed her arms, then tied them in front of her torso. He placed the hook of the block and tackle lift under her arm-tie and lifted her body to the upright position for its final rendering. Her blood-soaked hair hung down over her life-drained face. By some miracle, Marty was not yet dead. Her lips moved! David, ever the voyeur, placed his ear next to Marty's mouth. He heard the barely audible words which she whispered with her dying breath:

"Bob, darling, I pray for your happiness. My soul is going away. I will love you forever after death and for all eternity. I'm not saying goodbye, Bob. I'm saying love. Love and live, Bob! Live and love again. Go to Barbara. Find her and love her with all your heart. She loves you so much. I was wrong to take you from her. I could not help who I was. Forgive my body. My soul will find yours and we will be together again someday, I swear it. Good-bye, my love."

Marty imagined a monogamous lifetime as Bob's wife. In her final moments of life, that was what she wanted.

David stared vacantly at the barn's wall while he pulled on the rope and lifted Marty's body higher. Each pull reminded him that no one had ever loved him. That realization deepened his loathing of all those who experienced the love emotion. Marty confirmed what he had long suspected:

'I knew it! Now I am sure of it! That skinny Indian bitch still has eyes for Bob!'

He ordered his demented mind to remember that Barbara was his enemy. He vowed to murder her at the first opportunity. He then turned and stared at the lifeless body hanging before him.

A sudden revelation struck him. Like a bolt of lightning, it electrified his soul from the top of his skull to the tips of his toes. Sanity! It exploded into every cognitive cell in his nervous system. This couldn't be!

'I have not done this, have I?'

He gaped in wonder at Marty's lifeless body. His mind grappled with the realization that a body without blood can not live. Reality intruded on David's madness. His return to sanity made him tremble. He acquired the full comprehension of what he'd done.

'Horrors! What have I done? I have just murdered my sister!'

Simultaneously, an even more horrifying revelation intruded upon David's psyche: Marty was his last living kin. Now she was gone. His mother and father had long passed. He never regarded his wife as anything other than an ornament. She accompanied him in polite society and helped him disguise his true preferences. He had no children. Marty was the only human left on Earth that linked to his bloodline.

David stood transfixed. realizing the horror of his deed, not as it affected Marty's life, now disappeared; but as it affected his own life. His connection to kin of any kind was now completely gone:

'Neither Mother, nor Father had siblings. I don't even have cousins!'

That reality, the loneliness of it, horrified him. Before this day and deed, he could feel smug, believing Marty might possibly care about him, because of their blood connection. Even though that sense was ill conceived, in David's warped realities it was nevertheless real. The only blood related to his own he had just spilled into the earth, returned it to the womb of God. He alone, had done this deed!

One of David's most profound epiphanies ensued. His mind flooded with one overpowering thought. He needed to make amends. He needed to atone for his sin! Jewish guilt never ran deeper.

His insane mind attempted to first rationalize his heinous deed to God:

'Adonai, what have I done? Holy shit! I'm not sure I knew what I was doing. I'm not sure I did a good thing, but I might have done

a good thing. Anyway, I thought I did. I, sure as I'm standing here, was trying to do good by you. As you can see, I've murdered my sister; but I know you'll understand. I did it for you; not for myself. Honest! Yeah, I know I had a side hustle. I'll make a fortune when I claim her inheritance. But that's not why I did it. You see, she was not pure. She defiled you.

'Well, we both did, sort of. Yeah, we mentally tried to fornicate. But we didn't actually fuck, you see. We tried to fuck, but our minds couldn't quite get connected enough to get it done. Well, her mind was ready enough, all right; but mine wasn't. You know I can't bring myself to do it with women, don't you? So, you see, I needed to sacrifice her to you to purify myself, because I tried really, really hard to think about doing it with her. You understand, don't you? That's okay with you, isn't it?

'Please forgive me if it wasn't okay. I didn't have a heifer handy, and I didn't want to use one of my sheep because I need them for lamb chops at the company party; so, I had to use Marty. I know her body might not be exactly the way you've prescribed things, but try to see it as my best efforts, kind of like in an underwriting deal where I try hard to get it done. And I'm not sure I followed kosher procedures. Maybe I should had cut her throat before I took her fetus from her, not the other way around. Oh well, I don't see where it makes that much difference; hope you won't be upset with me. I never studied to become a rabbi, so you need to give me a pass on that. I tried!'

David stood silent, hoping to hear from Almighty God. When no word came, he panicked.

'Look, Don, don't be pissed. Come on, man! I'll make it up to you if you're pissed. You know I'll treat you good. Yeah, I promise. What I need from you is one of those indulgences, you know, like the Pope gives to Catholics who pay him extra money to pardon their fuck ups; or to get advanced permission from him to do something bad and unholy, like divorcing or jumping the line of succession to a

throne because some son is an idiot that needed to be murdered. You know, things like that.'

David was rambling nearly incoherently, searching for the right words, hoping to be heard:

'Listen, Don, this can't be that big of a deal to a big guy like you. If those fucking fish eaters can get side deals from their Pope, then you should be able to top anything they can do! Right?'

David paused his groveling to listen. But there was only more silence:

'Look, Big Guy, I'll give something extra to my Shul. Honest. Count on it. Tell you what: If this is okay with you, just stay silent and I'll understand that we have made a deal, okay?'

David stood silently, listening for word from God. Again, nothing came. Now, in David's tortured thoughts, silence became a good thing. David believed that he had turned the tables on the Almighty:

'Okay, good. Well, here's what I propose: The business will make about fifty million this year, so instead of giving the Shul ten percent, or five million, I promise you I'll bump it up to fifteen percent, or seven and a half million. That's a lot of dough and you know it! Okay?'

Again, David stood and listened in silence. Again, no word came to him from the almighty:

'Okay, great!' David clapped his hands. *'I knew you'd go for it! We are good, then. We have our deal. Even if what I did was okay with you in the first place, I'm still going to give you the extra five percent, just in case it wasn't okay. You'll see, I did a good thing here. You've got to be okay with me, either way; now that you'll be getting fifteen percent. Right?'*

Another interlude of silence followed. This time the silence made David a little unsure of himself:

'Look, you know I do more good things than bad things. You know that, don't you? You always get paid, right? We're good, right?

*I don't want you coming back and biting me in the ass over this,
okay? OKAY?'*

David paused to listen for God's voice expressing displea-
sure. Again, he heard nothing. This time, he was relieved by the
Almighty's silence:

'*Good. Thank you. I knew you'd be okay with this. You won't
regret it either. I promise.*'

David, now believing that he was good with God, whom he
affectionately knew as his buddy Don, set about to finish his gristly task.

Meanwhile, Tang, an exceptionally large and beautiful male
Monarch butterfly glimpsed the scene below. He had overslept. He
had a late start for the migration south and was now far behind
the kaleidoscope, trying to catch up. He was searching for Poon,
the love of his life. The two butterflies knew each other from the
time they hatched as caterpillars on their milkweed leaf. They ate
and grew and cocooned together. Recently, they had emerged
from chrysalis together.

Tang was crazy about Poon. His antennae quivered. He
detected her scent. His butterfly heart raced fiercely. He trailed
her pheromones to this barn. He was desperate to find her and
mate with her. He dreamed their bodies would join and copulate
in the brilliant blue skies above the Mexican jungle's canopy. Their
wings would flutter as one. He would embrace her body tightly to
his own, and inseminate her precious eggs. He'd watch her from
a branch above her, while she lay the next generation of Monarch
eggs on milkweed leaves below. When she finished her life's purpose, she would flutter up and rest beside him. Their mating then
finished; they would rest together until their deaths, accepting the
Spirit's promise of eternal peace.

But Tang was distracted. He had heard the spirit cries of
an anguished kindred spirit soul. It was Marty's soul. He could

not ignore Marty's human cries. His compassionate loving soul needed to comfort the pained soul that cried out from below. Tang was a very good and loving butterfly. He descended from his flight and landed upon Marty's ear. He heard her distress cries and her loving message to Bob's spirit soul. He understood that he needed to comfort her; explain the cycle of life to her; and the reincarnation of spirit souls to her. He understood how to ease her pain of death. He spoke into her ear; removing death's sting, and giving Marty peace:

"Marty, do not despair. Your soul will not die—not now, not ever. I am the voice of U, the Eternal Universal Spirit. I am here with the Spirit's message of comfort to help you with your passage through distress. After your body dies, your spirit and all its loving goodness and sensuality will instantly reawaken in the bodies of millions of women in new places on Earth; even in other worlds. In all your new lives, you will have a mother and father who will love and nurture you. You will have a beautiful appearance; and you will experience the same emotions that you had in your present body. In one of your new lives, you will meet a special someone who loves you as much as Bob loves you. Your new names will be Connie and Sheila. Your Sheila will fall in love with Danny. Connie will find love with Paul. Danny and Paul will love your new lives for all their lives. You will have beautiful children. And you will have other lives and other loves as well.

"Your new lives will live longer than this life you are leaving. You will be sexually active for billions of years in new universes, in many different bodies, and you will experience inter-universal travels and pleasures you cannot imagine. You will live the meaning of nirvana. Your families will adore you. Your happiness will be their source of happiness as well. There will be no sins in your new worlds; no violence; nothing to covet; no reason to bear falsehoods; only benevolent spirits to worship.

"You will be the loving source of goodness in your life as Sheila. Your surroundings will be identical to Earth's because you will live in a parallel universe to Earth's. In your new worlds, you will discover happiness beyond anything here. From your next universe, you will go on to countless other universes and you will never die. Come away with me now, Marty. Trust in my message from U. Believe in the magic of butterflies. Be unafraid to leave your earthly body. You are safe with me. I'm calling my friend, Horse of Death, to take you away. He will take you with him into eternity. It's your time, Marty. Come away, now."

CHAPTER THREE

'.... like the vampire she has been dead many times; and learned the secrets of the grave (Walter Horatio Pater: The renaissance, Leonardo Da Vinci)

'Death is a fabulous experience. It's your chance to explore new partners, preferences, and positions while the Spirit prepares your soul for reincarnation. Embrace, enjoy, make the most of it! (Rosemary Ness-Bitner, Author)

DEATH

Now *DEATH*, the mightiest horse of the apocalypse, appeared to Marty:

"Mount my strong back," instructed the spirit horse. *"Clamp your legs around my body; put your arms around my neck; hold your face next to my mane and embrace me tightly. I am taking your spirit with me; carrying your soul into eternity. You will sleep a brief, restful sleep.*

"When your soul reawakens, you will reenter many mortal lives. Be unafraid. I am the way to happiness. I am the Almighty. I am the swift and I am the 'I Am.' I am taking you to a wonderful place where your soul will reappear. You will again feel the joys of life and love. Mount me now. We are going to where life is reborn. Cling tightly to me."

"I am ready to leave Earth," whispered Marty. *"I'm coming away with you,"* Marty's spirit spoke to Death:

"I am unafraid. I have mounted you, my big magnificent horse. I am holding tightly. Bob, my dearest love, this mighty horse is my way to rediscover your spirit. Hold me while I journey, dear Bob. Love me always as I will always love you. Hold me in your heart. Never let me go."

Marty mouthed her last words on earth. A divine exultation swept through her mortal body and mind. Her soul embraced the Great Spirit of all Living Things. The Spirit held out its arms:

'Welcome to my eternal kingdom. You will go to your next lives from here. You may choose whether your new lives will be lived as a good person or an evil one. It is up to you.'

And Marty's soul responded:

'Tell me, Spirit; is love and making love good or evil?'

The Spirit answered:

'Love is always good. Making love can be for good or for evil. Which it is depends upon your reason for making love.'

'But, if I made love to be good to my lover and evil to my rival at the same time, then which is it?' Marty's soul sought clarity.

'If your thoughts while making love were thoughts of love and goodness, then it was love making for good; and even if your thoughts while making love were for evil, then that too may have been for good, because good often arises from evil. Sheila will be the name of a new body for your soul. That body will learn the history of your soul and the many murders you committed and why you committed them; and your spirit soul shall carry no guilt from your body Marty to your body Sheila, for there was no guilt in why you murdered while you were Marty; but Sheila must know your feelings so she can understand her own feelings. In your Sheila lifetime you will meet two earthly spirit souls that will explain why your soul is free of guilt for your murders.'

'But, why would they explain that?'

'Your soul needs to be free of guilt. You've had tough circum-stances in your Marty body, and your soul needs a reset. When

someone becomes trapped in a rut that's leading them nowhere, we spirits help them leave their miseries by giving them a reset. We're even working on a rush order for Hillary Clinton as we speak. She badly needs a reset. We're trying very hard to locate an extra-large reset button for her.'

'But, does good ever comes from evil?'

'One cannot know everything. After all, I'm not Johnny Carson's Carnac the Magnificent. I'm just a simple spirit. Yes, no, maybe. Who knows? Only the one who carried the baggage of evil knows; and why that soul chose evil is a choice only that soul understands. When a soul gets to that point of choice, it needs to make the choice. It's like Yogi Berra says: when you get to the fork in the road, take it! But if the choice chosen isn't working, then that soul needs to rethink the choice and adjust accordingly; but again, a soul that comes to realize it has made a wrong choice must not seek revenge upon others for its choice. Souls that seek revenge lock themselves into a cycle of tail chasing, like crazed dogs. They are a sadness to me. Those people need a kick in the ass. But souls that seek acceptance and learning and peace are joy to me. Make the right choice.'

'Then embrace me, dear Spirit. I am ready to learn your mysteries. I leave my body behind me now. Let my body provide sustenance to these lowly pigs and insects, and let my bones nourish the roots of hungry rose canes'

'Death awaits you, Marty. Look, here he comes now! He bows to kiss your hand.'

'My soul comes to you, sweet Master of Death. I open the door to your welcome eternal darkness. Wow! Your kisses are so tender. Ooh, I very much love your touch! I can feel your heat warming the inside my vagina! This could be a great experience!

'Ah Death, now you stand close before me! I see you clearly now. You are beautiful, dear Death. You are a most handsome fellow. Oh, please, I beg you, allow me to be your mistress and ply your underworld with my whoring. My soul rushes into your arms and *embraces your certainty. I kiss you; my arms entwine your body to my soul's bosom; your arms entwine my soul to your welcoming solace. I yearn to make passionate love with you and become one with you.'*

'We will, gorgeous hot stuff, we will. Come walk with me over this little bridge.' Death leads Marty onto a short, narrow bridge. She looks down and sees a raging torrent of molten lava.

'What is that, dear Death? Surely, we are not going there, are we?'

'Oh, that is the basement of hell. A river of molten lava that we call the fires of Belial runs through it. No, dearest sweetest love, you will not be going there.'

'Look Death! I see some hands waving at us from the molten lava! They seem to be begging us to rescue them. Shall we go down to the river and pull them out?'

'No, my sweet love. We must let the fires of hell consume them. They are the souls of pedophiles and child molesters. Mostly they are career politicians. We must allow the lava fields of Belial to consume them. My kingdom of death has no use for them. Let the lava eat their souls.'

'Oh Death, look again! I see many legs and feet sticking up from the molten lava! Who are those people and why are they upside down in the river of molten lava? Should we save them?'

'Oh, my dearest, sweetest, thoughtful Marty. Those are the feet of all the lawyers who end up down here. They are upside down in the river of lava because they are hell's bottom feeders. No, we do not save them. We must leave them to their work. They love sucking the bones of the dead. They are pleased here. They are simply continuing to do what they naturally did during life.'

'Where are you taking me, Death, if not to the river below?'

'Please, call me Suez, or simply Z, for short.'

'Why Suez and Z?

'Well, Suez is the mirrored back lettered spelling of Zeus. Zeus is My brother. Living people think he is God. We brothers pass human souls back and forth, like ships that pass between the Suez Canal from the Mediterranean Sea to the Red Sea, going from the Atlantic Ocean to the Indian Ocean, and vice versa. My friends call me Z. It's the last letter of the alphabet, you see. And, I am the last person their souls see before the Great Spirit of All Living Things calls them to their new lives again; so, Z is an appropriate name for me, you see.'

'I see. Thank you, Z. But where are you taking me; and why?'

'I am taking you to my chambers, sweet Marty. There I will charm you. I wish to kiss you and touch you; and fondle your lovely body everywhere. And then perform the most wonderful oral sex upon your sweet nether region's honey pot that you have ever known. I'm salivating over thoughts of you. You'll see. My tongue will become millions of soft, delicate brushes. They will lovingly caress your tasty cupcake and your highly prized clitoris. You'll be amazed. You will orgasm like a fountain spring of refreshing life-giving fluids that bubble up from the ground and flow like an endless river.

'Then, I will lovingly ply your soft, fragrant muff pocket with my splendid penis. I assure you; it is the most wonderful penis you will ever know. You'll adore how it feels inside you. It will come alive in your blood like a delightful songbird. And it will please every cell of your body, like no other penis ever has.'

'This sounds exciting, dear Death. I can't wait! But please tell me something. Why me? What is it about me that makes you want to treat me so special?'

'I've watched all your films, my dear. I've seen how pleased you are while making love. I am not some ordinary cretin, you know. We have cable TV down here! Are you afraid? Don't tell me that you've journeyed all this way to see me and have now, suddenly, become fearful of intimacy?'

'Oh, no! I'm not! I'm never afraid of intimacy. I love intimacy. I crave it. I always crave it. Do not doubt me, dear Death. My soul has not changed. My nymphomania used my body as its plaything; and now, my body has left me. But my soul lives. It cannot die. And what pleases it most will never change. In my heart of hearts, more than anything in life or death, I love to make love. I crave; I yearn for; I love erotic intimacy. I can't wait to enjoy intimacy with you, dear Death.

'So, let's do that, shall we? Let's cavort and dance; let's ravish ourselves until we exhaust ourselves with carnal pleasure. Let's enjoy our brief time together, before my soul must return to life!

'We will appreciate how much we love and need each other. We will dance together! We can waltz and tango! Teach me the latest macabre dance steps that are fashionable here in Death. You, Sweet Death, and my whoring soul, will enjoy our precious time together. We will laugh at those fools who failed to appreciate us.

'Please take me dancing. Let's go dancing, dear Z. Let's do,' Marty squealed. *'Let's drown ourselves in fun! Let's tempt the prophets, saints, and apostles! May we do that? Please? Pretty please? I will dress in a string halter that barely covers my nipples. I'll also wear a risqué micro mini skirt, sans panties. I'll anoint my vagina with oils and scents of freshest gardenia and lilac. I'll liken it to a dew-drenched rose bud yearning to open in the morning sun; eager to take in life!*

'Then, I want you to join me while I bounce my titties and buns to the beat of the music. I want to hear the drum beats vibrate through my soul. I want to feel the boldness and confidence that the blaring trumpets awaken in me. And I want to feel the lust of the saxophones in my bones.

While we fuck, dear Death, I want my vagina to tingle with the tempting notes of the soprano clarinets. And I desperately wish to

enjoy shameless, effusive orgasms while hearing the sweet vocaliza-
tions of the Ave Maria, sung in French.

'Come, dearest Master Death, let's see for ourselves if the teach-
ers of admonitions and restrictions can resist the lusts that they com-
manded humankind to shun. Will ancient misogynists who lived
when robes covered humans to their ankles abhor the welcoming
invitations of a comely femme; or would their souls prefer to arise
from their graves and make love with me? Will those testosterone
infested rule makers who ordered women's skirts not be shorter than
six inches above the knee adhere to their own rigid rules; or will
their souls rise and atone for their sexism?

'Would they curry my forgiveness by performing cunnilingus?
Shall we see if their souls can have an honest shameless relationship
with a woman? Let me dance and flaunt my profligate sex craving
lady bits over their graves, dearest Z. Let them see my joyful juice
box and breathe in my flower's flavorful scents. I'll bounce my titties
and twirl about; teasing their penises to life, while I charm you. Let's
see if my promiscuity can coax them from their slumbers. Will they
party and receive the sweet tastes of life they denied themselves while
they lived? Let's prove them hypocrites, all! Invite them to arise from
their graves and consort with me! Will prophets, disciples, saints,
imams, and rabbis lie in stilted stupor or will they arise like real
men? Shall we wager, dear Death? I bet I can fuck all of them.

'Will they resist my irresistible, deliciously decadent, fellatio; my
immoral salacious lips' loving kisses upon their penises' heads; and
my iniquitous, cum thirsting tongue's sensuous loving licks? I will
bet a longer stay in death that none will resist me. What odds will
you give me, dear Z? Might they join us in orgies and threesomes?
How delicious those thoughts! Let's tempt the prudish sensibilities of
the revered dead! Let me rattle their bones and set their souls free!
Oh, yes, dearest Master of Death, let's wake them! Let's be shameless
party animals! Let's have a riotous lascivious ball!'

'*I will not bet against you, Marty; but there is one special group here in my Valley of Death that requested your presence as soon as they learned of your arrival. They wish to do all manner of debaucheries with you.*'

'*Oh, I'm flattered. Whom might they be, dear Death?*'

'*The Lawyers.*'

'*What do you take me for?*' Marty's soul wailed. '*Do you think I'm some cheap, ordinary common slut? I'm insulted. I have my ethics and my standards. Lawyers! Why, they are out of the question. An honest working girl can never know when they are lying or telling the truth. They themselves do not know the difference. Lawyers! I will not fuck lawyers! Absolutely not!*'

'*I understand. I assure you, Marty, that I, Death, am different. I will always tell you the truth.*' Death lifted his head proudly, emphasizing that he was a gentleman.

'*Then, you and I must become lovers until the time I must leave you, dear Z.*' Marty touched his chin with her fingernail and smiled her most coquettish, dazzling smile.

'*I love having fun. And you know, I hate being bored. My soul desperately craves to know the fabled pleasures of your mysterious penis, you dear handsome fellow. I desperately want to make love with you, dear Z. I want to include you among my faithful unrighteous lovers. But, if you'd rather save fifteen percent on your car insurance, I'll understand. Please tell me that satisfying my nympho cravings deserves your masculine attention more than an advertising message. You wouldn't say no to me, would you? Please be a sweet spirit. Please sin with me, dear Master of Death. Allow me to discover if your cock is as fabulous as the reputation that precedes it.*' Marty reached out and took Death's cock in her hand. She began stroking it, bringing it to fullest hardness.

'*Here, allow me to bring your hand to my vagina, dearest Z. Oh, please, please, finger me and kiss me there. Yes! That's it. You are on your knees! You know what pleases a woman! I love how your soft lips nibble mine. You are soooo sensual! I love what you're doing. Oh, I do! Yes! I shamelessly do!'* Marty squealed with delight.

'Your lips feel so wonderful, dearest Z. Cup your mouth closely to my adoring vagina and make love with me. Let's the two of us flutter away together. Oh yes, please continue doing that. I can never get enough of that!

'I love you really good, G I; long, long time; I fuck you all night long, You will remember me. You will come back to me. I fuck you really, really good. You'll see. You sweet boy son, Master of Death. Marty teased Death pretending to be a Vietnamese whore.

'Ahh, your tongue is so loving; so good! My nymphomania has not died, just because my body did. It's my essence. Orgasms nourish my soul! Of course, you already know that. Oh, yes! That's it, dearest Death. I feel another one coming. Yes! It's so beautiful! I love it! I'm coming! Your tongue is so beautiful. Please don't stop! Never stop! Here in Death, you don't need to stop, do you?

'I'll love you forever, dearest Z. You big handsome man. Me love you long time. Me fuck you really, really, good. Not much money. Me love you special, all night long!' Marty's sing-song Vietnamese whore voice pleaded with Death. She wanted to fuck longer.

'Oh, goodness, dearest Death, this feels wonderful! I love you inside me. I feel your hardness; and you are so huge! What a magnificent, glorious penis you have! We must do this often. You make me feel love, you big handsome man. I LOVE making love with you. My special guest request is that we make love daily.

'Also, I much prefer room service, don't you know? Come to my room each morning. Oh, goodness, I do adore your penis. I must insist on daily room service. I could stay with you forever, dear Death. Your penis is truly fabulous. I want it to stay inside me forever! Yum! I love sucking it so much! I rue the day I must depart from you, dear Death.'

'As you wish, dearest Marty, I am at your daily service. I must say, I am delighted to serve you and have you here with me. So many women come here after their lives are finished. They mope about their memories, their marriages, and their families. They realize that their experiences and memories were nothing more than false imaginings. They reflect upon the truths of their lives; the fact that most people merely used them and wanted little to do with them as friends; that most of their so-called memories were results of forced events they didn't want to be a part of. Many of them rue that they had not lived a life more like yours, Marty. One righteous woman, whom I discretely loved, confided with me that she regretted not spending many more afternoons and evenings of her life with her panties off. Another who regretted her choices told me, unequivocally, that in her next life, she intended to become a porn star. You see why I say I am delighted to serve you, Marty? You understand that life should be about pleasure; not misery. You avoided the misery makers' traps. You are a love and a delicious pleasure!'

'The pleasures are mine, Death, my love. My soul will love you until it must leave you, dear Death. You opened the door and brought in light, out of my darkness. My soul will remember our fascinating interlude. And then it will depart you, as it must, dearest Death; to reenter life and the pleasures of living in the flesh. I patiently wait until my soul transcends you and resurrects in Sheila's body and rediscovers its carnal earthly pleasures. There it will enjoy love making as it did in Marty's life; and it will find its true romantic love; but it will never forget the erotic, other worldly pleasures of your company, my sweet Death.'

'Marty, I have news.'

'What news, dear Death? Is it good news or bad news?

'Here in Death, there is no such thing as good news or bad news, Marty. There is only news.'

'Well, what is it then? Tell me.'

'I received a call from U, the universal Spirit of all Living Things. You are to return from Death to the world of the living.'

'But, sweet Death, I don't want to return. I'm not yet ready. I've only been with you this short while! I love it here. I love our orgies and my threesomes with you; and I especially loved those times when you took me to visit the souls of the Saints and the Prophets. I'll always cherish those special times when I sat on their faces and helped them discover women's pleasures. I loved removing their shields of celibacy and helping them break their vows to their dogma. I loved taking their virginity and drinking the semen of their awakened sexuality. You saw how much I loved it! I didn't just drink it. I guzzled it. I helped them break their vows of celibacy. We had so many fantastic romps! Please let me stay with you, dear Death.'

'I'm afraid you must leave soon. Just a short while ago, U commanded your old nemesis Yolanda to reincarnate. He soul will enter the life of Cecilia. You are fated to meet her again and resolve your passions.'

'Yolanda? I don't know anyone named Yolanda. Perhaps U is mistaken?'

'No. U never makes mistakes about these spirit matters. You knew Yolanda only as Carl's wife in your previous life. You had such disdain for her you never bothered to learn her name. She had a burning passion for you. Her dying wish was to be your intimate lover.'

'Oh, her! The one who crashed and burned on Mountaintop Pass. Yes, I remember. She refused to have lesbian love with me.'

'Yes, that's the one. Her spirit atoned for her rigidity. She died praying to the spirits for her soul to join your soul in intimacy. U has decided that her soul will reincarnate into the body of Cecilia, or CC. She's a spectacular woman with an insatiable libido. You are to meet her in your next life as Sheila. You and she will have threesome love with a man named Hud. You will also know many lovers.

Pasqual will love you so much he will lose himself in thoughts of you. Your lesbian love will have constant pleasuring with Lotus Lulubell Wong. Your professional career will skyrocket after you poison your two detractors. And, you will discover true love.'

'Poison my detractors? I don't think I want to do that, dear Death.'

'Ah, you'll see. You did it before in the bodies of Bathsheba and Isabella. You advanced yourself and greatly enhanced your pleasures. You will again. It's an internal survival and self-preservation instinct. You'll feel elated after you dispatch your detractors.'

'Remember, in your new life you will search for true love. And you will find it. It will be a fairytale love you can cherish all your life.'

'But dearest Death, I love my time here with you. I do not wish to leave you! Can't you keep me here?'

'I'm afraid not, my lovely nymph. I'd love for you to stay. I loved taking you to the orgies. I delighted in untying your string bikinis, licking your delightful nipples, making love with you; and helping you grow your fan base here in Death. But I can't keep you here. U has commanded your return to life.'

'How long have I been here?'

'Death is not measured in terms of time as it is in life, my love. You've been here. Now you must leave here. Time only has meaning for the living.'

'But, where must I go to reenter life? Who must I become?'

'U told me a simple farmer's wife is pregnant. She will give birth to a baby girl named Sheila in a simple country farmhouse surrounded by cows and horses and sheep.'

'This sounds like an updated version of the Savior's birth, only with a woman baby. Is there a King Herod lurking in my future?' Marty stood aback and eyed Death warily.

'No,' Death chuckled, 'only peace and love. The farm where you will spend your childhood is in rural Pennsylvania near the waters

of two beautiful creeks, the Pohopoco and the Wild. You will not be an ordinary child; but a very special child that U is sending to save the world.'

'There you go again!' Are you sure there's no King Herod?'

'Now you're starting to sound like Ronald Reagan. Relax. You'll be tracking down a terrorist plot. It will be a real action-adventure experience. U assured me you will love it. You will be gifted with extreme intelligence. You will use your intelligence to undo a horrible evil that stalks humankind.'

'But, what about my sensuality? Will I lose that? Surely, U knows how much I love to make love?'

'No, you will not lose your sex drive. You will just apply it differently, that's all. U feels your soul in Marty's body has done many great things. You have freed the souls of many. You have released the sexuality of Billy and Donny, Darren and the four J's, Carl and his impossible wife, Fred, Big Ed, Dominick, the Prince, Marshawn, Josh, Travis, and hundreds of others. U feels your spirit soul has done enough in Marty's life. U likes to mix things up. Now U commands me. I must release your soul to its new, reincarnated life as Sheila.'

'I see. I understand I must obey the will of U. I shall miss you, sweet Death.'

'Never fear, Marty. I am never far away. You will return to me countless times in the journey of your soul. I will always be here for you; waiting to love you again. In the meanwhile, you can spend time with my brother, Sleep. Dream of our wonderful times together and of your life as Marty.'

'I understand. I am ready to leave now. Goodbye my love.'

'Let's not say goodbye, my sweet. Let's instead begin your next life now.'

'Oh! What's this? What's this, sweet Death? Oh, wow, I feel you shooting cum inside me, sweet Death. Oh, that feels so hot and so wonderful! Keep shooting! Oh, I love how you are making

me feel! Oh, wait! I feel things growing out of me! What is happening to me?'

'I have impregnated your soul, dearest love. I implanted the seeds of your new life. Your new life as Sheila will spring from the death of your soul's time as Marty. Your resurrected soul will seek the baby Sheila. The things growing out of you are the arms and legs of Sheila. You are still in your mother's womb, much like a butterfly is in chrysalis in its cocoon. Your soul is going into Sheila's body now. It will have all the love it had when it lived in Marty's body. You will carry my love with you as well.'

'But, will I still have the same urges to make love that I had when I was in the body of Marty? Will I still be promiscuous? You know how much I loved being promiscuous.'

'Never fear, my sweet love. Of course, you will still feel the urges that all women feel; and, yes, as Sheila you will be highly promiscuous. But you will attract men to you in a very different way than you did when you were Marty. In your new life you will become a highly respected, highly educated, professional career woman.

'Your allure to men will have a more subtle and mysterious nature than it did as Marty, but your allure will be every bit as compelling as before. Through trial and error, you'll discover that highly regarded professional men will throw themselves at your feet. They will adore you and desperately seek your consort. You will again discover true love.'

'Then, through my reincarnations will you still love me and understand my needs to love and be loved, within my own loving soul, dear sweet Death?'

'Yes, my love, my beautiful loving adorable darling. I love you now as I will love you forever, until the end of eternity. You will visit me often between the times you are dwelling inside the bodies of the living. I will wait patiently for your next visit with me, my truest love. Never fear to be with me. Never fear to know my love for you.

Come again soon, into my arms and make sweet love with me. I will always cherish your visits with me and I patiently await all your returns.'

'Then, good bye for now, dearest Death, I have thoroughly enjoyed my stay with you. I adore your splendid penis. You are a perfect gentleman.'

Marty's body had discovered its final peace. But the life of her soul continued to flutter on, pursuing its eternal journey of love and more love. Her resurrected soul had mounted the big Horse of Death and departed her body for the next segment of its journey, which began by first visiting the Master of Death, the handsome prince of darkness. In the kingdom of Death, she reveled in her promiscuous conquests of the underworld's souls. Her visit ended with its ascension from Death to join U, the Universal Spirit of all Living Things, and become reborn into the body of Sheila.

During metamorphosis between its resurrection and ascension, Marty's soul briefly traveled the Earth and visited Bob and Barbara. It made peace with Barbara and expressed to her its good will and wishes for her happy and loving life with Bob. Barbara and Marty's souls became understanding friends and a sister-like love bonded their feelings to one another. Marty's soul spoke several times to Bob, encouraging him to be at peace with the death of her body; to love and cherish Barbara for the remainder of the life that his body had on Earth; and to feel sureness in faith that his soul and hers would meet again in the reincarnated bodies of Danny and Sheila; and that the love their two souls discovered in the bodies of Marty and Bob would never end; but would live forever in eternity.

CHAPTER FOUR

'The will and high permission of all ruling heaven left him alone to his own dark designs, that with reiterated crimes he might heap on himself damnation (John Milton: Paradise Lost)

DAMNATION

Butterfly Tang briefly fluttered above David. He saw what David had done to Marty, and he became angry. He spoke to David's soul:

'You have done an abominable thing here today. There was nothing spiritual or Godly or forgiveness-seeking about what you did. You are a no-good son of a bitch! You have committed a heinous and evil act this day. It will haunt you for all your days and it will curse your spirit for all eternity. Your soul will wander the Earth is search of quietude; but will never find it. You are badder than a bad dog, David. You are hereby DAMNED and your soul is DAMNED! I have placed an eternal curse upon your soul. Yes, David. We butterflies are the Spirit's messengers. And we have the power to curse your soul.

'Your soul will be despised and reviled forever. Wherever it goes it will look over its shoulder in fear for its very life. It will not be welcomed for long anywhere it travels in its reincarnations in the universe, because today you have thwarted a searching. A beautiful loving soul sought to understand and discover love. She carried an

innocent loving soul to you; and you murdered her! You had no right to judge her or mock her. She was among my most wondrous creations. She was no threat to you, yet you took her mortal life to satisfy your greed. For shame! You no good son of a bitch!

'You live in a sickness of your own creation. You revel in your evil and you nurture it. You nurture hatred for others with your sociopathy. Your deeds have not gone unseen. We butterflies have found you out. You dwell in your loathsome self-pity and your petty revenge. You have no right to visit vengeance. You have no right to seek pity or attempt to sway feelings. Universal Spirit, U, decides such things, not man. We know that you know better. You can not fool us butterflies. You have disgusted and angered us. Shame on your soul! In your future lives you must try to do better, David. Try thinking of yourself as a golfer with a twelve-stroke handicap. You must work very hard to improve. Your behavior is not acceptable. Before you enter the kingdom of Death, David, your body must first pay for your sins. I will see to that.

'I hereby also curse your mortal body. By the powers of the Spirit of all Living Things, I hereby decree that you will experience two terrors. The first will be a terror from your past and the second will be a terror in your present. And know this: Your earthly body will meet an agonizing death! It will be far worse than the agony you have caused this well intentioned, loving woman.'

Tang gave comfort to Marty and dispensed his justice to David. His good deeds were finished. His antennae quivered. He detected Poon's hot scent. She was here! Poon's entire body trembled. Love's lust flowed within him. He desired only Poon. He needed her. He had to have her. Passion madness overwhelmed him. Being together with Poon was now Tang's only purpose in life. Holding her body to his and mating her now became even more important than his safety or his life. His wing muscles felt a renewed surge of strength. His mating drive lifted him high up, above the barn.

He needed to go to Poon. Now. His wings beat mightily and more rapidly, lifting him higher still. He reached far above the earth, his wings now pulling him swiftly and fearlessly through the sky. Instinct cried out to him. His response to Poon's scent was as old as time. He fluttered blindly, speedily forward, ignoring all risks and dangers to his life. Destiny and Poon awaited him.

He needed to father Poon's eggs. He flew harder and faster than he'd ever flown before. He ignored the excruciating pain that screamed from his muscles. He would soon fly over two thousand miles, fighting exhaustion and sleeplessness in his desperate, frantic search for Poon. An endless expanse of ocean passed below him. Other butterflies became weakened and fell into the sea. They would be eaten by fishes.

But Tang refused to tire and succumb to the sea. He flew relentlessly onward. Through headwinds and storms, he ignored his aching muscles. He did not allow himself to think of his pain. He only thought of Poon. He would seek her out among the millions of other female Monarchs. He would not allow himself rest until he found her. He needed to be inside her. No other male could have her. Only he could have her and know her.

His mind filled with thoughts of how beautiful she was, how brilliantly her wings dazzled in the sunlight when she fluttered; and how much he loved her. He could think of nothing else. He was blinded by thoughts of her beautiful wings and her glorious magic place. He wanted Poon, only Poon. Onward he carried his pain and his burning, yearning love. Onward, relentlessly, through endless scorching hot days and chilling nights, Tang flew.

CHAPTER FIVE

Wilt thou forgive those sins through which I run and do them still, though still I do deplore? (John Donne: Hymn to God the Father)

ATONEMENT

LATER THAT AFTERNOON

After David disposed of Marty's corpse and after he prayed for atonement for his and Marty's sins, he donned one of his late mother's dresses. He wore a woman's pair of walking shoes, and a wig made to look like Marty's hair. He drove Marty's car to a park-and-ride lot. From there he took a courtesy bus to the airport. He had assumed the disguise of a slovenly dressed woman, carrying a garish handbag. He calmly walked into the airport terminal. The cameras saw him. Their grainy surveillance film would assume he was Marty. He walked slowly, girl-like, from the terminal's north-side entrance doors to its south-side exit doors; then he exited. He hailed a cab and had it drive him to a gas station near his farm. At the gas station he sashayed into the ladies' room. Inside, he changed clothes. He walked out dressed like a man.

His women's clothes and the garish handbag were now stuffed into a large shopping bag. He walked the six blocks from the gas station to his barnyard. There he fed the woman's dress, the garish handbag, the women's walking shoes and wig to his hungry goats. They eagerly set upon the disguise items and ate them. The evidence of the woman who had driven Marty's car to the airport; walked through the airport; and taken a cab to the gas station was soon digesting in the stomachs of David's goats.

Walking to his farmhouse from the barnyard, David was joined by Dolly, his favorite sheep.

"This was a busy day, Dolly," he said to the animal. *"We accomplished a lot. We concluded the Marty episode. She did her job. She distracted Bob from doing corporate finance deals. His old contacts are stale now. We can't let ourselves become attached to our worker bees, can we Dolly? To be a successful chief executive one must understand how to use people; and when one is finished using them, they must be gotten rid off. An employee is no different than a piece of tissue paper, Dolly. No different; not really. They try to turn the business relationship into something more than it is. They try to be buddies, lovers; all sorts of goofy things other than being disposable employees; but they don't have the guts to be in business for themselves. They aren't worth wiping our asses with them. So, Marty's gone. That ends it.*

"But don't let today's events upset you, Dolly. She was only a Goy. Her mother is a Goy, so she was a Goy. Dad made a mistake conceiving her into the world. I corrected Father's error. But I kept my promise to her. She wanted me to fuck her, Dolly. So, I fucked her all right. I fucked her, big time! AHHH, HA, HA, HA!" David erupted in insane laughter.

David lay down on the grass before Dolly and started rolling over and over while laughing hysterically. His flirtation with insanity was growing stronger. His inner self had burst through his veneer of unflappable authority and expressed itself; first during the murder of his half-sister, Marty; and now, with his loss of behavioral control. Dolly saw David's madness; but she didn't say a word. She stood there watching him, while impassively chewing a mouthful of grass.

"Yeah, I really fucked her, Dolly. Ha! I fucked her, Dolly. Not how she expected to get fucked, but I fucked her good. Fuck her! And, I honored her wish too, Dolly. She said she wanted her life to have a happy ending and it did: FOR ME! HA, HA, HA! Dolly, can't you see, Dolly?

"I'm finally happy! I'm alone now, completely alone. My blood sister is gone. I'm back to how I felt when I was a little boy, rejected by my parents. It's the feeling I know best. I'm as ruthless as Joe Stalin, Dolly. Marty tried to get close to me, close to my power; so, I did exactly what Stalin would have done. I murdered her! The Mrs.? No, she's not close to me, sweetheart. She's just an ornament. Marriage helps me look normal to people. But we know better, don't we baby?"

David put his arm around Dolly's neck. Then, the two walked side by side.

"We stayed true to our Khuzarian heritage, Dolly," asserted David to his four-legged friend. *"We concealed our goal and disguised who we are. We tricked my slut sister into working for us, like Dad duped Susan. But we weren't stupid. Dad fell in love with a Goyim girl. Not me! I'm not stupid!"* David lifted his chin in proud arrogance.

"Marty no longer had a purpose," David rationalized his crime. *"Like all Goyim, she was only here to serve us. It was time to throw the used-up Goyim whore away. We're selling nationally now, Dolly. We can't build a national firm on the back of one whore. We're a high-class firm. We have high ethical standards. I did what I did to maintain our exemplary image."*

David's delusions of grandeur quickly melted before his ever-encroaching paranoia:

"Just don't tell Bob what you saw today, Dolly. It's our secret."

Dolly walked beside David, chewing her grass. Another paranoid thought entered his mind. Since childhood he was fearful that the rabbis would tell his parents he misbehaved in religious school. That risked punishment. Marvin could send him away to summer camp or force him to apologize to the mother of a child he bit. He never outgrew his dread of scrutiny. He needed to unburden:

"We must keep our secret from my rabbi," confided David to the black sheep. *"If he comes into our barnyard, do not say anything. Promise me you won't say one word. Possibly, our ritual flunked kosher. I didn't use a clean, sharp knife. My hunting knife doesn't make clean, razor cuts. The cuts were ragged. That's why Marty lived so long, before she died. I didn't use a healthy heifer either. The tribe doesn't even do animal sacrifice anymore. Only the ancient priests did that. No modern-day rabbi would do a sacrifice; let alone substitute a human for an animal. No chance!*

"Do you think I should have asked my rabbi what to do? Do you, Dolly?" David's paranoia caused him to distrust his dumb animal friend.

"There's a lot wrong with that thought, Dolly. He might have asked how I became so involved with her. Then he'd ask about our murders. Then what? Think! He might have asked me why I never took Marty to him so he could fuck her himself; try her out; give me his opinion.

"I know how his mind works. He'd put me down; call me a Yutz. He'd say I'm even more stupid than a Putz, like I'm a stupid Putz who is so stupid that I cut my prick off and sewed it back on backwards. He'd also call me a Schmuck, a Putz who's so stupid he doesn't even know what pricks and assholes are used for. Worst, he might call me a Hymie, a selfish, stingy Jew, because I never even let anyone sniff her. I always kept Marty away from the other tribe members.

"I don't like being ridiculed, Dolly. I'm a Mench! Hear me? I'm a Mench! I'm destined for greatness! I've had my bar mitzvah! My rabbi can't judge me. He has no right to do that! No one has the

right to judge me!" David loudly asserted his righteous dignity. His animals heard him. Sheep lifted their heads from grazing to look at him; hens stopped pecking and studied him cautiously; then, all animals carried on as before.

"Oh yeah, Dolly, I can see it. My rabbi would ask: Why didn't you bring her around; let me help both of you? Yeah, he'd hold his sharp chin and nose high like he does, then look down his nose at me. I can't bear to look up his nose, Dolly. It is better we say nothing. Trust me.

"Besides, I'm not a qualified slaughterer. I've never studied it, never done a kosher killing. I've never even seen it. I just look for the U on the food labels. I'm not sure I did it right. Please don't mention one word," he begged the sheep. *"Also, I don't think the Torah permits me to feed human body parts to animals. We're not allowed to sacrifice people in the first place. We could cause my rabbi some serious upset, so mum's the word, okay?"* He stared at the top of Dolly's head while they walked. He trusted her again.

She suddenly stopped walking. An attractive patch of grass caught her attention. She contemplated a mouthful. She stood, not moving, chewing the lush grass. David took her halt as a sign of disapproval:

"What else could I do, Dolly?" An alarmed David asked. His faux confidence was shattered. Again, paranoia gripped. His deranged mind imagined that Dolly might tattle; then a rabbi might tell his father. Marvin might possibly return from the dead! Father might order him back to military school. He dreaded that hellish purgatory. He had flat feet. He was overweight. He couldn't run as fast as other boys. He feared he'd stumble and fall; be laughed at again. He'd be forced to march extra hours; get assigned extra mess hall duty; ordered to wash other boys' dirty dishes; clean their dirty toilets.

'No! Not that! Not again!'

David shuddered. He imagined reliving summer camp hell. He turned around and stopped, standing in front of Dolly. He opened his arms widely, proving to his sheep that he held nothing back. He needed to persuasively plead his case. He slipped deeper into insanity while rationalizing his crime:

"Dolly, you know I'm smart, right? Well, I researched the torah carefully about this. I looked for contradictions and loopholes like I always do whenever I enter a business contract. I found the passages that forbid me to sacrifice your children, your sons, or daughters, by throwing them into the fire as an offering to Molech, the Pagan god. I never did that to any of your lambs, did I?"

Dolly stared into David's eyes with her understanding silence.

"No, I didn't. See? I carefully follow every rule, especially the fine print. Well, that sacrifice rule applied to the tribe at the time of the Greeks and Romans, while the tribe still ruled Carthage. But that prohibition about sacrifice did not technically apply to us and our sacrifice.

"First of all, we didn't do a Pagan sacrifice. We don't pray to Molech. See? Second, Marty was not my child. She was Father's child. Third, we didn't throw her into a fire to sacrifice her. We didn't use a fire! So, I think we're good, Dolly. We found a loophole! The only place we have a problem is the 'Thou shalt not kill' commandment. That's kind of a pesky commandment.

"But I found a way around it. Here again, there's another loophole, Dolly. We were supposed to sacrifice a red heifer if we touched a dead person. I think what the torah really means is if someone fucks a dead person. That would be bad if the dead person was a woman because one's seed couldn't get a dead woman pregnant and then one could not be fruitful and multiply; and that would violate the multiplication mitzvah, don't you think?"

Dolly looked at David with her vacant eyes. She continued chewing her grass.

"Well, as I explained to Marty, her soul was dead and that's the same as being dead, so it's only logical that I sacrificed a red heifer to atone for mentally fucking her. Okay? So, I got around the not kill commandment by invoking the sacrifice a red heifer commandment. See? But I didn't have an actual red heifer, so I used Marty instead. And I made her blemish free by cutting out her birthmark strand of red hair. So, I think we found an approved exception to the Thou Shalt Not Kill commandment, Dolly. Remember, there's always a loophole in every law; even the Torah's laws. There are always exceptions to everything. You just need to look for them and use creative interpretations. Right?"

Dolly continued staring into David's eyes. The sheep seemed to understand that David was trying to communicate something important. But, of course, the sheep didn't understand English. Or did it? David believed it did. And that was all that mattered to him.

"Look, Dolly, pay attention here. We needed to stay focused on what is important. The business needed to get rid of her. So, we did a good thing. And, she and I were both sinners. So, it was really efficient to both sacrifice her and bless her soul at the same time. So, we did two more good things, even though I'm not a rabbi and I don't have the powers to bless things. But, since we didn't have a rabbi handy, I took charge, like a Mench is supposed to take charge. That was another good thing. See?"

Through his maze of contorted casuistry, David rationalized murdering Marty to his four-legged confidant:

"That way: me and Marty both got forgiven by God. Pretty smart, huh Dolly? I killed two birds with one stone! I remembered to ask God to forgive my sins and forgiveness for screwing up the sacrifice by using a human instead of an animal. We might even get totally forgiven for what we did today, Dolly."

David hoped that by using the plural pronouns *we* and *us*, instead of *I* and *me*, Dolly might believe that she was equally responsible for Marty's murder; thus, less likely to divulge his heinous deed to a rabbi.

"Hopefully we will get lucky with God, Dolly," he spoke in optimistic tones. *"I'll pray for both of us, next time I go to Yom Kippur. I'll make doubly sure God isn't upset with us. Hopefully God will know we tried our best. Rabbi said I should always try to please God.*

"I think we did okay. We probably performed a historic first. We might make the Guinness Book of World Records, Dolly. Maybe, we made history! That makes us special, Dolly. Maybe, some day, when I think it's okay to tell the world what we did here today, I'll explain everything. Since it was a historic first, we might get a historic preservation site plaque placed on your barn, Dolly. You'll be famous!" A sense of elation swept over David. He felt like he got away with something; much like he did when he was a little boy who stole cookies from a cookie jar.

David smiled and nodded to the sheep:

"Just promise me that you will never breathe a word of this to any rabbi, Dolly. I don't think any of them would be happy about this. That would not be good." Guilt seeped back into David's consciousness. It continued to haunt him.

Dolly's head went down again. She was intent about chewing grass. David knelt beside the animal. He put his arms around her neck and sobbed while he buried his face in her woolly neck and inhaled her musty scent.

"Don't look at me that way, Dolly," implored David. *"Her sacrifice had nothing to do with you. I'll never sacrifice you. I love you. I had to get rid of her. Don't be sore with me."* David pleaded with the sheep for understanding.

"Her mother would have nagged me to keep her in the firm because of the agreement that we made, but I didn't want her anymore. Marty had a personality disorder, Dolly. She may have had mental issues." He looked at the sheep and touched the side of his

head with his index finger, indicating where Marty's problems resided, further justifying his deed.

"People who work for the Firm must have excellent mental health. We can't have nutty people working with the public, Dolly. Marty's mind wasn't right. It was upside down, ... especially today. Ha, ha, ha!" David rolled on the grass, making his insane laugh.

"Didn't you see that was funny, Dolly? I made a joke!" He held Dolly by her ears, taking the sheep into his confidence, seeking her camaraderie and good will in committing the murder. The sheep seemed to be in a heightened state of alertness now. She always became alert when David grabbed her by her ears. The poor animal was alarmed. But David believed her heightened alertness signaled that she was paying close attention.

"That completes the first part of my plan, Dolly. Now it's time to move on. She got a terrific deal from me. I always did my best for her. I always treated her first-class. I prayed for her future in the world of the spirits, I prayed to God for the forgiveness of her sins, and I sincerely thanked her for her service. I did for her what every good employer should do for their most trusted, most valuable employees. I'm a wonderful example of a chief executive, Dolly." David nodded his head to Dolly. He affirmed to the animal that Marty's murder was a positive policy decision for the Firm's human relations. David's chest heaved. He felt gripped by guilt. Tears rolled down his cheeks and fell onto the ground.

"I'm not a bad boy, Dolly, honest. I'm a good boy. Sometimes I hurt people and that makes me feel good; but afterwards, I know I did something wrong. But I can't help it. You know I can't help it, Dolly. I know you know that. I love you, Dolly. I know you understand me." He kissed the sheep's forehead. He believed that the sheep accepted his rationalizations. The two of them resumed walking toward the house. Dolly turned away to reach for a fresh

clump of grass. That alarmed David. He feared the sheep had again rejected him:

"Please don't be upset, sweetheart!" David again knelt before the animal and pleaded with her. He sniffled. More tears came to his eyes.

"Listen Dolly, I only pretended to fuck her. Honest!" He sobbed while holding the sheep's face in his hands.

"Marty needed to believe that her wildest dream came true. She needed to believe she could fuck me, Muscle Boy, and Bob. She needed to think she could control our entire company with her cunt. But that was never going to happen, Dolly. She had her mother's blood. She did not have pure Jewish blood. So, naturally, I tricked her. You watched me use Muscle Boy in my stead, Dolly. You saw that I didn't do anything with her sex part. She meant nothing to me. Honest! I never cared for her like I care for you." He begged the sheep to believe that his love for the animal was beyond question.

"I apologize if that sacrifice upset you." He gripped her ears again, and looked sincerely into the animal's eyes. Dolly returned his gaze while chewing her grass.

"Honestly, Dolly," David pleaded. *"She was disgusting; not beautiful like you. I never would have entered her female part. Honest! Listening to her talk about whoring made me certain that I needed to get rid of her. She had an upside-down view of life."* He chuckled again. By disparaging Marty, David sought to ingratiate himself to Dolly. His delusional mind had become incapable of distinguishing between human life and animal life; or between romantic human love and animal fornications.

"Dolly, we're just getting started. These things take time; but we are making great progress. We successfully bribed Wilson and his congress to get us the Federal Reserve and the Income Tax. Everything else is now falling into place. We will soon be taking back the lands of the Krai steppes from the Slavic hoards who stole them from

us. We'll get even with the Tzar and all the thugs who followed him, Dolly. I'm going to personally see that we get back the lands taken in the pogroms. Yes! I'm going to see you grazing on our ancestral land, Dolly; the land my great, great, great, great grandfather walked away from; when he walked for six thousand miles with his chair and all his worldly belongings strapped onto his back.

"I've even talked with Don about my plans for revenge, Dolly. He told me that he will promote me to Colonel in the Tiny Hat Army. He will let me lead our charge into Russia to retake our historic lands."

Dolly lifted her head. She stared silently at David while chewing her mouthful of grass. After a while, the sheep's silence disturbed David:

"What's that you say, Dolly? You're telling me that I'll get killed? You're saying that the Russians have tanks and armored personnel carriers and artillery and missiles and fighter jets? You think they can stop me from getting our land back?" David held Dolly by her ears and stared into her eyes to make his point. *"Don't let little details like that worry you, baby. We're going to win this fight. We're unstoppable! Remember, we've got thousands of Cadillacs!*

"I'm going into the house now. The wife isn't home. But I have had a hard day and I'm tired. I'm going to watch a good fight; then I'm going to go to bed. I need rest. You sleep with the other sheep tonight. I'll bring you into the house tomorrow night."

David kissed the black sheep's forehead a second time. Then he disappeared into the house.

Three days later the phones in Plaintown were abuzz with the latest gossip about Marty.

First gossip:

"Did you hear what Tina and Leona saw? You didn't? Well, let me tell you. This is crazy stuff. They were on vagina patrol duty, trying to catch Marty fucking a husband. So, they followed her. It was

on a Saturday. Yes. She went to David Sustack's place. They watched the whole thing from the grassy knoll in the meadow near his barn."

Second gossip:

"Did she fuck him? That would be weird. I heard he was gay."

Third gossip:

"I know she works for him. That would be just like her to fuck her boss. She's disgusting. No morality at all. Not a twinge of guilt or a second of hesitation over fucking another woman's man. It's casual and normal for her. No concerns for consequences. None. How are hard working women supposed to get ahead when they need to compete with a woman who does that?"

First gossip:

"No, no, no! Listen! Tina said Marty lay naked on hay bales in the missionary position for about two full hours while David rubbed her legs and stared at her Vag. They were getting bored, watching the two of them; but then David put this exquisite diamond chocker neckless on her. He left her for a few minutes then came back with a handkerchief for her nose. Leona thinks she needed to blow her nose.

"Hay bales can cause allergies. She probably needed to sneeze. This is where it got interesting. After he blew her nose David kissed her everywhere. He kissed her mouth, her arms and hands and her legs and feet, her breasts, her tummy and even her Vag. Tina said he kissed her like he was a crazy person; kissing her everywhere like he did. But then he settled down and just sucked her nipples for the longest time. Leona said he acted like an infant that wanted to be close to his mommy. Tina said it looked like he worshipped her."

Second gossip:

"Marty has that effect on men. But did he fuck her? That's the sixty-four-thousand-dollar question. Did Tina think he was trying to become not gay by fucking her? Tell me!"

First gossip:

"Tina thinks he fucked her. But she wasn't sure. He stopped kissing her after a while. He stood up and closed the barn door. Tina and Leona couldn't see anything after that. Marty just laid there in her missionary position while David closed the door. Tina thinks she was waiting for him to fuck her. That makes sense. She has no morals whatsoever. She just expects men will fuck her; and she wants them to. That's what's normal for her. Why, in one of her prn movies I saw her teasing the cross by slipping it into her vagina and then smiling and laughing about how sacrilegious she was before she began licking it, and before she began fucking several men. She's proud that she's ungodly and unholy. She's a determined sinner. So, I'm sure she got David's penis inside her, even if he is gay. Anyway, after the door closed, Tina and Leona stayed and watched the barn for a while. But they couldn't see anything. They heard David's pigs squealing about something. Then everything went quiet. They waited a while longer but they didn't see or hear anything else. They figured Marty seduced David and the two of them were inside the barn; fucking the whole afternoon away. Leona and Tina were too afraid to open that heavy barn door and look inside; so, they went home."

Third gossip:

"That's it? They just went home?"

First gossip:

"Yes, they went home. Oh, Tina mentioned that David's roses looked especially vibrant this year. She was tempted to cut some roses for herself and take them with her when they left, but she decided not to do that, in case David came out of the barn. So, they just sneaked away."

Second gossip:

"David does have spectacular roses, doesn't he? Frank Zell's flower shop sends a truck out to David's every few days to harvest his best long stems. I know, because my husband, Melvin, buys me a dozen roses from Zell's every week. Zell told Melvin that David's

roses are the best. I love how perky they are, how they sit up proudly on my dining table; especially how beautiful they are when they fully open. They are the best. They assure me that Melvin loves me. And they make me feel sexy. I love David's roses."

Third gossip:

"You are lucky to have Melvin. I envy you. I wish Melvin would talk to my Harry about Zell's roses."

CHAPTER SIX

Your bait of falsehood takes this Carp of truth (Shakespeare: Hamlet)

PATS

Bob was at his desk when he heard the door handle move; its slow downward motion was nearly imperceptible.

'*That's David. He never knocks first, likes to let you know it's his prerogative because he owns the Firm,*' thought Bob. But it annoyed Bob that David dispensed with common courtesies. Bob rationalized David's behavior as like a man's who was looking in on his '*son,*' but he knew that didn't quite explain it.

Everyone noticed the creepy way David opened doors. Some said it was due to his quirky personality. Others joked about it, saying David was mentally off center. He opened doors so softly he often went unnoticed by those on the other side. He often stood silently, watching, and listening behind a barely opened door, before entering.

David opened Bob's door a barely noticeable half inch. He peered inside and listened for a moment before he entered. This was his routine entrance, his silent pantomime act. It only lacked the ghoulish theatrical music that chills audiences.

'*He missed his calling. He should have been a government spy,*' thought Bob. His eyes met one of David's looking through the slightly cracked door.

'*Yep, that's him.*' Bob grinned. '*Always sneaking around, looking in on people, listening.*'

It had been a week since anyone at the firm had heard from Marty. Bob wasn't making as many sales calls as he normally did when he was in Plaintown. And he hadn't been on the road. He was transitioning. His renewed love for Barbara still had not erased his feelings for Marty. That would take time. He still had deep feelings for Marty. He understood her nymphomania. She was a troubled woman. But beneath her 'devil may care' attitude about men and her affairs, was her need for love. And that need had bonded him to her. He couldn't just let love go. Hour by hour, his concerns for her well-being grew. He was baffled and hurt by Marty's unexplained behavior. Mostly, he missed her terribly. Now, this morning, he agonized that he hadn't heard from her. His thoughts ran non-stop on his mental hamster wheel.

'*Did something I said offend her?*' Bob wondered. '*No,*' he concluded. He went over everything they said to each other the past few weeks. He couldn't recall saying or doing a single thing to upset her. He dismissed that possibility. Besides, she was a thick-skinned; fun-loving, outgoing sort of woman. If something bothered her, she would have spoken to him directly, face to face.

'*Was there foul play?*' he puzzled, '*But who would want to hurt her? Could someone from her past, a former lover or an estranged wife, intent on settling an old score, have harmed her?*' That possibility seemed implausible to Bob. Marty had been with him an entire year. She never mentioned feeling threatened. Yet, thoughts of foul play dogged him.

Marty had taken time off before. But never this long without calling anyone. Barbara and Susan were attuned to changes in office morale. They both noticed Bob's mood change. There were office whispers that Marty had fallen in love with Bob. Some staff members speculated that marriage gave her cold feet. They opined that she was too footloose to become a married woman; and likely balked at tying herself down. No one visualized Marty as a motherly, stay-at-home wife. She was a free-spirited butterfly. She often slept at Bob's place. And he often slept at her place. But she lived alone and closely controlled her privacy. That was essential Marty. The arrangement enabled her to manage simultaneous affairs.

Had Marty linked up with an old flame? Was she spirited away for a romantic vacation? Was she focused on making love at a romantic resort in Europe or the Caribbean? Had she eloped with a European prince or a wealthy Arab sheik? Was she ever coming back? Office staff members squealed as they speculated about the possibilities. Rumors ran rampant.

Just like that, she was gone. Her absence seemed plausible to the women who knew her the longest. No one bothered to call the police or file a missing person report. That would give the Firm unwanted publicity. But no one knew, for certain, the reason for her mysterious absence. She hadn't dropped any hints that she was leaving. The situation felt odd; even unsettling and a tad frightening.

But David was cavalier and non-plussed. He carried on his routines as if nothing changed. He assuaged staff members' concerns, chalking up Marty's absence to her penchant for carousing. He decided it was time to focus his attention on Bob. Today he sought to replace Bob's anxieties with jealousy. He would plant seeds of doubt.

He slipped into Bob's office. His stealth movement resembled someone trying to sneak unnoticed past a police stakeout. Quickly and quietly, he closed the door behind him. In his flair for the dramatic, David made every entrance appear to be an urgent, extremely secretive matter.

"Hello there!" David smiled his cherry salutation. *"It's been a week since anyone has seen or heard from Marty,"* he remarked. *"I*

thought I'd ask you if you know why she's not calling into the office or why she's staying away. Did you two have a disagreement about something? Did she mention anything about running off?" David wore a genuinely puzzled look on his face.

"I haven't heard. I have no idea why she hasn't called. I thought we'd hear from her by now," Bob replied. He was obviously despondent. Thoughts of Marty were always on his mind. He couldn't compartmentalize them. Worries about her invaded every aspect of his life. He agonized, sending his thoughts down what ifs, and dead ends. Nothing comforted him. Her absence tugged at his heartstrings, trapping his mind in thoughts of her and his hopes for their future lives, together.

"Do you know who saw her last?" David continued his charade.

"No. Barbara said she saw her about a week ago," replied Bob. *"Marty took some of her office things home with her. She told Barbara she'd be staying home for a while. I haven't heard anything after that. Shouldn't we call the police?"* Bob's voice betrayed his anxiety.

"Well, I thought of that," David tiptoed past Bob's logical inquiry. *"I talked to Susan about it. She thought we should hold off; take a little more time, just in case Marty's off somewhere and needs privacy. I haven't done anything. I figured if her mother isn't worried, we shouldn't be either. Women have a better sense for these things. I guess we should wait until we hear from her."*

"Why do you and Susan believe Marty wants privacy?" Bob pressed for an answer.

"Well, you don't know her as well as we do; or for as long as we have," said David, skeptically shaking his head while drawing Bob into his confidence. *"She's had some lovers in her past. She's a beautiful, spirited woman who tends to attract men. And she has been known to go off with one man or another and stay away with him for some time. She has a history of being quite the...... romper, you know."* David imparted the word romper into Bob's mind

slowly, emphasizing it while shrugging his shoulders and looking chagrinned.

Bob didn't like hearing about Marty's proclivity for love affairs, but he had to ask: *"Just how long has she stayed away with a man in the past?"*

"Hard to say, for sure; what with holidays and long weekends," said David matter of factly. *"I'd guess maybe ten days or so would be within the normal range of her absences. A week or two or even three weeks away wouldn't put her beyond her past romps."*

"This is above my pay grade. I don't know what to think," said a confused Bob while shaking his head. *"You and Susan decide about calling the police. I'd like to know that she's all right, though. I hope you two don't sit on it for too long."*

"Okay. Thanks for sharing your thoughts," David spoke in a reassuring tone. *"Try not to worry about her. You know how it is with some women. Men just kind of come and go into and out of them—into and out of their lives, I meant to say. Sorry. They get excited about a new man, but after some time he gets a little familiar or stale. Then, off they go after a new one. Some women never know what they want. I guess that's why we men call them cunts; heh, heh."* David's little chuckle conveyed his vulgar thoughts. *"By the way, I noticed your sales have slowed down some. Is that because you miss having Marty around?"* David was ready to move on from discussing Marty's absence. It wasn't like him to skip a beat.

"I think so. I'm very fond of her. She is a great help to me."

Both men told each other only half-truths. Bob wasn't about to tell David he intended to marry Marty, especially now that she might be off with another man somewhere. No man likes admitting his girl was cuckolded away. There was also David's thorny executive memo about office love affairs. Bob had clearly violated Firm policy. David concealed his knowledge about Bob and Marty's plans to marry for a different reason. He was Marty's murderer.

"How about coming over to my place in the morning and meeting me at my barn?" David's voice turned suddenly chipper. *"There are some things I'd like to talk over with you. I like being in my barn, away from everything. It's a quiet place to think and work."*

Bob often met David on the way into work, when he was in Plaintown. They had a routine. They met for an hour in the morning to discuss the markets and everything that might possibly affect securities' prices; politics; economic policies of the Federal Reserve; cyclical factors affecting various industries; new technologies; women's fashions; weather; and anything incidental to the markets. David's invitation to meet was a relief to Bob. He knew he needed to put his thinking in order. He trusted David to help him with that.

The barn was sited far from the house near the western edge of David's western property. It was down slope from the house but high on a small rise above the duck ponds. Rain water didn't pool around the barn. It ran off and seeped into the duck ponds. The barn was in disrepair. It was a huge, ramshackle structure with old, weathered plank boards for siding. The boards were sun bleached gray and paint peeled. Faded traces of original red paint showed on some side boards. Colorado's intense high desert sun had long ago blistered and peeled the barn's original bright red. Faint patches of it bravely held out against time and the elements. Here and there, patches of original red peeked through newer layers of sun-blistered, peeling gray.

The roof was gray shingled, and in terrible disrepair. It had bullet holes in it from David shooting barn pigeons from the back deck of his house. Pigeons perched on the barn's roof became targets for David. Sometimes he hit them. He fed the dead pigeons to his pigs. He didn't bother patching the roof's bullet holes.

The barn roof also had a sizeable square hole in it, at the back of the barn's farthest distance the house. It was a water-rot hole.

It wouldn't take much to patch it. A two-foot square piece of ply-wood, some caulking, and an hour's labor would repair it; but David preferred to ignore it. The barn represented death and decay to David. He liked it the way it was. The barn's failing paint and its compromised roof reminded him that, like his barn, life was also a temporary structure. Death and life's progression toward it fascinated David.

Whenever David worked in his barn, from time to time he paused whatever he was doing to look up at the sky. He gauged the speed of passing clouds and the chances of rain or snow. He didn't bother listening to radio or television weather reports. Those took the surprise and the wonderment out of living close to nature. He liked nature and the simplicity of his barn. He also never wore a watch. He considered time watching and appointment keeping unnecessary distractions that intruded on one's abilities to think. Thinking was David's all-important activity. The barn's roof hole served its important purpose. From the position of sun's rays on the barn's floor David could closely gauge the approximate time of day, should he care to know.

The following morning, Bob pulled into David's driveway. He spotted David working in his barn; wearing his customary bib overalls, rubber knee high boots splattered with animal dung, and big straw hat. He'd obviously been working for some time before Bob arrived. Bob wore a blue two-piece suit and black wingtips. He joined David in the barn. Bob had never met David inside the dilapidated structure before today. Bob noticed its huge wooden entry doors were mounted on steel roller wheels which slid on steel tracks. One person could push them open or close without much effort.

Bob went into the barn. It took a minute for his eyes to adjust to the shadowy darkness. Naturally curious, he looked around. The barn had eight gated stalls, enough to hold eight horses or twenty sheep. In the back, opposite the side with the roof hole, was an indoor wooden shed. Its door was closed and padlocked. Beyond the shed was a small tractor. Next to the tractor were various implements for turning earth, cutting grass, and lifting things.

Up by the front sliding doors was a wall rack for assorted hand tools. Bob noticed a garden rake, a pick axe, a shovel, a post hole digging shovel, a machete knife suspended by a lanyard, several electrical extension cords, several hand saws, and coping saws; and a chain saw. Beside the rack was a large black anvil and a black mallet. On a ceiling rafter, near the front doors, a huge pulley and chain-fall hung down halfway to the floor. Bob noticed that an electrical line with a four-socket outlet appeared to be new additions to the barn. The outlet was mounted beside the wall rack. David stood by the front barn door. He tipped his straw hat to Bob after Bob was inside the barn, out of the sun. David was out of breath; perspiring heavily.

"Hello there!" chirped a cheerful David. *"I've been moving these hay bales closer to the front door of the barn. On wet mornings I just push them outside with my feet and close the barn door. That way the animals can get to the hay under the barn's overhang. They can eat without getting wet. And the inside of the barn doesn't get wet. On warm nights, they stay outside. When it rains or snows, they can stay dry under that open air shed over there, but they still need their hay. The bales stay dry under the barn roof overhang. Anyway, could you help me move some of these bales? I want them placed right inside the sliding door."*

Bob happily obliged. Soon, both men grunted in unison, lifting bales, and moving them close to the front barn door. After two bales, David took a break. He sat on a bale looking outward from the barn toward the house. Bob went to the back of the barn to get a third bale. As he slid the bale away from a stable wall, he noticed something red. It was a tuft of hair about eight inches long. Stooping down to pick it up, he saw it was attached to a dime-sized, circular patch of dried skin.

'*This must have something to do with the animals. A fox probably got in here and got its fur torn. It's curious. I'll hang onto it. I'll frame my fox picture and put it in with the framed picture. It will add a nice touch,*' thought Bob. He liked foxes. He often noticed them searching for mice in the meadows around Milltown. He returned to the task of sliding the hay bale toward the barn door. He put the hair plug into his pocket and forgot about it.

David joined him in the back of the barn. The two partners resumed lifting and grunting in unison as they positioned four more bales near the barn door. Their work finished, they took their seats on the bales and looked out at the barnyard. The goats played on a nearby dirt mound. The sheep were off grazing on grass stubbles—except for Dolly, the black sheep. She stayed close to the barn door. Occasionally she looked up at the two of them and stared, as if to make sure they were still there.

"*I have a few things on my mind,*" David began. "*First, there's Marty. I can tell from some of the expense reports that came in that you two spent a lot of time together when you were on the road, even on weekends—and you weren't selling on weekends. I don't judge people. But you are like a son to me; and I just don't think you should get too moonstruck over a gal like that. The fact of the matter is Marty is not a good partner kind of woman. She's a slut. There's something you need to know about sluts. They have a hard time staying loyal to one man.*" David looked at Bob with widened eyes, as if giving a warning.

"*You weren't thinking about marrying her, were you?*" He tested Bob for a reaction.

"*Well, what if I were?*" Bob bristled. He didn't want to lie about his intentions but he didn't want to admit them either. "*Even if Marty has had lovers in the past, people can change. We developed special feelings for each other. Besides, you're the one who encour-aged it by sending her on the road with me. What did you expect? She's got a brilliant mind; she's widely educated, sensitive, loving, and she's damn beautiful. It's hard to take my mind off her."*

Marty thoughts stuck in Bob's gut. He was a helpless fish that swallowed a hook. Try as he might, he couldn't shake those thoughts free. His emotions tugged him every which way; kept him trapped in a romantic fantasy land. He knew Barbara loved him. He had just professed to Barbara that he loved her in front of the faux offices of *'Monument Printing,'* whatever that was.

And he did love her. That was the truth. He also knew that Barbara's love was the right kind of love. It was love he could part-ner with and build a stable life; a love that brought children; and happy times together. And a lifetime of enduring memories.

But he couldn't quite make the emotional leap from Marty to Barbara. His feelings were immersed in his memories of erotic love making, pillow talk and imbedded passion. He suffered a male's version of nymphomania. He'd romanced Marty all over the country, made love with her five or six days every week. They'd laughed and frolicked together; seen, and done things together; explored intimate positions and made jokes together. She was an integral part of his life. He knew her ways. He'd become accus-tomed to her being with him in their bed at night. His feelings were still attached to Marty.

Reattaching those passions to Barbara would take time. His emotions were trapped between the two women. There had been no in-between time to let his feelings sort out. His heart needed a natural, measured transition; instead, Marty's sudden departure handed him a rupture.

He loved Barbara from that first day he saw her. Now, he finally had her. But Barbara demanded monogamy; and no Marty. That demand required that Bob cut his ties to Marty. He respected

Barbara. He loved the brilliance of her mind. He wanted a life with her. It would be a wonderful life. He knew that.

But he needed to bite through the line that tied him to Marty and time to swim away from her. Cutting that line didn't feel right or natural, despite Marty's apparent lack of fidelity to him. He was accustomed to Marty; her ways; her looks; her intimacy. He was not able to bring himself to break away. Love is a lot like a pasture cow that way. It meanders around like it doesn't know where it's going; nor does it care. It refuses to walk in straight lines and make logical decisions.

His mind often lapsed into fantasy. He still imagined a married life with Marty and a home filled with their happy children. He often longed to hold her closely in his arms; kiss her; make up with her, no matter what she did; then hold her even tighter, closer. He was steeped and slow cooked in his impossible irony. And, he didn't know that Marty was already dead!

David recognized romantic thoughts of Marty were lodged in his protégé's mind. Bob behaved as a man vexed. Sales were paralyzed. Not what David expected from his racehorse salesman. Intervention was needed to get Bob back on track. A kick in Bob's ass would only alienate his young partner. David understood finesse was needed.

"*I understand,*" comforted David. "*These things happen. People fall in love. But Marty's problem, if you call it that, is that she falls in love with every man, married or not. She has a way about her that drives men crazy. Sometimes she has several men after her at the same time. I don't know how she does it. I mean, I don't know how she manages to keep them from knowing about each other; but she does.*

"*I have an extremely high regard for Marty. Before you joined the Firm, she was the Firm's most valuable employee. And there's a sound business reason why I've always treated her with the utmost respect and dignity. Her mental acuity amazes me. Yes, she's stunningly beautiful and charming and all that goes with it. But what sets Marty apart from all other women I've ever encountered is the way her mind works.*

"You see, Marty has a very flexible, adaptive mind. Most women don't. Marty correctly perceived that America's morals were changing, and she adapted herself to that change. Few women can make an adjustment like that. Marty was quick to understand that most men are interested in women for the possibilities of having sex with them. Most men simply do not care how well a woman cooks, cleans house, or mothers children. Most men don't care about a woman's political leanings, her hobby interests, her social causes, her opinions about anything. Most men simply are interested in knowing whether a woman likes sex. By that I mean, does she welcome opportunities to fornicate and perform fellatio? Does she love to fuck and suck?

"Marty correctly intuited that the morality pendulum was swinging from Victorian times, when women wore pantaloons and bustles; when their behaviors were guarded and reserved; when their very survival depended upon finding an eligible male who would provide for them, to our modern times, where the pantaloons and bustles have been replaced by G Strings and Napkin bikinis. Marty realized that more men preferred the company of a bad girl, a girl who welcomed sex, to a good girl, a girl who married, cooked, cleaned, and bore children. She understood that the stigma of being a prostitute or porn star was disappearing from our culture. She got ahead of this societal shift by doing pornography and prostitution right out of our office. Marty has no inhibitions or moral hang ups. She's the ideal American woman success story. She loves to fuck and suck. I simply channeled her natural inclinations towards sales. It's a wonderful arrangement."

"So, you and she turned the Firm into a whorehouse? I that what you are telling me?" Bob's tone reflected that he was miffed and a bit cynical about the way David was denigrating Marty.

"Don't delude yourself. Every business is a whorehouse."

"But they don't all operate as fronts for prostitution."

"I disagree. In my world view, they do. Their advertisements are a form of pimping for the sale of the product or service. It's about extracting money from the public; same as our business. I'm just more matter of fact about it. So, when I have a world class asset, like Marty, I do my utmost to treat her with whatever she requires. The Firm's staff takes care of all her needs. We manage her appointments, arrange her accommodations and security, cover her hotel, travel, medical and personal care expenses; essentially, anything Marty needs or wants, Marty gets, free. When she's happy, I'm happy. Nothing is too good or too much for her.

"So, Bob, what I'm explaining to you is that, right now, Marty is probably away somewhere, fucking and sucking a man or several men. And she's likely very happy to be doing that. So, don't begrudge Marty her happiness. If you're going to be involved with her, you need to accept her as she is. Heck, you may even come to love her for being the way she is. From my limited research on this subject, I can tell you that most men would prefer to be married to a porn star than some goody two shoes, home with the kids, kind of gal. Most men would even applaud her promiscuous goings on and want to be a party to it. It's a phenomenon. It's more than a subtle change in mores. It's a complete displacement. With the birth control pill and access to abortion services, women are now free to pursue their pleasures and peccadillos. And society now applauds them for becoming porn stars. It's breathtaking stuff, Bob. Get used to Marty being away from you, Bob. She's likely very happy. Some man is probably pumping semen into her right now, as we speak. Be happy for her happiness. Don't get yourself worked up over it."

"And you're okay with this? It sounds so incredible!" Bob's face wore the look of dismay.

"Of course, I'm okay with it. I'm a businessman. I need to be flexible. There's nothing wrong with what Marty does. She loves doing

what she does. It brings in business. What's not to like? I encourage her to do more and more of it.

"Look, every now and then we get calls from upset wives claiming Marty is stealing their husband. We just listen. Then we tell the wives we've got nothing to do with what consenting adults do. We tell the wives to go back to sleep. After a while the husbands' get tired of Marty. I'm telling you this because you need to forget about her. She's probably off on the other side of the planet in some exotic hotel with one of her dozen boyfriends. And you can't afford to get your Kopf fedrayed. That's Yiddish for getting your head mixed up over some whore."

"Just stop it, okay?" Bob's blood pressure was rising. *"I don't want to talk about it anymore. Maybe I made a mistake. Let's just leave it at that."* Bob's emotions clung to what once was. He didn't know Marty's bone chip remains were already fertilizing the rose bushes that bordered David's barnyard.

"I understand," reassured David. *"Anyone can have romantic notions about a slut. It's natural enough. Women get into men's heads. That's what women do. That's how they are. It happens. Don't worry about it. It will pass. I've always wondered why Marty never made a run at me. I guess I'm just too ordinary, or maybe too old. I'm not young and handsome like you. Maybe she just figured an older guy like me couldn't keep it hard enough, long enough, to keep it interesting for her.*

"How was it? Could you keep it up?" David enjoyed eliciting images of Marty's whoring behavior. *"Did it help you keep it erect, knowing that she fucked all those other salesmen; or did knowing that about her make you want to hurry and wash yourself off?"* David sneered, as if he smelled his shoe after stepping in a dog's mess.

Bob recoiled. David's vulgarities were hurtful. But he had to admit that David was making a valid point. Since Marty's disappearance how often had he froze while looking at his phone, attempting to make a sales call? How often had his thoughts drifted away from business and locked onto Marty? Had he not sat and stared at his phone for long minutes at a time, imagining he was holding Marty's tushy cheeks in his hands, kissing her honey pot? Had he not often pictured her sitting naked on his lap, kissing him with her long, soulful French kisses?

Had he not come to think of her as a woman of pleasures? And had he not come to adore her for being the glorious whore that she was? Had he not felt joy for her while imagining she was pleasuring herself with other men's penises and tongues? Had he not felt guilty about concealing these thoughts of Marty from Barbara? Had he not told himself that he needed to snap out of his thought paralysis?

But he was stuck in it; mired in it; drowning his thoughts in her arms, her kisses; and her fabulous, heavenly honey pot. Marty held his feelings in her imaginary arms. And he knew he could not break free:

"That's all I can take, David, all right?" Bob's anger showed. *"Let's leave the subject. I'm sure we have more important things to talk about. What else is on your mind?"*

David understood that Bob clung to his feelings about people after they were gone from his life. Bob was softly human that way, unlike the insects that David identified with. Understanding behaviors was David's strong suite; the source of his tenacity. He had correctly identified love and sentiment as Bob's weakest traits.

Adult Bob related to events in the same ways that he had related to events when he was a little toddler, like the time he desperately tried to cling to Nevin, the dead man whom Bob believed was his father. That same needy emotion now bonded Bob to Marty. Despite her profligate immorality, she was a source of stability for Bob. She was there for him. She gave him intimate love. He couldn't bring himself to let her go.

'*He needs her,*' thought David, resolving himself to his task. To get sales back on track, he needed to turn Bob's thoughts away from Marty and crush his love for her. David knew his task would take time, resolve, considerable effort, and clever planning. He began by placing his hand on Bob's back, letting it linger there, momentarily. David reflected, while his hand patted Bob's back:

'*I'm doing what any good father would do when he sees his son distraught, believing that the love of his life is somewhere far away, fucking her brains out with another man.*'

"Life is on my mind, Bob—your life. Life is about time," assured David nodding his head. "*Time is the most precious thing God gives us while we're here this short while on Earth. I think about you quite a lot, Bob. I think about your future. You are uniquely blessed with a great opportunity to build a huge company and make a vast personal fortune. You will be tremendously successful if you'll keep a few things in mind.*

"*What I'm about to tell you is extremely important. Take my thoughts and words into your heart; bind them to your mind, and think of them when you go to sleep and when you wake up. Few men have the benefit of these thoughts. I'll give them to you because you are like a son to me. You are also my best, special friend.*"

"*This is to help me forget Marty, right?*" Skepticism rode Bob's voice.

"*No, I can't make you forget her,*" said reassuring David, while shaking his head and wincing, as if sharing heartfelt empathy for Bob's turmoil.

"*She is a woman, okay; and you are a man. This is about the heart. No man can change another man's heart about a woman. But you will come to forget Marty in time. That is how the mind works. After what she's done, you now know you can not trust her. Besides, the Marty's of this world are a dime a dozen, Bob. When you are on the road by yourself wholesaling products to brokers, you'll meet dozens of whores like Marty.*

"The world is full of fuck-crazy sluts who want to get a successful man into their bed. They hang around sports stars, movie stars, successful businessmen, and political leaders. They all want the same thing. They want to bed a man who will take care of them. Your biggest challenge will not be forgetting Marty; but avoiding new entanglements with the women you meet on the road. Your best defense is to keep moving from city to city; never stay in the same place too long. No, these thoughts are not about forgetting Marty. They are about helping you become a complete man with a great purpose.

"Most men go through life aimlessly. They are clueless because they have no purpose. Others take guidance from wives, who simply want their man to bring home a monthly paycheck. Those men are worse than clueless. Orientals call them 'salary men.' I call them dopes.

"But you are not like other men. You have talent beyond measure; and you have the benefit of my wisdom and guidance. You will be a Mensch among men; a leader." David's voice rose as if he was a boxing coach urging his man to prevail over an adversary. *"You will be the tip of the spear for the firm; our Kidon. Your presence and your words will lead other, lesser men to follow you and do as you tell them."*

"That's cool, David, thank you for the compliments," replied Bob. *"Say, tell me something. Why does that black sheep follow you around like she does? I notice the other sheep kind of stay off by themselves, but that black sheep always stays close to you."*

"I don't know why she does that. She's been like that since I got her as a little lamb. I brought her home on a cold snowy night and kept her in the house for a few weeks until she was strong enough to be outside. She's kind of taken to me, I guess. I call her Dolly. I guess she thinks she's special.

"But getting back to our subject, Bob, what I think we need to do is take a period of time, during which I will give you lessons on how

to think like a man. You've never had the benefit of that. And you need that to become successful in this world.

"What I propose is that, when you're in town and before you go into the office, you swing by the barnyard in the mornings. I'm usually out here with my animals. That's a good time for me. In the mornings, my mind is clear. I feel relaxed. I do my best thinking then, right here in the barnyard. What do you say? Would you be up for some executive coaching?" David gave Bob an assuring, fatherly look, convincing him that he had his best interest at heart.

"Sure, I'm all for that. I look forward to it. Thanks," said Bob.

"Good, it will be healthy to take your mind off romance. Compartmentalize that female stuff. Lock it up for a while and learn some things about the world around you. Otherwise, you will go through life running on emotions, like silly women do. Women don't understand how the world works. Don't let them influence you.

"These executive lessons won't take much time. When we're finished, you'll have the correct perspective about things that matter for men. I want you to be careful.

"I must caution you. You might get smoke signals from Barbara, the skinny Indian girl. I see how she notices you. She's a beauty. I can't figure why Marty would run away and give that squaw a chance to lure you into her teepee." David smiled a knowing smile and gave Bob a few more pats on his back.

CHAPTER SEVEN

What is better than wisdom? Woman. And what is better than woman? Nothing. (Chaucer: The Tale of Melibius)

Women are much smarter than men. They understand people and the way the world works. Men simply don't. Never let a man tell you otherwise. (Rosemary Ness-Bitner, author)

LESSONS

An intensive period of executive mentoring sessions began, whereby David sought to groom Bob for executive management. David asserted that the key to business success required an understanding of how to view the world and its actors, as they all played their respective roles in life's grand mosaic. By lesson topic after lesson topic, David imparted his pearls of wisdom:

Time, the First Lesson, according to David:

"Time is God's greatest gift to you," began pontificating David.

"You need to make the absolute most of the precious little time you have on Earth. When Adam made his colossal mistake of listening to Eve in the Garden of Eden, God punished him by commanding him to atone for being stupid and listening to a woman. He ordered Adam to work his ass off for the rest of his life. That's the world's first mitzvah, the very first order God gave to man was that you must work your ass off, so that must be really important. Also, you need to learn this key lesson from that bible story: Adam would have been much better off if he had never listened to Eve in the first

place. So, never listen to women. None of them know anything and they always fuck up your thinking. If you listen to women, you'll spend the rest of your life regretting that you ever listened to them in the first place; like Adam lived to regret it. It's okay to eat apples, though. They are good for your digestion.

"Anyway," continued David, "you need to be working every day because Adam listened to Eve, except when God gives you a day off every week. That's called Shabbat, or Sabbath. You get a break. You're supposed to go to Shul, if you're a Jew, like me, or I guess the rest of you are supposed to go to church or do whatever it is that you do when you get a day off. But, think about it: taking that day off or honoring Shabbat puts you in conflict with that first mitzvah. You're not supposed to get time off. You're supposed to work your ass off, remember? So, be careful. Even God tries to fuck with your mind and waste your time.

"You must always be on guard against wasting time because God is everywhere. Now I know for a fact that a lot of guys skip out on Shul to go to football games or just lie around and watch TV. I'm not sure if God takes you to the woodshed for not going to Shul, but he might. You've got to watch out for God. If you don't listen to him, he can really fuck with you. So, your first executive lesson is about time management. We need to concentrate on it. And I've got some great thoughts about it.

"Look, God lets some guys get away with watching football and goofing off on Shabbat. They don't pray all day and God doesn't kill them for being slackers, so it must be okay with God if you get the jump on these slouches by working on the Sabbath. That way, you're honoring the very first mitzvah to work your ass off and you can get ahead of the slackers who take the day off.

"That kind of contradicts the mitzvah that you're supposed to go to Shul on the Sabbath, but there's also a way to get around that. See? On Yom Kippur, we Jews get to atone for all our screw ups for

the whole year. There's a brief period in the service, right near the end of the High Holy Days, where the rabbi yells out:

'The gates are closing!'

"*That means you have a limited amount of time to get your ass to the Shul and pray for God to forgive your screw ups for the whole year! It's like getting the two-minute warning in football.*

"*I time that gate call to the minute. At the last three minutes of service, I barrel up to the Shul in my Cadillac and I skid the car to a screeching stop right in front of the synagogue's security guard. I jump out of my car, put on my yarmulke—that's Jewish for skullcap; then I scream to the guard:*

'I've had a life and death emergency, but I must get inside before the gates close!'

"*I throw him my car keys, and then I run like a banshee into the Shul. I'm always there, just in the nick of time. My rabbi is closing the curtain on the holy of holies, where he keeps the Torah scrolls. From the back of the congregation, I bow my head and scream:*

'Forgive me, God!'

"*I get on my knees and act sorry when I do this, in case God is watching.*

"*Then the gates close. But that's okay. I know I've made it. I'm good for another year. I've atoned. I'm forgiven. See? I don't need to go to Shul again for a whole year. The big plus about doing religion my way is that I don't waste time listening to weekly services. That's time I can use wisely, studying stocks.*

"*And, there's another plus. My car is the safest car in the parking lot. The guard watches my car because it's parked right in front of the Shul's entrance. Since I was the last guy in, I'm also in the back of the congregation. That way, I'm also the first guy out. I run out, jump into my car, and I blast out of there before the crowd jams up the parking lot. I don't waste time trying to get out of the parking lot. I race to the delicatessen where all the other Jews go. I get there first, every time. I'm first guy in line. I order a huge pastrami sandwich and I break the fast before everyone else. The point I'm making here is that you've got very little time on Earth to make money. So, if you can find little ways to cut corners to give yourself more time, then cut those corners.*

Another simple time saver is taking showers. You should just skip them. You'll save a good fifteen minutes every other day by throwing on deodorant instead. Think about it! Fifteen minutes a day times one hundred and eighty-two skipped showers on business days gives you an extra 3.79 days a year to do something important, like making sales! Over ten years, that's an extra thirty-eight days! Think of the advantage you get with thirty-eight extra sales days every ten years!

"Even when you go to the grocery store, make every second count. For instance, think objectively about those plastic bags they have on those little stands around the produce. They expect you to waste your time whenever you pick something up, like a bunch of carrots or a head of lettuce. They want you to get the carrots, and then walk around looking for a plastic bag. You're expected to take a bag and put your carrots into it. Then you're supposed to walk to the lettuce, pick out a bunch of lettuce, walk to the bag rack again, take a bag and put your lettuce in it. Listen. Don't waste your time being stupid. Remember, you are the customer. And the customer is always right. So, just grab the entire roll of bags off the first bag rack you come to; and carry it with you in your shopping cart.

"If there's a line in front of you at check out, don't waste your time standing in it. Only stupid people stand in lines. Walk to the service desk, hand them some cash for whatever you think your groceries are worth, then just walk out of the store with your groceries. The store expects you to waste your valuable time checking out every item. They like keeping track of their inventories; but that's their problem. It's not your problem. You don't work for them. You

work for you. So, just throw them some money and leave with your groceries. Let them figure it out.

"Apply relentless scrutiny to everything that wastes time. You don't have to shave every day. You don't need shoes that lace up; you can simply slip into loafers. You can eat sandwiches instead of going to restaurants. See? There's three simple ways to save time.

"Examine your driving habits. If you consistently drive ten miles per hour above the speed limit, chances are no cop will bother you because the cop makes more ticket money by nailing the guy who goes twenty miles per hour over the speed limit. Drive peppy on the gas pedal instead of driving like you're a slow-motion barge. You'll rack up extra minutes of time for making sales.

"Stop signs and red lights are there to be nuisances for dummies. They slow you down. At a red light, slow a little, look up and down the cross street. If there's no cop and you can beat it across the intersection before oncoming cars hit you, just go for it. You'll save a full minute or two. Beating five red lights every day gains you five minutes a day. Three hundred days of driving a year saves you twenty-five hours for making sales! See how fast the minutes add up?

"Driving in stop-and-go traffic is also a huge waste of time. Traffic wouldn't be stop-and-go, bumper-to-bumper, if there were no communists. The commies make silly rules about driving carefully; stopping when you have an accident; exchanging insurance cards, licenses, and registrations. All that paperwork is designed to waste your time and slow you down. If you have an accident, just give the other guy your phone number and take off. Let somebody else figure it out. If you're caught in traffic and there's a clear sidewalk or a shoulder lane, just drive on the sidewalk or the shoulder. Use those emergency shoulder lanes. They are there for people who value time.

"Unfortunately, the commies are taking over the country. They want you to drive toy plastic cars, powered by batteries, instead of real cars. Get an old Cadillac, one of those battlefield tanks they made in the 60's or 70's; or, buy an old Ford pickup truck. Those old Caddies and Ford trucks last forever because you can get parts for them. But the reason you need one is to scare the other drivers who see you coming. They'll fear you'll ram them if they get in your way. I own an old Caddie. It's a great car; a beast. I took a sledgehammer to its rear passenger doors; banged them in; smashed them really bad, so people can see that I don't mind having accidents. My car scares the crap out of people. That helps me cut in front of lines. My car is a valuable time saver.

"Here's another driving tip. On freeways there's a shoulder lane. You're supposed to stay off it unless there's an emergency. Well, an emergency is how you define it. Don't let the cops define it! You define what an emergency is. Squandering the gift of time creates emergencies. Suppose somebody is late to work because of traffic. Then maybe something doesn't get built on time and somebody ends up dead or injured, or maybe somebody can't get to a doctor's appointment on time and the doctor gets upset and goes off and plays golf, and then cancer doesn't get diagnosed in time. See what I mean?

"These communists want to screw up the entire world. You must stop them. Say 'no' to them. Defy them. Do not let them waste your time. There's always a way to beat them. Freeway traffic is one example. The ways you beat freeway traffic is either use the emergency shoulder, or turn on your headlights, blow your horn and ram into the back bumper of the car in front of you. Wave your hand wildly and scream while you do this. Other drivers will get out of your way. You'll save time.

"When you drive and someone cuts in front of you, just speed up and pass him so you get back to being the first in line. Your time is always more valuable than the other guy's time. I remember this red-neck cowboy. He had a brand-new pickup truck; it was one of those huge 'king of the road' jobs. He passed me; so, I passed him. Then he made a huge mistake. He tried to pass me again, so I rammed into *the side of his big fancy truck with my old Caddie. That got him. He went totally crazy. He flashed his emergency lights and waved me to pull over, which I did. He pulled his truck in front of me, kind of half on the shoulder of the road and half in the driving lane. I sat in my car and waited for him.*

"He got out of his truck and started walking back to me, like he was some kind of a super macho-man. He was wearing his cowboy boots and hat and carrying a baseball bat. I figured the guy was an image obsessed asshole moron. He thinks he's going to smash my windshield; maybe my head too. I waited until he got really close. Then, I gunned the car and drove straight at him, like I was going to run him over. You should have seen him dive off the side of the road. I blew the horn and flipped him the bird as I drove by. He was screaming and swearing. I just drove away. That was the end of it. I haven't seen him since. I didn't let him waste my time.

"There's one other important thing about driving. Occasionally, a cop will follow you and flash his lights. You know you're about to get a ticket, right? Tickets waste time, right? Well, there's a way around tickets. Prepare in advance. Buy ten or fifteen candy bars, take the wrapper off one and always keep it on the front seat next to your wrapped ones. Got that? I see you are nodding your head. Good.

"Once you know the cop is right behind you, slow down. Drive very, very slowly, almost imperceptible slowly. Slightly weave your car back and forth on the road, like you've barely got control of the car and it's hard for you to stay in control. It's okay if you bump into other cars or scare them off the road. Got it? Okay. Then, look for something to run into as your car slows down. Find a tree or a telephone pole, or someone's parked car.

"You need to go really slow while you do this, so you don't hurt yourself. Ram your car into your target. If you can't pull over because

you're on a freeway, just kind of gradually scrape your car against another guy's car. He'll stop. Stop near his car. Then, when your car stops, just fall over on your passenger seat, and rub the candy bar all over your face around your lips and make a big mess. A chocolate bar is perfect.

"When the cop comes to your driver's side window, just lay quietly on the seat. The cop will open the door and shake you. Act groggy, like you've just passed out. Then mumble: 'sugar, sugar, sugar.' Repeat that word 'sugar' a few times. Then, feebly point to a candy bar. The cop will think you have diabetes. He'll panic. He'll shove a candy bar into your mouth. You eat some of it, and then you slowly act like you're coming back to life. You thank the cop for being such a savior. Tell him he's wonderful. Tell him he saved your life. Cops love hearing that.

"Tell him you're sorry to inconvenience him from his important work. Cry a little. Tell him you've noticed there's something wrong if you don't get sugar occasionally. You've meant to see a doctor about it, but you haven't had time to see one. You've been working hard to make money to pay your back taxes to the city that employs the cop. You're trying hard to be a good citizen so the cop can get paid so he'll have money to feed his wife and kids.

"The cop will feel sorry for you. He'll cry, along with you. Offer him one of your candy bars in case his sugar ever gets low. He'll gladly let you drive away without a ticket.

"A great way to reduce wasted time is cutting in line when two lanes of traffic are trying to merge into one lane. The commie time wasters will always be happy to sit in the longest, slowest-moving lane. The correct move is to pull out of the slow lane, get into the fast lane or pull onto the shoulder; then, race ahead of all the slowpokes.

"Here's where having my old Cadillac is a huge advantage. Most drivers will let me get back into line when I've reached the front

because they're afraid I'll smash into their new plastic-toy, electric car if they mess with me.

"One objection to having an old clunker is that they use a lot of gas, but they really don't. The gas other people waste by sitting in line in their new mileage-efficient cars waiting to go nowhere is a cost for them and a time-saving opportunity for you. You just roar right up to the front of traffic lines and jam yourself right in there. Sure, some people will blow their horns at you. They're jealous because they didn't have the chutzpah to cut in line themselves. They blow their horns and scream to impress their wives. Ignore them.

"Always carry a ten-foot piece of surgical hose, a hammer, and a screwdriver in your car. If you forget to stop at a gas station and run out of gas, you can always stop next to one of those little plastic gas-powered cars. Punch a hole in its gas tank, and siphon off some gas into your car. If you get good at this, you can avoid gas stations entirely. That saves even more time."

Bob looked askance at David. *"It sounds like you make a lot of friends driving like you do."*

"Nah! I don't care about friends. I don't have friends; don't need friends; and don't want to make friends. Friends slow me down. They have ideas about things. But their ideas are never as good as mine. That reminds me. Avoid slowing down while you are driving, like when you come to an intersection and there's red lights stopping you, and you are back behind the first car at the red light. Well, say you're going to be turning right, or left for that matter, onto the cross street.

"You've got a choice. Sit there like a schnook or take the bull by the horns. If there's no building on the corner; only grass or small trees and shrubs, you don't have to sit there and suffer. Waiting is intolerable. That's accepting communism. Turn your car's wheels into the curb and gun your motor. That jumps your car over the curb. Cut across the corner and get where you're going while the

schnooks wait for the light to turn green. It's the Occam's Razor principle."

"I always thought Occam's was about using the fewest assumptions to solve a problem, getting the most likely answer that way." Bob corrected David.

"Well, you'd be wrong about that, or Occam was wrong. It doesn't matter. The whole point of Occam's Razor was to solve the problem. Get things done, see? My ways get things done."

"Okay." Bob shook his head in slow dismay. Arguing with David was pointless.

"Getting stuck in a long line of cars because some repair crews are working on the road and they've closed traffic to one lane is another situation you need to know how to manage. Most people just sit there patiently and wait for the line to move along at a snail's pace.

"But that's a huge time-wasting mistake. Make a hard right turn onto a neighborhood street. Race down the side street. Make a left turn at the first cross street. Race through the neighborhood for ten or twenty blocks. Turn left again and race back onto the road ahead of the schmucks who waited in line. You save time by using this tactic."

"But little kids could be playing on those side streets. Shouldn't you drive cautiously?"

"Hell no!" David bellowed. "Never slow down just because it's a residential neighborhood. That's just more communism. If some little kid is playing in the street, that's democrats teaching the kid to be irresponsible. Those kids have democrat communist parents who haven't taught them to respect the rights of drivers. Cars rule the streets.

"I'm not telling you to run over the kid. You shouldn't do that. That might cause trouble. It might also be expensive. There's a simpler way. When a kid is in the street, just drive around him. Bounce the curb and drive your car through the kid's front yard.*

"Don't even slow down. The kid won't notice anything. You might tear out some bushes and flowers, maybe knock the kid's toys over; maybe put tire track ruts through the yard, but that doesn't matter. The important thing is saving time. The key to executing this maneuver successfully is taking the curb one wheel at a time. Don't knock your car out of alignment."

"That's quite a lesson. I never would have thought of it." Bob was dumbstruck at the lengths David would go to avoid slowing down.

"I'm teaching you valuable tactics," assured David. *"The more you use my methods the more you'll appreciate them.*

"Here's another one that keeps you ahead of communist time wasters: intimidation. Add it to your repertoire. We've discussed time wasters for a while now. I want to make sure you're getting the concept, so answer me:

"When you see a bunch of people running a marathon to raise money for breast cancer, crippled kids, multiple sclerosis, or to commemorate a historic event, like the Boston Marathon, what do most people see?"

"Well, everybody sees a worthy cause and public participation, a community bonding sort of thing." replied Bob.

"Exactly," exclaimed David, *"but that's not what's really going on. Those are communist community organizer programs designed to dull peoples' minds and lull them into la-la land. The real goal is to disrupt commerce, snarl traffic, and keep people from thinking about making money; making them more dependent on the state. They want people voting socialist because socialism legitimizes theft from hard workers and giving free stuff to lazy communist shitheads. That's insane. It's not what God wants. It's about destroying the work ethic and justifying lazy dependence."*

Bob's glance filled the air with skepticism. *"But these things are done on weekends, when people aren't working."*

"You've missed the point," scoffed David, *"Torah says we're supposed to work for six days, not five. God worked for six days. Who*

do these people think they are, anyway? Do they think they deserve a bigger break than God? God worked his ass off for six entire days; then God rested. He didn't run marathons on his day off. There's nothing in the Torah about God running marathons. So, you see, those events are about justifying idleness. That's all communism is: idleness. Now that you know what you're up against, here's how you deal with it:

"In my car's trunk are two red flags on little flagpoles. I also keep a flashing red emergency light that plugs into the car's cigarette lighter. On the passenger side floor, I keep a bullhorn. When I see a marathon or a parade; anything designed by communists to slow me down, I take them head-on.

"I get my flags out of the trunk and put them in holders mounted on my car's inside roof headliner, just inside the car's rear windows. Those flags stick out, making the car twice as wide as it is. I plug my red emergency light into the cigarette lighter and stick it on the car's roof. Last, but most important, I grab my bullhorn. Now I'm ready to take on the commies. I flip on my flashing red emergency light and my car's emergency flashers. Then I blow my car's horn and drive straight at the commies.

"When I get right on top of them, I roll down my driver's side window and yell through my bull horn: 'Clear the road! Clear the road, NOW! This is a civil emergency! Your life is in danger! Get off the streets, NOW! Go home, NOW! Lock all doors and windows to escape radioactive fallout! Take shelter in your basements, NOW! Cover your children with lead shielding and put up ten gallons of fresh water! Run! Run NOW! Run for your lives! Ahhh, the Russians are here! They're here!'

"I have all of this written on a little three-by-five card which I keep in the glove box, so when I come up against communist crazies, I'm prepared. I know exactly what to say. I have another variation of my 'Get Off The Road Now' program, based upon an imminent

meteor impact. I tell them to get into their cars and drive out of the city as fast as possible. Come to think of it, I should get ones made up for a tornado strike and a Chinese attack, too. Anyway, can you see what I'm talking about? Your time is more important than their efforts to waste it."

"What happens when you do these things? Doesn't anybody get hurt?" Bob thought what he was hearing was unbelievable.

"Nah. It's fun to watch them scramble. They run like cockroaches when you flip the lights on. Commies! Too funny! They pretend they are important. But they aren't. They're useless dead wood that prevents society from working smoothly. I've never run over any of them. But I should. They're worthless.

"After they run away, I turn onto a side street, take down my flags and flashing light, and go where I was going. Sometimes cops show up, but everybody is so hysterical and incoherent the cops just scratch their heads and leave to get their donuts. But if the cops ever stop me, I've got that covered. I'll just tell them I heard there was a big disaster on a shortwave radio transmission that somehow got picked up on my car radio through a freak atmospheric disturbance. That should work.

"The way I see it, I'm keeping God's law, except for driving on the Sabbath when I do this on a Saturday. For gentiles, Sunday is the Sabbath. That means I don't have any Torah rule violations when I run at them on Sundays. So, I'm good with God. If a cop stops me on a Sunday, I'll tell him these people attacked my religion, which requires that I work on Sundays, and they intentionally blocked my way. As a citizen, it's my right to use the road to get to work.

"Once a cop stopped me. He threw up his hands and drove away. So, I'm sure what I'm telling you is okay with the police, the Highway Patrol, FBI, CIA, NSA, the Homeland Security manuals, U.S. Army intelligence manuals, the Outer Space NASA Planetary Discovery Regulations Manual, the French Foreign Legion Marching Orders,

the South Pole's Penguin Regulations, Martha's Vineyard's Illegal Person's Get Off Our Lawns' Manual, and the Universal Dog Catchers' and Cat Neutering Manuals. There are zillions of communist rules designed to waste your time. But there's always an exception. Think of that exception and save time. Think outside the box. God gave you time. Communists have no right to waste it. Thinking like I think will make you hugely successful."

At the conclusion of Bob's first lesson, David again patted Bob's back. Bob departed with the understanding the two would meet up for drinks later in the day. Driving on the downtown freeway Bob's thoughts again drifted back to Marty. His eyes burned from lack of sleep. He had lain awake nights, wondering, and worrying about her. Sleep deprivation and fatigue caught up with him. He perspired. His hands shook. Passion dreams intruded on his consciousness. His car drifted out of its lane.

A horn blast! An alarmed driver! He nearly caused an accident. The other driver shook his fist, reprimanding him. He took the next exit, drove a few blocks to a side street and parked. He leaned his head back on the headrest and closed his eyes. Frustration and desire consumed him. He was too exhausted to go forward. Thoughts of Marty were all he had now. She danced in his imagination. Marty was embedded in his soul. Her memory held his heart. He was beholden to her.

He sensed she was waiting for him; but where? She had to be there, waiting; if not in this life, in some future life. He insisted that was the truth. How badly his heart and soul ached for her. He whispered her name:

"Marty, Marty. Are you there? Can you hear me? Are you somehow with me in my mysterious realm of thoughts? I don't know if you can hear me; but I'm determined to reach you. I miss you.'

Tonight, he would make another try; try even harder than before. During his lonely nights, he tried to connect with her spirit soul. He felt that he had come close. He believed he felt her presence. He was certain she was nearby. She seemed close to him; then with him; in his arms again; but he couldn't hold her in the flesh; he couldn't touch her. But he *felt* her presence. She was there, all right. He knew she was with him. She was alive in his mind! Then, he would relive those precious moments, hours, and idyllic days when they were together; intimate.

That was his source of love now; his happiness. He had to have this source; allow himself these obsessive moments. Barbara had made him wait. He had accepted that. Then, he and Marty found each other. Now, he couldn't let Marty go. But she was gone!

Yes, gone. But not from his mind. He refused to move on. His mind hung onto memories of Marty; everything she said; every kiss they shared; every touch; everything they did, together. He believed if he continued loving her with every fiber of his being and soul, she would return. Magically, this hellish separation would end.

He tried to love her so much that his love alone would bring her back to him. He loved her that much. He fell into an ethereal love state; loving her without shame, doubt, or reservation. He loved her immensely; unconditionally. Whatever she did; why she had gone, he didn't care. Her intimacy captured him. He was hooked; but good. He could not shake free of her; nor did he want to; not ever. He would have her! David could not belittle his love for her. David could not deny him his obsessive mental happiness, even if she was now only a figment of his imagination, sitting beside him, here in his car. Yes, his mind saw her now. She was here. She appeared from out of his exhaustion. He imagined holding her close, kissing her.

"You really are here, aren't you?" he whispered. He rolled his head to look at the empty passenger's seat. The mind does funny things. Marty's image appeared. She was as real as life.

"Yes, I am here," spoke the figment. *"I am my soul. I will never leave you."*

"I want to hold you again." He spoke to her figment as if she had materialized in the flesh.

"I know. Hold me. I want you to. I want the same thing. And we will have that again; but until then, you must hold onto our memories." Bob wrapped his arms around his imaginary figment.

"I love holding you. I hold you in my memories."

"I know. I know your thoughts. I love how your memories hold me." Then the figment put her head back on the head rest. She sat there, facing him, smiling. She was beautiful and at peace.

He closed his eyes and remembered the many times he had undressed her; held her in his arms; how wonderful her naked flesh felt in his arms; how aroused he became while she sat naked on his lap; how his heart leaped and fluttered when she brought her mouth against his and kissed him with her soulful tongue-searching kisses. He thought back to the countless times he had rubbed her back and kissed her flawless white skin; worshipped the wonder of her being; all the times he had massaged her shoulders and neck muscles; and the wondrous feelings he had for her while he kneaded her muscles; the gratitude and appreciation he felt for the many times her beautiful shoulders and neck and mouth worked patiently to bring his penis to erection and deliver its cum into her loving mouth. She was Love's Goddess.

He thought of their love making. How wonderful it was; always heavenly! He saw it all again now. His mind relived what they did together. He would kiss and gently bite her cherry button nipples. She would laugh and giggle and tell him he was sending chills all through her body; making her feel like a naughty girl who was getting wet and anxious to make love. He would then kiss her butterfly wings on both sides of her upper thighs. He would place his hands on her legs beside her sex and hear her purr her giggling purring sounds while she smiled at him. She would flex her buttocks to lift her honey pot higher, presenting her love desires to him. And she would say to him:

"I'd love you to lick me. I'd love you to find my clitoris with your tongue and kiss me there until I come. Please kiss me there. I want your tongue inside me."

Other times she would hold her vagina open with her hands while she smiled. Then she would say:

"Am I making you hard, Bob? I hope I am. I want your penis inside me. Here," she would say as she took his penis in her hand: *"let me feel your penis touching my outer lips. Oh, that feels good, Bob. I feel you now. Let me rub you all over my sex. Do you like that feeling? Do you want more of me? I love the way you feel against me, Bob. I want you inside me. Let's make love, Bob. Let me guide your penis deeply into my sweetness. Ohhh, that's it. I feel you now. Come all the way in. Yes! You're so hard! You're making me feel wonderful! Let's go slowly for a while. I love how you feel against my clitoris. Yes, that's it. That's wonderful. Mmmmmm. Come close to me. Let me hold your face and kiss you. Hold me tightly against you. Let's go slowly and sweetly like this until you come inside me."*

She would kiss him with her searching tongue, run her fingers through his hair and her hands up and down his back, and she would squeeze his ass. He would move more quickly now.

"Yes, that's it, Bob," she'd say. *"We're one now. I can't ever get enough of you, Bob. I love you. I love you. Oh, Bob, fuck me, fuck me harder! I want you to come inside me, Bob. I want you to give me everything you have inside you. I want you to give it all to me. Ohhh, that's it! Ohhh, I can feel you shooting now! Mmmmmm, Mmmmmm. Yes, yes. Oh my God! You're really shooting! Ohhh that feels so wonderful! I feel your hot cum gushing into me! Oh, keep coming into me, sweetheart. Give me more. I want everything you've got. Fill me up with all your cum. I love it! Love it! Yes, yes, yes,"* she

would whisper, *"I do love it! I love it so much! Oh, that's so good! That's it! Push hard into me. Oh, that feels so wonderful! You are beautiful, Bob."* Then she would whisper again: *"I love you, Bob. I will love you forever. We will always be together."*

And he remembered their afterwards times. They would lay side by side, their naked bodies touching, still embraced, still kissing with soulful kisses, staring longingly into each other's eyes, touching, and kissing each other's faces, letting their fingers play upon the other's foreheads and noses; all the while giggling their love giggles and smiling. It was all so good; so wonderful. As his penis shrank and fell out of her, she would hold it in her hand and fondle it and his balls, all the while kissing him and telling him how wonderful he made her feel and how much she loved him.

She would then sit with her legs folded in front of her and lean back on the pillows with her vagina wide open and exposed. She would sit there, holding her vagina open, like an amazed child, watching his cum flow out. She giggled in wonder while talking incessantly about their love making and his cum; reliving every moment of it. Marty was sex obsessed. There was a craziness about her obsession; but he loved it, all of it.

"Look at all the wonderful cum you gave me, Bob. It's so beautiful and thick and creamy! See the way it flows so slowly from my vagina. I love seeing your white cum on my pink vagina lips. Does my vagina please you when she displays your white cum oozing out of her? Is she more inviting to you before you come inside her; or after, with your cum flowing out of her?"

"Either way, Marty," he would answer, *"she's lovely before and after sex. Seeing cum pooling inside her and oozing from her gives me a sense of awe, like she's triumphant, like she's defeated all the prudes in the world. To me, she's more glorious after sex than before."*

"I'm so glad you told me that. I've always felt that way about her. I think when she has cum pooled inside her, oozing from her, and

smeared all over her outer lips, she's at her glorious best. Tell me, my love; does seeing cum coming from her give you any urges?"

"Yes. It makes me love her more. I want to kiss her and give you orgasms all day long when I see that, even though you've just had one; but honestly, Marty, whenever I see your vagina, I am smitten. I feel beholden to her; like I must please her and you in every way I can, to the best of my ability. I want to make love with you and her every way imaginable. You hold my heart in your hand and she is glorious, like her name, 'Gloria' implies."

"I'm so happy we please you, Bob. I need to know these things as a woman. Tell me: do you like the colors of your white on my pink? I mean do you feel like I feel when you see that combination? I believe it's the most beautiful sight in the whole world, don't you? It's creation, Bob. We just produced creation. Do you know what I'm thinking when we're having sex, Bob?"

"I don't know," he would answer. *"I only think about how much I love you, how thrilled I am to hold you and to be with you. What do you think about?"*

"Oh, I think about our love, too, Bob; but I also think we should be butterflies."

"Why butterflies?"

"It's the creation thing we just did, Bob. Just imagine for moment that you are a big Monarch butterfly and I am a very sexy, fuck-happy female Monarch Butterfly. Then imagine that I have hundreds of little butterfly eggs inside me. Imagine that the sperm in your white cum carries millions of tiny creatures that want to get my tiny eggs pregnant. I think a lot about this. I believe we are strongly attracted to each other for a reason. I believe we have the spirit of butterflies inside of us. I think we want to be with each other in life cycle after life cycle and we want to have sex together every chance we get. Are you understanding what I'm saying, Bob?"

"I guess so. Butterflies live to fuck. And so do we, right?"

"No, silly, what I'm trying to say is that maybe we make love so much because we have a purpose, like the butterflies have a purpose. Maybe we make love because nature wants us to create life. Would you love to create life with me, Bob? When I look at your beautiful cum inside my vagina, I get this profound feeling that I'm seeing creation. It's a meaningful, incredibly beautiful feeling. I don't understand why hundreds of artists don't paint pictures of women's pussies with cum pooled inside them. By my way of thinking, that's the most beautiful sight in the world.

"Here, I'm holding my pocket mirror up close to my vagina so I can see your semen better. I love watching it flowing from my vagina. I want you to watch it with me. My goodness, look at all your cum, Bob. You are amazing. If we were butterflies, we'd have enough cum here for thousands of baby caterpillars. Isn't that a beautiful thought? Just thinking that way makes me want to have another orgasm."

"Yes, sweetheart, it is a beautiful thought."

"Bob, I've never had this much cum inside me in my whole life. I love what you just did inside me. I love how you pounded me hard and fast like you did while you were thrusting deeply into me. And I love the way you stayed deeply inside me while you came, and how you just kept coming and coming. I love what we just did, Bob. There's nothing better in the world than what we did. You are a wonderful, beautiful lover. If you and I were butterflies I know we would find each other and make hundreds of baby caterpillar eggs. I just know we would. We'd be inseparable. You are a beautiful man. I can't live without you, Bob. I can't ever be away from your wonderful penis. I love you, Bob. I really truly love you."

She had squeaked with a child-like pleasure as she spoke those words. He wished she was here with him now so he could hear her voice again. But her voice was only in his memory.

He recalled more from those blissful moments: how Marty would scoop up a portion of his cum and take it into her mouth, laughing happily like a playful child the whole time. She would open her mouth to let him see his white cum on her pink tongue; then run her tongue all over her lips in that delicious sensuous way only she could do. She was at her uninhibited happiest. Nothing about the things she did seemed vulgar or ugly; only mirthful and joyous. She was in love with the act of love making. She wanted their sex to always be beautiful, like breathtakingly beautiful mid-air butterfly sex.

Bob believed David was completely wrong about her. She was never a whore when they were together. She was a devoted, giving, loving woman, who loved only him. He felt her love in his soul. And he knew it was real and true. They had something special.

Watching her rolling his cum in her mouth and on her lips never failed to arouse him. She always opened her mouth while she did that. That seductive invitation to kiss her teased his lust even more. Her tongue and lips always moved slowly; always in control. She would then smile seductively, as if to proclaim there was no other woman who could offer him comparable erotic pleasures. She was sure she was right about that. She knew she was a gorgeous sex pot. She played to her strength. When she saw Bob's testicles begin to roll, she would take his balls in her hands. She loved to feel them roll, making new sperm. Often, shortly after their coitus, she told him she wanted to make love again. She was expert at understanding men's balls. She knew when they were ready.

She would then kiss him on the mouth, touching her shameless tongue to his and stroking his tongue with hers. And then she'd kneel over him, down by his knees.

"I want to make love again. We must. If we don't, I'll lose my mind," she would say with her mirthful laugh while fondling his balls. *"I want to make love until I come so much that I forget where I am. I need your penis back inside me, Bob. Let's put our little big man into his happy home, "*she would say.

Then she would lean back; proudly shove her luscious breasts outward. She would pick up a bottle of vodka; wash her mouth with the alcohol; and lovingly suck his penis. He never had to ask her to suck him. She just did it. She loved doing it. He always responded instantaneously, coming back to full hardness. She then tease-brushed her hair over his legs; driving him crazy for her. She made a hair tent above his penis when she did that. She would then kiss his penis; and mount it. She was never forceful; always gentle; watching his face patiently until she felt his penis was secure, deeply inside her vagina. Then she would rock her pelvis, rolling her vag back and forth against his erect penis with her slow rhythmic motion; gradually building herself up to her wild, twerking and gyrating frenzy.

And, this time, they would make love longer than they had before. Bob would stay hard longer than before, because he'd already come before. Marty would make non- stop love all night through. She loved sex that much. She didn't stop; only paused. During those pauses, she squeezed his testicles with her hand; writhed, squealed, whispered, and moaned:

"Yes, Bob. Oh yes, Bob. Fuck me. Keep fucking me. Ohhh, that's so sweet; so nice. You are so wonderful darling. You are marvelous. You please me so. Mmmmmm, Mmmmmm. Now, feel me. It's about to happen. I'm going to come again. Yes, here I am. I'm in a special place now. You're so good to me. I'm going to purr for you."

Then he would place one hand on her stomach and his other on her ass; helping her rock her clitoris; helping it swell, while it pressed hard against his stiff penis.

"Oh, FANTASTIC! You're hitting my clitoris just right,"

She screamed while running her hands through her hair. She was so hot she couldn't contain her frenzy.

"Ohhh, yes, my gates are opening," she moaned.

"Yes! Yes! I'm coming now," she squealed. *"I'm flowing and flowing and I'm not stopping. Purr, purr, purr. Oh, this feels so Gooood!*

Yes! Oh, fuck me, FUCK ME! Oh, Bob, you are so wonderful!"

She whispered now in a softer, more heavenly whisper. *"I love you so much. Oh, how I love you. Mmmmm. I love how you fuck me."* There would then follow silence.

Then, she would break the silence with her scream:

"Fuck me harder now. Oh! I'm coming so much! I love you, Bob. I truly do love you. I will love you forever. You are wonderful, Bob. You're such a splendid man. I'll love you forever."

As if by a miracle, he would come inside her, again! She felt his new warmth flow into her. That confirmed her right to demand him a second time. Her Cheshire cat smile devoured Bob. Her eyes told him she was proud that she understood his balls as well as she did. She laughed her triumphant pleasure-filled belly laugh and smiled her most lustful, satisfied smile. She told him he amazed her; and she praised him; telling him what a splendidly strong, devoted stallion he was.

Her eyes blazed with lust pleasures. She loved what they were doing. There was a magnificence beyond joy about it. And it always happened so naturally; so easily, like they were meant to do this every day and evening, together; forever.

"Your balls can produce an endless supply of cum for me. Can you see them turning, Bob? Those two little fellows must really love me. Do you think they love me? Could you please inform your marvelous penis that I want it to deliver all their cum directly to my cervix? I want to reserve their whole supply. I want their lifetime's supply; every drop they can possibly produce, exclusively for me; and no one else! Tell them that everything they make is all mine; forever!'

And Bob would dutifully promise her that he would give his penis its instructions, and that he would make frequent deliveries of her requested product. She'd kiss him and hug him when he promised her that. And she would often say *'I love you'* to him.

They would often make love this way a third time during their intimacy sessions, until Bob was spent. When they finished, she'd playfully kiss him while holding his balls.

"Could I please have another out of office appointment to love you again in the near future," she would purr coyly. Her eyes were the essence of serenity and childlike innocence when she made requests like that. Honest love radiated from her face.

And he would tell her she most certainly could.

Then they'd lie there, side by side, kissing each other's faces and staring into each other's eyes until they fell asleep in each other's arms. He remembered that special moment when Marty revealed her inner soul to him. She was a beautiful innocent child that day; saying beautiful innocent things:

"What do you think about while we're making love, Marty?" he asked while he held her in his embrace.

"Oh, I think of many things, my love. Before you enter me with your penis or your tongue, I think I am spreading open a holy altar for you. I'm thinking I'm inviting you to come inside me and be intimate with me. And I'm thinking how wonderful it will be if you'll accept my invitation. I'm thinking I want our love making to be very special and I want your thoughts to be inside my thoughts and my thoughts to be inside your thoughts, like we are praying together in the most holy of holy places.

"And when you stimulate my clitoris, I think we are so lucky to be together in our special intimate relationship, communing through love making and professing our commitment to each other, like what religious people do while they are in church because I believe what we do together is sacred.

"Then, when you come inside me, I think our love unleashes a force more powerful than Niagara Falls; I think our love can move mountains. And when I see your cum flowing out of my love temple,

I think what we have together is so wonderful and beautiful that even Niagara Falls can't come anywhere close to the majesty of what we have. Do you ever have feelings like that?'

"Yes, very similar feelings. I always feel like we've done something wonderful and good together.'

"I'm glad. I believe that, some day, artists from all over the world will see love making the same way we do. They paint so many scenes of naked women, and portraits of women's faces; but I've never seen a portrait of a woman's vagina held open with glorious streams of cum oozing from it. I think they are failing to capture the most wondrous, most marvelous, loving portrait of all. White cum flowing from a woman's love temple is the world's most beautiful thing, by my way of thinking.

"Sometimes I think I should leave sales and become a full-time porn star. Sometimes I think I would love to have men touching me everywhere, kissing me, biting my nipples, fingering me, and fucking me. That's how much I love sex. What do you think?'

"I think you would make a fabulous porn star. You'd have millions of fans. The whole world would love you.'

"Don't worry, Bob. It's just a thought that I hatch occasionally. If I ever did that, I'd make sure it would never interfere with us. I want to marry you and have your children. If I were a porn star, that should not change our relationship. Sex work is just like any other work. And what porn stars do is exceptionally beautiful and spectacularly glorious. They get a bad rap, like they are somehow lesser stars than movie stars in R rated or PG rated films. The world has everything backwards. What porn stars do is more beautiful and more meaningful than what actresses do in R or PG movies. Watch a few porn movies and think about the emotions they elicited. You'll understand what I'm telling you.

"Women who make porn films should not be called whores."

"No? Well, what would you call them?"

"Actresses, film stars; but not whores. Whores are people who pretend to be someone they are not and take money for it. Women who do porn are completely honest about what they do. They are loving, sharing, caring, good hearted women. They put their whole heart and soul into their work so their viewers receive great value for their money. They are conscientious and fun loving. And they help people become mature about intimacy and uninhibited over ridiculous preconceived misconceptions.

"Think about all the violence and criminal plots that the mainstream studios and TV networks sell. It makes people accept violent behavior. Sex is different. It doesn't kill anyone. Sex doesn't make people blow up buildings or shoot each other. Sex needs to become mainstream family entertainment. It's wholesome and good for everyone. Full length explicit sex movies should become the norm for family entertainment. What's wrong with a child seeing people making love? Nothing. What's right with a child seeing murders and mayhem? Everything. Violent movies and video games should be relegated to specialty venues.

"Porn stars should be elected to congress. There needs to be a tidal wave that washes away rigid values. Religions and temples that worship sex goddess porn stars need to be accepted, in the same way prostitution worship was practiced in the days of Baal, before men got their hands on religions and convinced everyone that monogamy was right and worshipping fertility and sex was somehow bad. There's no logic in that theology. The guys who spew that monogamy and adultery stuff are just wrong. Modern theology perpetuates wrongheaded thinking. There needs to be change. Porn stars should be ranked at the highest levels of society and honored in every community.

"Movie stars pretend to be someone else in their movies. Their movies are rip offs. Those movies don't stay with people. They don't

touch peoples' souls. But porn movies and porn stars do stay with people. They imprint images of love and help people reflect. Those images embed beautiful imprints in people's minds. Porn stars are modern day goddesses. They depict life and creation. Their work is glorious and wonderful."

"Why do you think that?"

"Because they inspire people to make love; and often; and with many different partners. That helps people lose inhibition and pho-niness. It encourages procreation; and life. Intimacy is wonderful and good. It's wonderful knowing that many people in your circle genuinely love you."

"And that they all love fucking you, right?"

"Well, yes. I believe so. What porn stars do is beautiful; more inspiring than a church service; more majestic than the Grand Can-yon or Niagara Falls."

"Artists paint the Niagara and the Canyon."

"Yes; but artists paint nudes of women, too; thousands of artists, painting thousands of women every single year. There's majesty in the female form."

"Agreed; no argument. You are majestic."

"I'm glad to know you think that. I try to please. Bob, do you think we could find an artist that would paint a portrait of my vagina held wide open with your cum flowing out of me, after we've had sex?"

"I'm sure we could."

Marty had been lying back, propped against the hotel's pillows when she asked him that. Casually, unconcerned, her legs spread widely opened; mingled ooze of juice squirts and semen dribbled out. Their joined creation progressed. Gravity pulled it downward, spilling it onto the bed's duvet. It puddled, then soaked through the duvet into the comforter which became its repository. Bob remembered thinking in that moment:

'How profoundly different Marty is from my mother! Mother would never have soiled a beautiful piece of linen. She would have cuffed me if she ever caught me participating in anything so egregious, even by accident. But Marty, who enraptures me with these feelings of love and passions for sex that I have never experienced before, is a very different sort of woman. I know her well enough to not mention the soiling to her. She does not care one wit about it. She doesn't put on airs. That isn't it. I am seeing her authentic mannerisms. She knows exactly what she is doing.

'She is much like a cat, marking its territory. She doesn't care that the hotel will have extra expense because of our soiling. She knows what she is and what the hotel represents. She is a sex goddess, enjoying a love making experience. The hotel is merely her servant and enabler. The arrangement permits her to use the hotel; and its room service; and its maid and linen services, as she pleases. Her pleasures become their expense. Marty is shameless that way. What would be unthinkable to Mother is ordinary practice for Marty. Her mind is poles apart from Mother's. Marty is an incorrigible whore; but I love her. How can I not love her?'

And Bob did love her, for all her ways; not just for the sex; nor for how she thought about herself and her place in the world; but in her every day thinking about what mattered and what didn't matter. Love, romance, high living, erotic romantic love making mattered to Marty. Nothing else did. Whoever bore the cost of her peccadilloes did not concern her. Whoever suffered emotional damages from her philandering did not trouble her in the slightest. Love making; erotic romance, never ending, never tiring, always interesting, always more creative, and imaginative than the time they had made love before mattered; seeking ever greater pleasures in all her ribald, romper ways that guided her life, mattered. That was this woman he loved so deeply.

'*She is so unlike Mother.*' There, that thought described it all. That was it! That hit the differential on the button. That's the why in the why he loved her. Character, morals, attitude toward life, he loved her ways about these qualities because she was the *opposite* of his mother.

Not until much later, after Barbara had pointed out the extent of Marty's involvement in pornography and her involvements with many other lovers, would Bob realize the true nature of her personality. He would then wonder:

'*How can it be possible that this woman, who loves me so sincerely and tenderly during the times we are together, is the same woman who relishes performing in the most ribald, lascivious erotic scenes in the world of pornography? How did sucking and fucking other men's penises become her joyful purpose in life? How does she compartmentalize her feelings about each of her lovers? And how is she so able to convey those feelings with the appearances of complete innocence and heartfelt sincerity? Does she have no soul? Or, have I seen and loved a soul that has no conscience; no moral compass?*'

Bob would ponder those questions for the rest of his life; but always, based on the relationship *he* had with her, he would conclude that she did truly love him and that she did have a soul. His compassion for her affliction grew stronger with his deeper understanding of her disease and its needs. And with his greater comprehension of nymphomania and its behavioral effects, he cherished and loved Marty, and his memories of her, even more.

Honest, innocent immorality defined Marty. Nothing about that trait was fake. Her cherubic glowing face and infectious smile convinced everyone that her whoring expressed her genuine love; so much so that while she committed her morality crimes, people automatically forgave her. They reflexively accepted her sociopathy; even embraced it and loved her for it. After all, she personified wholesomeness and loveliness. How could any indiscretion be held against such a bonhomie femme fatale; so pure and sincerely honest about every immoral deed she performed? People forgave; nay adored, the immoral nature of the sex goddess they knew as Marty. They loved her.

Guiltlessness more aptly described her serpentine conduct. Like snakes must devour rodents, fowls, and other reptiles to live, Marty needed seductions to feed her nymphomania. Snakes feel no guilt or remorse over their predations. They are natural acts that must be done. Marty knew no guilt or remorse over her seductions. They were acts equally natural, to her, as a snake digesting a mouse. Her demeanor and absence of continence about her lascivious romps betrayed no awareness of her improprieties. Of her immoral rightness, her conscience never had doubts. Even were she to be charged with her murders, her conscience assured her that she would never see jail time. She was confident a judge or a juror could be successfully bribed. She appreciated that she was widely known, loved, and adored. Surely, at least one juror would find her misdeeds excusable and look the other way; perhaps even become a lover. She was supremely confident that no jury would ever convict her of anything.

Thusly self-assured that she would never face consequences for her misdeeds, Marty answered her greater motive. She sought to add fuel to her immoral conduct. She was driven to meet the increasing demand for her pornography. She challenged herself to create and perform some act or film scene that would be even more lascivious, more ravaging, more explicitly tantalizing than anything she or any other porn star had ever done before. She appreciated that her viewing fans cheered her debaucheries; many obsessively so. She appreciated that many reveled in the news that she destroyed yet another marriage. Her anarchist fans applauded her unconstrained ribaldry. They adored her cavalier, unbounded revelry. Her serpentine mind received a constant stream of positive fan mail and film sales feedback; reinforcing her commitment to become more immoral and more pornographic than ever before.

After Barbara's clues about her, Bob purchased several of Marty's films. He marveled at her performances in the many scenes; ranging from lavish hotels to offices, hideaway homes and raw nature settings. He noted her unbridled enthusiasm; her eager thrusts; her bantering with her partners; her exhortations to release their semen inside her; her explicit screams and compliments at how many cocks, or dicks as she sometimes called them, were stroking her orifices; thrilling her to pleasured rapture. Her fondling of numerous testicle sacs, sucking many penises, and fornicating with many partners became seamless mental collage, spinning in his mind. He lost track of what she did in which movie; which positions she assumed; which scene she was in; and with whom she was copulating with. The spinning collage became a blur in his mind. When he closed his eyes, he saw endless, fast moving image frames of Marty's nipples being kissed and pinched; her vagina being licked and stroked; her positions blurred; seemingly endless streams of semen flowing from her vagina and onto her tongue. Every part of her body; every variation of every scene and position seared its memorable impression into his memory. His limbic mind was flooded; drowned in Marty's unapologetic, incorrigible wantonness.

His attentions returned several times to a particular scene in one of the films. He watched it, then went on to watch a different film; but something about that particular scene drew him back to it. It bore testimony to the eloquence of Marty's fellatio. She lay prone on a bed of soft, fluffy white pillows. She is the viewers' supremely reigning goddess, positioned majestically, gloriously above the entire celestial universe that labors eternally beneath her divinely insatiable desires. She is attended to by two small girls wearing white robes and angel wings. They kiss her forehead and cheeks, and brush her lustrous hair. One girl presents a large, ripe, red cherry to her lips. Marty kisses the cherry before she takes it into her mouth. She is ready to receive her lover.

The scene progresses to a close-up study of Marty's face and body. She is relaxed and self-assured in the rightness of the immoral acts she is about to perform. The positioning of her body upon the pillows messages that she is the glorious immoral goddess whose glorious debaucheries encompass the entire world, which struggles in banal ignominy beneath her breathtaking, insatiable whoring. She is the beautiful, heavenly purveyor of pornography; the pinnacle Siren of Lust who inspires romance and freedom; the one who causes men's hearts to sing, and who inspires their minds to write poems to honor their love and desire for her.

She awaits on her pillows for her partner while the camera pans to her lips. The camera now lingers; filling the film's screen with Marty's beautiful lips, those lips that her fans have previously witnessed kissing hundreds of partners and sucking hundreds of penises; lips that will soon perform the most eloquent fella-tio sequence ever captured on film. The camera knows that the fans have seen these lips perform before; but that doesn't matter. Each performance is new and beautiful; more intriguing and tan-talizing than anything their sex goddess has done before. The fans know that is the truth; their truth. They love her and everything she does.

Marty now purses her lips; moistens them with her tongue. The camera pans out to capture her full face and her confident, innocent smile. Clearly, her messaging tells the viewer that her lips are their conduit to heavenly nirvana; and her partner's path-way to guiltless, sinful bliss and freedom. Her coquettish smile invites him to cast off his yolk of all things that oppress him and surrender to her; to love her; to adore her as his change agent. The viewer looks upon her as the one to whom and for whom he will give up everything. She is the spark that ignites his limbic mind. She is the catalyst that causes changes in men's lives.

The penis approaches her face. She smiles; beholding it in obvious awe and adoration as her hand reaches under and supports its testicle sac. She then commences to lick its shaft, bringing it to its fullest hardness. And then, her lips kissing its grateful head, her enjoyment of sucking begins in earnest. After pleasuring the penis, she intuits when it is ready. She opens her mouth and smiles while receiving its creamy ejaculation. She opens her mouth, displaying her triumph over morality; then burbles the penis's semen as if to defy all things religious and holy; flaunting her casual, gleeful whoring as the antidote to unenlightened morality. Then, a transformation of sorts appears to take place. It transpires! There, on Marty's face! Bob sees it! It is distinguishable from all that has gone before. Marty is more than pleased with herself and her partner. She's more than pleased that she has extracted all the penis's semen. She is communicating more than her victory over mundane morality; more than her corruption of yet another male partner. It's in her expression! It's a radiant glow; a shining outward; a silent, perceptible communication that tells the discerning viewer, especially Bob, that there is something far more demonstrably heinous and wicked about this woman; this love of Bob's life; this heralded, unrepentant sex goddess.

Bob captures the message and takes it into his heart. He now knows that there is something more than desires for explicit sex that compels Marty to perform pornography. Bob only glimpses a hint of what lies beneath his lover's sex addiction; but he senses that the something more, whatever it is, is what Marty lives for. He intuits that she lives not for him; nor his love for her; but for some other, ultimate behavioral driver.

His curiosity causes him to examine the film sequence more closely. He pauses the film and views it, frame by frame, seeking a clue. There, about halfway through the penis's ejaculation erup-tion, before Marty sucks the remaining semen from it, the camera changes position to capture the penis's ejaculation from below. Bob notices that there is a poster on the wall, above the level of the bed. It is grainy and somewhat blurred in the film. He enlarges the film. Then, using a magnifying glass, he studies the poster. It is an advertisement for kitchen knives. A weirdness? It shows a woman holding a large blade in her hand. She is about to carve a prime rib roast with the knife. The company brands itself as:

'Purveyor of the world's most serviceable, longest-lasting knives, with the sharpest, most durable, unbreakable obsidian blades; sharper than razor sharp and much stronger than steel.'

Marty's communication of some deeper need that needed sat-isfying, and the poster ad for obsidian kitchen knives, tweaked more than idly curiosities in Bob:

'Why the shining glow from Marty's face? It was more illustri-ous; more serene and heavenly than her other smiles, after she had received ejaculations from her partners. Did the shining glow come from the set's lighting effects; or did her radiant illumination come from within her?

'Was she trying to silently communicate some secret?

'Was she trying to express that she had some compelling need that was even greater than her nymphomaniac needs to fornicate and perform oral sex?

'Did Marty somehow intuit that I would see this film, someday?

'Why was that knife poster in the scene? Did Marty want it in the scene? 'Was it a disguised plea for help?

'Was it something she wanted me to discover; or was it a mes-sage for everyone?

Bob had no answers to his questions. He felt chagrinned; asked himself what could he possibly know from looking at that film scene that he didn't already know? Without hearing what

Marty had to say about the scene; without her interpretation of the meaning behind the shining glow that exuded from her face; and without her explanation of the reason why the knife poster was in the scene, his speculations would be hopeless. He filed away his questions in his mind, thinking that perhaps someday, answers would be revealed to him. He returned his attentions to Marty's other films.

Through them all, there was one overriding constant: her childlike innocence and honest heartfelt belief in what she did. Her character was genuine. That plainly showed. The serenity on her face, after her orgasms, and the sincere compliments and love she showed her partners was authentic. Her immorality was convincingly expressed because the serene innocence and rightful rectitude of every sex act that she performed was the real her.

Bob acknowledged that he was observing his real, unvarnished, uninhibited true love. And he loved her. He knew the real her was enveloped within her disease condition. And he accepted it. All of it. And he arrived at an acceptance love for the disease that lived within her, because he understood that it had become an essential part of her. He could not bring himself to pass judgment on her conduct. He knew he had no right, no moral authority, to do that. He held her guiltless, the innocent victim of an intractable disease process.

His love now became spiced with a bittersweet touch of pity for her morally compromised condition. And he loved her even more than he had ever loved her before. While watching that film, he had achieved the ultimate, faith-based depth of love for Marty's immorality; feeling that same loving adulation that worshippers of the Christ experience when they contemplate his suffering upon the Cross. But what did his ardent spiritual love matter now? He could no longer have her; kiss her; touch her. He could only confess his love to his own memories and imagination. She was gone.

Part of Bob's mind knew that he would always go on loving her, even after he finally found his true love with Barbara. Over coming years his limbic zone would settle upon his new obsession: Barbara, and their life together. The tornado whirlwind of Marty had taken him to the heights of human passions. Then it had dropped him hard and cold. It left him to cope with his altered self. It would eventually blow itself out and fade in his memory, but never completely leave him.

But this idyllic Caribbean night, months before David meddled in Bob's love life, after he and Marty had shared a baked sea bass and had sipped lemon tea; when the sun dipped below the ocean and the twilight hour had just begun; Marty had smiled her innocent child like smile to his eyes, while her index finger slowly circled the rim of her tea cup. She didn't need to say a word. Bob knew what she was thinking. He understood what she wanted. That night would mark the beginning of his whirlwind.

That night in Barbados was when Marty gently revealed her proclivity for nymphomania.

"Maybe, we could ask around and see if someone would be willing to do that. But whichever artist painted me nude would have to sit and watch us making love first. No doubt he or she would want to join us in the love making, wouldn't you think?"

"Yes," Bob agreed, *"I suppose so. That would only be natural. But it might be fun too, don't you think?"*

"I'm serious. How would the love of my life feel if he were there watching me fucking another man or woman? Would you like seeing me moan while another man's penis entered me, darling? Would you feel excited seeing me suck another man's penis? If I'd cause you to have a jealous rage, I absolutely would not do it."

"Sweetheart, if you were happy and enjoying yourself, I'd be thrilled for you. I'd love you even more knowing that you were so secure that you wouldn't have any inhibitions about making love with others. I think we should look for our special artist."

"Okay, you are a love. I'm glad you'll let me play. Then we will find our artist. I hope we can find a very handsome one with a very wonderful penis. I think I'd have wildly erotic feelings, knowing you were pleased and excited to watch while I fuck another man; or, if I was with another girl and you saw us kissing each others' pussies. I believe that would thrill me out of my mind, sweetheart. You're so understanding! I'm such a fortunate woman to have your love. I totally love you, Bob. I love you more than I've ever loved anyone. I'll love you all my life. Do you love me the same way I love you, Bob darling? I mean, do I mean more than anything else in the world to you, like you mean to me?"

"Yes, of course you do. You are my precious love. I love you. You are more precious to me than all the gold and all the silver and all the jewels in the entire world."

"You're so sweet, darling. Then, would you do something very special for me?"

"Yes, of course. What is it?"

"I'd like you to kiss my toes."

"Why, baby? What is it about toes?"

"It's a feeling I have. You've kissed me everywhere else. I need to know you love all of me. I know it sounds crazy, but I need to feel that when I'm walking my toes are kissing you back, and you are always with me. Please, humor me. I want to feel your love every time I take a step."

"Okay my love. I'm kissing your toes. I love you everywhere, all of you, everywhere."

"Now, please I have one more request of you."

"Yes?"

"I'd like you to kiss me everywhere else. I need to feel your kisses."

And Bob did kiss her everywhere else. He began with kisses to her forehead, then her eyes and lips; and then her neck, then her nipples; and then, lower still, he kissed her stomach and her lower abdomen. And then her thighs; and still lower until his kisses entered her and disappeared inside her sex; and then he lingered there, kissing gently, lovingly, the sweetest part of her.

"That was beyond wonderful, my love. Could you feel how much I loved what you did? Could you taste my love for you when I gushed?"

"Yes, I felt you. I tasted your love. You were wonderfully precious. I love you."

"Do you? Do you love me more than any other woman in the world? Tell me you love me that much. Please tell me that. I think I'd die if you didn't love me that much."

"Yes, a thousand times yes. I do love you. I love you more than any other woman. I love you more than all the other women in the world combined. If God took the best of all of them and made one woman out of the best ones; that woman couldn't hold a candle to you. You would shine brightly beside her. The glow from your love would melt her into a puddle of nothing."

"Really, do you mean that?"

"Yes, love, I mean that, every word."

"Then do you love me more than you could ever love Barbara? Do you think you love me that much?"

"Yes, Marty. I love you, not her. I could never love her as much as I love you. Why are you even thinking this way?"

"Because I know she loves you. And she's very beautiful and very smart. A woman knows, Bob. She loves you, all right. She thinks I don't know, but I know. And I don't want her to have you. I want you all to myself. I want to make love with you every day of my life. I want to grow old with you, just the two of us. Can you understand that?"

"I guess so; but I've told you it's you that I love."

"You mean it, don't you? You're being honest, aren't you?"

"Yes, I do, honest."

"Then, hold me close. Hold me very tightly and tell me you love me."

"There, I'm holding you close. I love you."

"No, hold me much tighter than that. Squeeze me like our lives depend upon how tightly you can hold me. And don't let go of me. Hold me tightly and never let go of me. I need you to hold me close like that and I need you to tell me you love me."

"What's wrong? You're afraid! What are you afraid of, tell me?"

"I sometimes hear these voices and I have these dreams. I dream I'm being very bad. I dream I'm in an orgy making love with over a dozen men; and I'm loving every moment of it. And I sometimes dream I'm murdering people and having an orgy after I commit murder. People are watching me commit these murders. They paid money to watch me kill other people and have orgy sex after I do that. And I wake up frightened, wondering if you'd still love me after I did all those immoral things for real. I wonder if I'm a terrible person. And, if I am, could you still love me if I was such a terrible person?"

"Yes, a thousand times yes. Of course, I would love you. I love you unconditionally, no matter what you do. Here, I'm squeezing the stuffing's out of you now. That's how much I love you. A thousand times, I love you. I'm kissing you. Are you all right? You're crying. What's wrong?"

"I'm a woman. That's what's wrong. And I'm a woman who desperately needs you by my side no matter what I do, no matter how naughty my nymphomania makes me be. Can you understand that about me? And I'm a woman who loves you very, very much, much more than anything else in the world. Can't you understand that?"

"Yes, I'm sorry. I wasn't trying to make light of your feelings or your needs. I'm truly sorry."

"It's okay. I just got frightened that I could somehow lose you and I don't ever want to lose you, okay? Please don't tell me I'm just being a silly woman, okay?"

"Okay. You're never going to lose me. You're not being silly. Love is very important. It's the most important thing anyone can have. I'll always be there for you, no matter what, okay?"

"Okay. Just hold me close and keep kissing me and keep telling me that you love me. I need you to tell me that. I'm very frightened right now. I'm so scared, Bob. I can't tell you why I'm scared. It's just there. It's so real. I need to hear you saying that you love me, okay?"

"Okay."

"Bob"

"Yes sweetheart?"

"Bob"

"What sweetheart?"

"I need to say something."

"Say it."

"I need you, Bob."

"I know. It's okay."

"But I mean no matter what I do or whatever I need to go through I couldn't do it unless I know you're there for me and that you love me. I don't have anyone else, Bob. Without you I couldn't go on living. I mean that. It's true. I don't think I could. You won't think I'm being a hopeless mess for telling you I feel this way, will you?"

"No darling......, of course not."

"Bob, I need to tell you something. I want you to know this because we love each other and we should have no secrets from each other. You love me because of me, don't you? I mean you don't love me for my money, do you?"

"No, of course not. I love you for you. Honest."

"Then I need to tell you something. Marvin was a very intelligent man. He understood people very well. He used that intelligence to make a great deal of money. He was on the rationing board of the Roosevelt administration and he was an advisor to the President. Between Kristallnacht in November of 1938 and the deportations of Jews to the death camps in October of 1941, Marvin put in place an underground network inside Germany. From 1939 until January of 1944, Jews who had a family member that they wanted to get out

of Nazi Germany could use Marvin's network, for a price. Marvin's trusted operatives were paid bribes to pass a Jew along until that person got to Switzerland; then, the network got them out through Spain or Italy or Denmark. Payment had to be in jewels. Jewels were smuggled out via the network to Marvin. Marvin then made escrow payments to Swiss banks for the Nazis who took bribes to let a Jew pass through the checkpoints. The network made all the necessary papers for the Jew to change identity and gain safe passage. Then, as the war ended and for years after the war, Marvin used his established rat lines to get Nazis out of Europe. And Marvin made a second fortune."

"This is far out stuff, Marty."

"Yes, but I swear what I am telling you is the truth. I'm not making this up. This is not fiction. It's true. I have seen the proof of it. There's more. Marvin amassed in today's dollars over five hundred billion dollars' worth of jewels. Before he died, he arranged for Mother to have custody of the jewels. He knew Mother and David hate each other."

"Yes, he got that right. I can see it."

"Well, what he did was give Mother's service company custody of the jewels. That company bought land which is where David's farm is located. Marvin separated the mineral rights below ground and gave them to the service company. The surface rights and the farmhouse were given to David."

"So, David didn't buy the farm, like he tells everyone?"

"No, he's lying about that. David lies a lot. Get used to it."

"If you know that, why do you work with him?"

"He and I have certain understandings that I won't get into. It's not anything you need to know."

"You're sure about that?"

"Yes. But, here's the interesting thing. Marvin bribed the local mayor and the county commissioners to get a water well permitted

for the property. Then, Marvin had two huge duck ponds dug on the property. Those are not ordinary duck ponds, Bob. They are thirty feet deep. At the bottom of each pond, Marvin had a deeper hole dug another ten feet down. Into each hole he placed five steel chests filled with jewels. He then had a small shed built over the water well and placed a pump on it. This pump shed had locks that prevent anyone from interfering with the well. Are you following me?"

"Yes, sounds far out, crazy! Are you making this up?"

"No, I swear to you, my love, this is the honest truth."

"How big are these chests?"

"Huge. Mother said they're like steamer trunks, three feet long, two feet wide and one foot deep."

"And they all contain jewels?"

"Yes, filled to their brims. Mother said Marvin had amassed most of the jewels of Europe; more than the Portuguese took out of Gao."

"Where?"

"India."

"Oh. Why ten separate chests? Why not just dump the jewels down the holes?"

"Mother said that was Marvin's Jewish thing."

"Huh?"

"He had mental cross currents about his religion. Guilt; respect; tradition; preservation thoughts. And he had issues with all the restraints; all the stuff you're not supposed to do. It made Marvin a little neurotic. Mother told me the ten chests represent a Minyon in Marin's mind; like ten male Jews coming together to pray a service."

"But there are millions of jewels?"

"Yeah, but Marvin wanted them in ten chests. Like Mother said: 'Marvin was neurotic about his religion.' She thought, in his mind, it was his way to atone that he couldn't do more than he did. So, symbolically, he thought the ten chests represented combined prayers

of millions of Jews that another Shoah will never happen again. That was a very upsetting time for Marvin, even though he got fabulously wealthy because of it; and even though he and Mother had fabulous sex practically every day and night during those war years."

"And this is all true? You're not making this up?"

"Yes; all true. When we're back in Plaintown, I'll show you some papers I keep in a drawer. Mother gave them to me. There's faked passports; faked visas; faked travel papers; all with the Nazi stamps and seals on them. And there's letters of gratitude to Marvin from Jews who got out of Germany, thanking Marvin for their lives. It's very emotional stuff."

"So, the chests are still there, under the duck ponds."

"Yes, Marvin thought they were safer there than in a house or a bank."

"Because.........?"

"Because, after the chests were placed in their bottom holes, those holes were earth filled to the level of the bottom of the ponds. Then, Marvin activated the well pump and the ponds slowly filled with water. After the ponds filled, Marvin transferred the property's mineral rights to Mother and the property's surface rights to David. Are you getting this?"

'I think so. So, the duck ponds in David's barnyard are not about geese and ducks acting as alarms to keep intruders away from the house, then, are they?'

'No. Yes, they serve that purpose; but their real purpose is to alarm Mother if David ever has them removed or if the water level in the ponds falls. You see, that would tell Mother that David is trying to get to the jewels; or that, somehow, he got past the pump locks and shut down the water well that feeds the ponds. Marvin viewed the jewels as sacred treasures of the Jewish people, to be accessed and used again only in the event of another Nazi-like holocaust. Marvin was very concerned that what happened in Germany will also

happen in America. He believed antisemitism would rise up again; this time in America; sometime in the future. He was fearful that all American Jews will be murdered."

"That's pretty neurotic, Marty."

"No, Bob. Not neurotic if you're a Jew. It happens periodically when societies get stressed. Marvin was very sensitive to risks and risk avoidance. And he valued life above everything else; far more than land or jewels or gold."

"Jesus! This is heavy stuff, Marty. So, those jewels just sit there, available to bribe the next generation of Nazis; Nazis that spring up in America and start murdering Jews again?"

"Yes, until after Mother dies. They belong to Mother because they are below the surface. They are part of her mineral rights. She keeps remote cameras on the neighboring property which she owns and rents. The cameras watch the ponds with a continuous feed. Sometimes I believe Mother does things just to torment David. I think Marvin told David about the jewels; even gave some of them to David. But the major portion of the jewels were Marvin's gift to Mother with her pledge that she'd use them to help Jews escape America when the time comes."

"And your mother believes that time will come?"

"Yes, she does; because the Nazis are already here in America. They are in the U S and in the Americas. Mother believes, as Marvin did, that the Nazis will arise again. They have a compelling ideology that blames Jews every time their progressive socialism scams collapse."

"Well, then what happens?"

"At that time, Mother's estate, through her will and Marvin's will, are sworn by agreements to turn the jewels over to one of Marvin's most trusted temple's rabbis. But, here's the thing, Bob. David can not have any of the jewels. That's Marvin's way of tormenting David,

because Marvin did not believe that his son was an honorable Jew."

"And Marvin was?"

"Oh yes. Absolutely, he was. Marvin was a committed Zionist."

"But the Nazi rat lines?"

"Well, you'd need to understand Marvin. He saved many Jews. But Marvin also forswore vengeance. He told Mother that vengeance only begat more vengeance and the cycle of vengeance would never stop unless someone simply stopped being vengeful. He believed in understanding and forgiveness. He believed that people can be rehabilitated; even Nazis. He thought there might be some good ones; like when God told Lot that he would spare Sodom if there was a good man in the town. Marvin believed that some Nazis and Nazi children would become good, moral people. And he believed it was right to give them that chance."

"For a price, right?"

"Of course. Marvin was also a businessman."

"What if Susan dies before the Nazis have their great comeback?"

"Here's the interesting part. When Mother dies, her estate, that's me, gets one tenth of the jewels before I turn them over to Marvin's designated temple."

"So, you will become a multi billionaire?"

"Yes. I am Mother's estate representative. I suppose I could run off with all five hundred billion worth of jewels if I had a good, trusting husband whom I could share them with. And that is why I have waited this long to tell you this. I needed to know that you honestly loved me first, even though I am a whore and a prostitute and a porn star. I needed to know that, despite all my human flaws and my views about morality, that you really do love me, for me. That commitment of your love, for me, is more important than the jewels or all the money in the world."

"And, I do love you, for you. Honestly and absolutely, I do."

"I know you do. I love you the same way, Bob."

"So, the barnyard is a source of eternal frustration for David? He can't get to the jewels. He knows they are there, right? But if he tries to steal them, your mother nails him; and he gets thrown out of Marvin's will, right?"

"Right. Now you understand Marvin. Marvin hated David's guts."

"Oh, man, what a convoluted family relationship!"

"Yes. It's based on paranoia and hatred; not on love and trust. I want our lives to be based on love and trust, even though I have my nymphomania condition. Do you understand how important honest love is to me, Bob? It's the only thing in life that has any meaning. Whether someone is rich or poor, love is the only thing that matters. A woman must have love. Absolutely, she must have it. She must know that she is loved. Love is everything."

"Yes, I do understand; and I do love you, Marty. I love you with my whole heart and soul."

"I know you do. And that is how I also love you, Bob."

And then they held each other tightly and kissed with long soulful kisses. Bob whispered *'I love you'* into Marty's ear until she fell asleep. Serenity came over her face. She was an innocent trusting child, living in a woman's body.

'What is it about her that's so different?' he wondered. She was so different from anyone he'd ever known. She was outwardly so sure of herself and so trusting; but just then, so frightened and insecure, like a child afraid of the dark. Most people need to believe in something greater than themselves. It might be a religion, a political party, their military service unit, a team, a family, their country club, or neighborhood; something. But that was not Marty. As he nodded off to sleep, he realized what it was about this woman that fascinated him so.

She only believed in love and in herself. Her childhood taught her that she was the only person whom she could count on. He respected her for that. She had no other needs than that need to believe in herself. That and knowing that he loved her. That she could always count on his love was Marty's bed rock need. He knew she had just revealed something profoundly important. Some people would call their relationships: *soul mates.* He now understood that they had that. It was something even deeper and more closely binding than love. It was dedication; eternal spirit love of like souls; reincarnating, certain, endless love. Marty wanted his soul joined together with hers; forever. He felt good that she wanted that. He wanted that too. That night, Bob slept soundly.

His thoughts and his soul would go on loving Marty and her soul, forever; even after he finally discovered the loves of his life, in this life, with Barbara and their children.

Recalling their conversation from that night, Bob considered David's perspective about Marty. He believed David was terribly wrong. Marty was a sensitive, loving, complex woman; not a base, unprincipled whore. David angered him when he disparaged her. The Marty whom Bob knew was not consumed with carnal passions like blood-lust crazed Aphrodite; nor was she the destroyer of men's morals or devourer of descent families; and if she did, he didn't see it. She did not gloat and laugh about what she did; at least not to him. She simply reveled in her debauchery, naturally. He hadn't believed that she sneaked away to secretly whore behind his back. He never suspected her for the romp she had with the bikers, or her weekends away for affairs and porn filming. She had told him that she was off visiting her girlfriends or looking at new things for a woman to wear. That's how well Bob hadn't known her. He had looked at her angelic child-like face many times that night. He adored her. She was magnificent at managing her affairs.

Bob couldn't or wouldn't see those underlying deceptive traits in the Marty he knew. He believed she was kindness personified; a devoted loving partner. She cared deeply about the feelings of others. She had often told him how deeply she cared about his feelings. He believed she only mentioned her desires to fuck others in front of him to casually let him know that she wished to please him by performing erotica to stoke his passion fires. He interpreted her utterances as loving, caring thoughts; never as expressions of selfishness or self indulgence.

He could not then imagine that his gracious, beautiful Marty was capable of a malicious thought toward anyone. She was his ideal partner: Sweet, caring, kind to everyone; loving freely, passionately, openly, and honestly. He wanted to join their lives in marriage. He imagined having children with her. He was convinced she would be a perfect nurturing mother. Now, sitting in his parked car, remembering her professed innermost feelings, his love flames reached intensities which he'd never known before.

It was inconceivable to Bob that she'd chosen to be away from him. There was no reason. He had told her that if she desired sex with others, he'd be accepting, even pleased with her. He'd assured her that he only wanted her happiness and would never be possessive. He would not be controlling like other men. He knew in his gut that they belonged together, even if she did have other lovers, as David had intimated. It was simply wrong for the two of them to be separated like this. His heart ached for Marty. He wanted her to come back to him. Only she could satisfy his maddening, unrequited passion; this horrible emptiness. Only she could fill that nagging void.

Bob's mind was in a terrible place. He couldn't grieve. He didn't know whether Marty was alive or not. He couldn't be angry.

He didn't know why she left or where she was. He could only hurt and ache inside. It wasn't fair. He didn't understand.

He revisited their past year, forensically examining every moment he remembered. Painfully, he dwelled on what they did during the times they were together: on the sands of Assateague Island; under the stars in the Shenandoah Valley; on Bar Harbor's Cadillac Mountain; on the sands of Barbados; in every hotel they stayed in; every dinner they shared. He related those places to every outfit she wore; every tilt of her head; every flutter of her eyelashes; every pursing of her lips; every teasing twist of her fingers through her hair; every suggestive wiggle of her hips. He saw her putting on her stockings, panties, and bra; and observed her, tantalizingly, taking them off. She brought out Bob's voyeur longings without fail, especially while she smilingly slipped her stockings and panties off.

He recalled how she smacked her lips with her signature smack-pop open-mouthed kiss, after putting on her lipstick; every winsome smile she flashed; every breath she inhaled or exhaled. He blissfully remembered how he adored her eye shadow; her blush; the way her smiling happy cheeks made her earrings dazzle; even the seductive way she slowly placed morsels of food into her lovely mouth. He held each of those images in his mind, hoping that remembering them would make them become real again; wishing that he could once more press his face deeply into her soft, scented breasts; lose his mind in her closeness; wrap his arms around her and hold her more tightly than he'd ever held her before.

Her butterflied vagina often danced in the forefront of his thoughts. It enticed, seduced, and beckoned him to partake; kiss; enter; love; and copulate deeply, endlessly, and forever. It was as vivid now as it was that first day when she'd first reached out her hand and lifted his head. His chair-leveled eyes then saw her creamy, smoothly waxed honey pot. His desires had flared instantly.

He was smitten. His mind was mesmerized; his heart lusts were hooked. His obsession was instantaneous. He remembered the majesty of her revelation; her implied promise of wonders that were beyond anything he had ever known or contemplated.

Now, smitten even more than he was then, Bob ached inside. He craved everything about her. Her voice echoed through his mind. Her laughter and giggles returned to his memories. They lived their imaginary lives within his thoughts. He could often hear her voice clearly, as if she were there, beside him, talking, whispering to him while kissing him. His memories placed her next to him, in the flesh. His life had become a surreal blend of imaginary figments and reality, a delightfully pained blur that he could not untangle. His breathing was often rapid, oxygenating him to a euphoric, nearly unconscious state. Yes, his soul mate was still with him. She would always be with him. He knew that was the truth.

Now, in his car, he looked at his imaginary passenger on his right. She possessed him still. She was smiling: more beautiful, more self assured than he'd ever seen her. He wanted to reach over and put his arms around her and hold her; place his mouth to hers. But before he could do that, her apparition spoke softly to him:

"We'll be together again, Bob. You must believe me. Our souls found their true loves. A soul is like the Aspens' root. It grows into a body, a tree; then when the tree dies it grows into another tree. It lives beneath all that we see. My soul loves yours, Bob. My root is now carrying my love into the body of a woman named Sheila. My soul lives within her body now. It waits for your soul to join her. The spirits told me your soul and your new body will join my soul there, in the body where Sheila lives. Our love will flame anew. We will be lovers again.

"My consciousness is now being absorbed into the consciousness of the universe where it will become part of the consciousness of the

eternal cosmos that was, is and will be. Your consciousness will also join the eternal cosmos; there it will find mine, and we will discover our love again and again, an infinite number of times. Love is the only constant, Bob. Love never dies. Do not be afraid of death, Bob. It's merely a part of life. It is a vacuous and meaningless contrivance that the Earth's misogynistic religious hierarchies use to capture and control human minds; but death truly is a meaningless concept. Love is the only eternal meaning. Life is the carrier of human love. Always allow your life to know love. You, your consciousness, and your love will have my love again. And my consciousness and my love will have your love again. I am speaking from beyond bodily death, Bob. And I understand that of which I speak.

"*You will know you are with me again by the way you feel when you are with me. You will tell me that you will love me all your life and you will swear by it. You will. And I will tell you that I will never leave you. I will tell you that again and again. That is love, Bob; and love is the eternal constant of life; and it's the only thing that matters. Do not be afraid to go on with life, Bob. Never despair. My soul is with your soul now and it will be with your soul always until the end of time. I love you.*"

"*Then I will find you and come to you, wherever you are. I will be there,*" said Bob. "*And I will love you more than I ever did before and know you better than I ever knew you. My lust for you burns within me, like a furnace fire that I yearn to fuel with even greater passions than we knew.*"

"*Bob, there are things I haven't told you. Before I met you, I was promiscuous and I had many lovers.*" The apparition spoke contritely.

"*I don't care what came before. Nothing could taint our love. I love you. That's all I know or care about.*"

"*I must confess my feelings, Bob. Hear what I have to say. Before I met you there was no place on Earth that I'd rather be than on my knees with my mouth around a penis, or lying on my back with a penis deep inside me. I was a promiscuous, shameless immoral whore and I loved every minute of my experiences."*

"I don't care, Marty. I love you."

"Let me speak. Whenever a penis lusted for me, I could not deny it, nor did I ever want to shun it. I craved to please it and make it lust even more for me. I wanted it to come back to me again and again. I loved sex and I thanked my spirits that they blessed me with my shameless lust for the penis. It all started as a refuge for a little girl seeking love. That little girl was me. I was often truant from my senior classes so I could be off with a boy's penis making love to it. Penises became the focus of my studies."

"Marty, none of those things matter to me, I love you."

"I know you do. That's why I must finish by saying what I must say. I grew to love sex and lust after penises, until my lust consumed me. I became totally obsessed with nymphomania. I couldn't stand being away from a penis. I couldn't help myself. I had an addiction that I couldn't shake and I didn't want to shake it. I wanted it to grow stronger because I loved it so much. Few people would ever understand it, but it's true. It's a real disease and I had it bad. I was obsessed with having sex, all the time.

"Then I met you. You were the love whom I sought and needed. I changed, Bob. I'm sorry it came so late for me, for us, but you must know that, in the final moments of my life, I did change. I love you now in the same way that you love me, with no thoughts of others. I am ashamed it took me so long to know that." The apparition lowered its head. A tear ran down its cheek.

"It's okay, Marty. I understand. It doesn't change how I feel about you. I love you."

Bob knew Marty had been with him, sitting beside him in the car. But, as suddenly as she had appeared, she was gone. He closed his eyes to hold onto his memory of her. He was furious that he was trapped inside his car, his office, his world. He wanted to tear all those confining barriers apart, go to her and race into her arms. But where was she? And with whom? Was she even alive?

"*Oh, dear God, please bring her back. I miss her so much,*" he whispered to himself.

His turmoil tumbled downward to that darkest place; where thoughts spin wildly:

'*Why did the apparition tell me to be unafraid to go on with my life? Has Marty left me? That could not be! How could the apparition know such a thing? What is happening? Am I going insane? Did Marty and I not know each other's souls? Had we not discussed our childhood abuses; how her mother's abandonment drove her to depression, promiscuity, and whoring; how my mother's endless beatings drove me to rage, depression, and my urges to fight? But together, we discovered our love and with the blessings of our love we had worked through all that. Hadn't we?*'

Never fully understanding nymphomania, Bob believed their love was stronger than any other force or factor in their lives. He trusted in that love and believed in it. They'd found each other's' souls through love and their love triumphed over all their obstacles. They'd sworn to each other that they would marry. What bond could be stronger than that? So how could Marty's apparition tell him to move on with his life? What did it know that he did not? Had she become tired of him?

Surely, she could not believe he had tired of her. How could she possibly think that? What final moments of her life was the apparition talking about? What could it possibly know? There had to be some mistake. He had always been dutiful to her. His passions for her were stronger than they'd ever been. They'd grown stronger with each day he was with her. His ardor for her burned hotter now than it ever had. He'd performed cunnilingus with her hundreds of times. He'd kissed her face and neck with adoration kisses more times than he could count. His yearnings to savor her passions never waivered; his yearnings for her only increased a hundred-fold more, every time he shared intimacy with her.

'So, what was it,' he wondered?

What had her apparition meant? How could he ever move on without knowing what happened to Marty, or where she was, or with whom; or why she was not with him? And where was he supposed to move on to, or whom was he supposed to move on with? Obviously, that was Barbara. He loved Barbara. He knew from somewhere inside himself that Barbara was his true destiny in this life. But they had not consummated anything. They'd shared kisses and promises. He believed their love and marriage were fated to happen; but he could not simply close his mind's door on his love for Marty and walk away from the many dreams that they had shared together; not without knowing what had happened to her.

His feelings seemed steeped in madness. They pegged wildly between yearning passions, fears, and hopeful anxieties. He tortured himself with fruitless searching. What was the reason for Marty's absence? Why must he and Barbara wait longer? What were these mysterious secrets which Barbara knew? Were the things Barbara had told him about Marty, true? Would Barbara make up an entire fiction about Marty's life? No, that didn't make sense. That would be out of character for Barbara. Of all the people he knew, Barbara was the most honest and truthful. But, why was he seeing this apparition of Marty? Was David's crass simplistic reasoning about women correct after all? David's opinion echoed and reechoed through his mind:

'All women are nuts…… All women are nuts…… All women are nuts.'

He'd heard David voice that opinion a hundred times, as if it were the gospel truth. He'd dismissed the disparaging comment as David's incurable misogyny. But now, he wasn't sure. Perhaps

David was on to something? He considered that possibility. But that didn't mean that he had to let a woman drive *him* nuts. But it was not a woman that had spoken to him. It was only an apparition. Wasn't it? Maybe it didn't mean anything at all? Maybe he should just ignore its message?

'*Yes, I will simply ignore it.*'

He would not let David or some imaginary ghost shake him from his logic. David *had* to be wrong about Marty. She would *never* go away from him just to tease him crazy. She wouldn't do that. She loved him. He was certain of it.

He craved Marty's essence like a herd bull craves the taste of estrus. He yearned for her passion, her thrusts; her writhing and her exploding orgasms in his mouth. Their souls connected in those moments. Their bodies reveled in them. He knew her innermost feelings of womanhood then. Their intimacy was a sensation that could never be equaled; of that he was certain. He missed that unbridled gushing wildness which she brought to their love making and he ached to taste her hot liquid lust again. It was all so deliriously wonderful. He wasn't ready to accept that she was gone. Even Barbara's taunting, implying that she was a much better love-mate than Marty, had not yet dislodged his thoughts of Marty. He wanted answers.

He was in no condition to make sales calls or do much of anything. He could not keep mind on the business. It dwelled in another world, in other times and places. Today it returned to Barbados. The moonlight was shining brightly through their hotel window. He remembered it as if it was yesterday. They'd had lemon tea and sea bass in a quaint little bar overlooking the magical sun set on the Atlantic. Then they had returned to their room before dinner. Marty had removed her black cocktail dress and black silk panties. She was especially playful this night. The moonlight illuminated their room as if it were soft daylight; making everything ethereal and magical. He turned around from his dresser and saw her in the way that he would remember her forever. She spoke as she laid back, her hair splayed over the pillow:

'Let's have desert to finish a splendid day,'

She smiled while motioning him to join her on the bed. She was positioned on the edge of the bed with her legs spread widely apart. Her butterfly wings glistened and shimmered in the softly streaming beams of moonlight. He framed that picture of her irresistible sexuality in his mind then. And now he recalled it; vividly. Her feminine wonderment was smoothly waxed. He adored it. He was smitten by the sight of it. And he salivated for its tastes.

His obsession for Marty's peach was akin to a cat's obsession with fresh catnip. His nostrils captured her wafted scented oils as she invited him closer. Her fingers parted her creamy white mounds to display her irresistible outer lips. The soft moonlight illumined her anxious juicy purse. It was a soft, opened heaven; welcoming him to lose his soul in her blossom flower. She seductively rubbed her fingers over herself, smiling widely; inviting him to come to her, bury his face inside her velvety peach; kiss her slavishly, adoringly, there; and surrender all his nights and morrows to her delicious immorality.

Bob knew he needed to get his mind off his dream fantasy and return to the office. But he knew that today would be another unsuccessful one. He didn't *want* to be at the office. He wanted to be back in Barbados, with Marty. His mouth watered, remembering back to that night. He would give anything to bury his face once again in Marty's glorious peach and dreamily lick her clitoris until her orgasm flowed. He wanted to do again with her what they did that lovely night in Barbados. He imagined he was again kneeling before her and immersing his face; once again lifting her up high above his head with his strong arms; then holding her delicious flower over his face as he lay her down on that bed.

She had shrieked and giggled. She was with her lover; obsessed. And she had loved it; loved him passionately when he dominated her in that possessive way. Now, sitting in his car, thinking, he would give anything to be able to relive that special night. He would again caress her vagina with his tongue for hour after hour while she released orgasm after orgasm onto his face; and then he would enter her welcome flower, make love with her, filling her with his semen, again and again. They had missed desert that night. It didn't matter. Their love making was better than anything the hotel could offer.

He stopped his car beside a bed of blooming roses. He lowered his window for fresh air. He decided the office could wait. He wanted to linger with Marty's spirit. Then, a battalion of playful Monarchs appeared. They fluttered amongst the roses; landing upon them; lifting skyward again; returning to a flower again. They fluttered from flower to flower, probing them like they were choosing between red, yellow, white, and pink; and then settling themselves down upon the roses, tickling each flower's anxious pistil sex with their thirsty proboscises. One butterfly seemed to notice his presence. It left the colorful happy riot and landed on his partially opened window. It opened and closed its wings rapidly and faced him, as if enticing him to continue his dream. He smiled at the cheery insect. Confident that he would not harm it; the butterfly jumped onto his arm. Again, it opened and closed its wings rapidly. He again smiled at his little friend and wondered:

'Could it be? No, it couldn't be; or could it?'

The butterfly then did something that sent chills through his spine. It crawled up his arm until it reached his cheek. Upon his cheek it deposited a teeny droplet of clear liquid paste. It crawled back down his arm, fluttered over to the top of the opened window, facing him again while rapidly opening and closing it wings; then it fluttered off to rejoin the other Monarchs. He watched it disappear in their kaleidoscope above the roses, leaving him to his thoughts:

'*That little creature carried Marty's spirit. I'm sure it did. It was saying not to worry, that I'd meet her again; perhaps soon; perhaps in another life. But it also told me to be happy in this life. It's gone, enjoying its life and it wants me to do the same. That's the truest form of love: wishing your loved one the best, after you are gone. That butterfly was Marty. She just did that. I know I'll see her again. How wonderful, to know that!'*

He touched the droplet on his cheek. It was real; not his imagination. He promised himself to never betray his love for her. He would defy her apparition. Wherever she was, whoever she might be with, he would think of her always and return his thoughts to her again and again. He loved her. He could never stop loving her. He promised himself that he would *will* her to come back to him with all the powers of his thoughts until she finally returned. He swore from his soul to hers that he would forever love her. If she was with another man, he would love her regardless; welcome her back and love her even more.

No man ever obsessed over a woman more than he. He drove on with an empty, sinking feeling in his heart. He'd find a way to live without her for yet another day, unable to think about her without interruption until evening. He felt his heart was torn from him. His reason for living was floundering. Should he confide his thoughts and feelings to Barbara? His instincts told him that would only hurt her. He didn't want that. He needed time for his emotions to settle themselves. They were captured like fish on a hook line. They needed to shake free of Marty. But how?

Readers with no interest in money matters may prefer to skip David's lesson on money.

MONEY, DAVID'S SECOND LESSON

When Bob arrived for his second lesson day, David beckoned him to come to the barn and sit down on a hay bale with him. As soon as Bob did so, David launched into his second lesson:

"Money is the second greatest gift that God gave you, after time, which is a terrific gift if you don't waste it. Without time you wouldn't have been born because being born took time. And you also wouldn't need to know anything because you wouldn't have time to learn anything in the first place. So now you need to learn about money, which is the next most important thing after time, about which you now know everything. But, before you can know what money is, you first must know what money isn't. When a man gets a paycheck, does that mean he's made money?"

"*Yes.*" Bob answered quickly.

"*No, it doesn't,*" corrected David. "*He hasn't made any money at all. When you go to the store and pay for something with a check or cash or a credit card, are you paying with money?*"

"*Yes.*" Again, Bob answered quickly.

"*No, you aren't,*" corrected David a second time, "*there was no money exchanged in the pay check or in the transaction, none at all.*"

Bob cocked his head and looked at David as if he saw an extra head. "*Well, are all these people, who work for a paycheck or who buy stuff with a check or cash or credit card, just nuts?*" he asked.

"*Well, yes, they are nuts,*" replied David. "*As a matter of fact, the entire world is nuts. I'm the only person in the world who has a sane mind about money.*"

"*How so?*"

"*Dad explained it to me. Woodrow Wilson is the problem.*"

"*But, he's dead.*"

"*Yeah, but he signed up the country for the Federal Reserve and the Income Tax and we're still stuck with them.*" David was excited. He spit out his words and drooled when he got like that.

"*But people don't think they're stuck. They like things the way they are.*"

"*That's going to change. The Fed will print so much money that their printed debt chits will become worthless. That's how they will inflate away the nation's debt. Noah tried to warn us about the Federal Reserve.*"

"*He did? I don't think there were banks in Noah's time! Wasn't his arc about saving his family from an immoral world?*"

"*No. There will always be immoral people. That's missing the point of the story. Do not smart ass me. I know what I am talking about.*"

"*Okay David. What was the Noah story about?*"

"*It was God's way of warning us about the Federal Reserve!*" David became animated, waving his arms wildly. He was about to launch one of his rants. "*God knows more than you know, smart ass. God knew there would be a Federal Reserve in our future before we even had banks. He knew that bankers would use their money lending mechanisms to create credit and charge interest for the credit. And he knew that, over time, the money these bankers created out of their credit generation would not be backed by gold or silver. God knew the bankers would issue 'cheat' money, or 'fiat' money as soon as they could get away with it, because 'cheat fiat' money is the most profitable money for them to issue. So, what God told Noah is really God's message to everyone. God is telling all of us that the bankers will run amok creating money in an unbacked, not backed by gold or silver, money creation scheme. God was not talking about a flood of water. God was talking about a flood of worthless 'cheat fiat' unbacked paper money. God wasn't talking about building a physical arc and loading animals into it. God was talking about loading up your household with real money, real gold, and silver; so, you could survive the inflationary storm of excess 'cheat fiat' money the Federal Reserve System banks would create."*

"Why would God care about the kind of money we use?" Bob chided David with his skepticism.

"When will you learn to shut up and appreciate wisdom?" David became rankled.

"Sorry. I apologize. But it's an honest question."

"Okay, apology accepted." David was mollified. *"So, here's your honest answer. God created gold and silver. That took a lot of hard work on God's part. There were tectonic plate movements, volcanos; all sorts of geological stuff that God made happen so we could have honest money, because we need to dig up money where the volcanos left it in the ground. So, God feels insulted by bankers who issue 'cheat fiat' money instead of real gold and silver money. So, God was telling Noah and anyone else who has the sense to listen to God, that the bankers will run amok and print 'cheat fiat' money until they send the economy into a runaway inflationary crack up boom which will be followed by the most horrific depression ever. Most people will be wiped out by the flood of 'cheat fiat' money and most people will drown in their debts and depression that comes with it. But if you can be smart, like Noah, and listen to God, you will build your ark of gold and silver money; and you will survive the flood of 'cheat fiat.'"*

"So, what happens after this 'cheat fiat' flood of money causes a grand depression?"

"People will not stand for it. They will want a change."

"To what?"

"To gold and silver backed money, the original money that Ben Franklin put into the constitution. See, Ben was smart. He figured

if money was honest the people would control the government and if money was dishonest the government would control the people. He visualized government like a three-legged stool, legislative, executive, and judiciary; but he knew the scheme of co-equal branches would fail unless the stool had an honest foundation to sit upon, which was honest gold and silver money."

"But that all got changed."

"Yeah, Wilson changed it. He was a dirty filthy cock-sucker. We need to dig up his body and throw it off a cliff."

"Why? He's dead!"

"Doesn't matter, everything is fucked up because of him. Everything that's wrong with America is Wilson's fault."

"But, David, he's dead!"

"That's not the point. We need a scapegoat. He's the one that needs to go off the cliff."

"But, in Jewish, your religion, the tribe used a live goat."

"Doesn't matter. It's his fault. He needs to die twice. And you need to stop back talking back to me and listen to me, because I know more than you do."

"Okay. I apologize."

"Good; now listen. Dad loved the song 'Louis, Louis' by Richard Berry. People think the song is about a lovesick sailor at sea, anxious to get into his girl's panties. Dad thought otherwise. He believed Berry expressed Congressman Louis McFadden's frustration with that wrongheaded Federal Reserve law. His song tells people to go back to how things were; back to honest money; back to silver coinage; back to how Kennedy wanted people to stay in control of the bankers. Dad told me the bankers got Kennedy murdered."

"Do you believe that?"

"Yeah, it's the only thing that makes sense. Dad always asked: Que Bono? Who benefited? After Kennedy was murdered, Johnson became president; bankers controlled the people with fiat money; the military

industrial complex got lots of freshly printed fiat money to fight the Vietnam War; and socialists got money for Great Society programs. The war and the social programs were gigantic wastes of wealth but they got the bankers more wealth and power. The military industrial complex machine got lots of profits; the socialists got programs to milk; and the American people got hugely screwed and sons and husbands got killed. Dad said McFadden tried to warn us about it.

"Berry's song pissed off the bankers. The bankers got Hoover's FBI to investigate Berry. The FBI portrayed his song as an assault upon morals. That was a ruse.

"The FBI didn't care about morality. Slimy, filthy, cock-sucking blackmailer J. Edgar Hoover oversaw the FBI. The bankers who run the country didn't want the public to understand the real meaning of that song. The public still doesn't understand the meaning of that song. Dupes still believe it's an immoral song. The bankers are great propagandists. They work the media extremely well and they use morality scams to deflect attention away from the real bedrock issues. It's classic bait and switch propaganda playbook basics."

"So, what's the lesson I'm supposed to learn from a song and stuff that happened years ago?"

"Behaviors, Bob. You need to learn behaviors. Champions for the people face uphill fights in a banker-controlled faux money country. People would rather believe liars who promise them free stuff than think about why anyone would ever give away anything for free. Social programs are not there because the government likes its people. They are there to buy votes and maintain power."

"But that happens everywhere. You can't change it. I can't change it."

"I know we can't change it. But get ready for it. The people will believe the liars without thinking, then the liars will tell them to blame someone else when things go wrong. Most human brains prefer sleeping to thinking."

"What's that got to do with money?"

"Simple, Americans are not going to know what money isn't until the day comes when they no longer have a country. Americans are a hopeless, lost people. They are being eaten from the inside out. China owns our political class. China is coming for America. They will conquer us. Meanwhile, a vampire squid banking system sucks Americans' wealth away and turns them into powerless debt slaves. This explains why a whore like Marty does so well. People and families are being torn apart by the system's stresses. They must run faster and faster; work harder and harder to pay the bankers and fund all the debts and government programs. Countries and interest groups are like neighbors squabbling over minor turf wars. There's rising road rage; burglaries; arsons; assaults; murders; and white-collar crimes. Everybody tries to cheat everybody else because a dishonest currency breeds dishonest people. People want instant relief from stress. They want instant gratification. They get drunk. They call whores, like Marty, so they can get laid and forget things for a while; things like that."

"Okay, I get that you like bashing Marty; but what's the lesson?"

"Don't sass me, Bob. I'm helping you here."

"Okay."

"I've explained what money isn't. Americans don't have real money. Real money isn't paper," David was happy to ply this subject. *"It's not a credit card balance. It's not numbers in a checking account. It's not what the government wants you to think it is. The dollar is not real money. It's a piece of the country's debt obligations, a debt chit that may never get repaid. It's a fraction of the debts that the country owes. The dollar is not redeemable in gold or silver. The non-money paper dollar currency is a fractional ownership of debts. You, using common sense, would not make the loans that the bankers make. They make loans for hopeless causes; political causes;*

causes that make no economic sense. You would never take back questionable debt paper for the rat holes that these loans disappear into. But bankers do make dumb-ass, politically motivated loans because repayment is guaranteed by the income tax. Repayment is based on political slogans; not reality; not economics. I'm afraid this grand experiment in socialist insanity will end badly. It's communism. Communism always fails badly."

"So, what should I do?"

"When you get paid, cash your paycheck. Then buy gold and silver coins and bury them someplace where no one can find them. Do not make a record of where you bury them. Bury them in lots of different places, and never mark where those places are. Never leave a record anywhere. You don't want anyone to find your records and go digging up your gold and silver."

"Well, that's kind of what squirrels do with nuts, David."

"Yeah, I know. That's because squirrels are smart."

"But they forget where they bury their nuts!"

"Some squirrels remember some places. They survive that way. That's the point."

"There's got to be a simpler way, David."

"No, there isn't. You better do as I tell you. America is going to hell, fast. The government must issue new debt to pay the interest on debts it has already issued, because the tax on the nation's income is insufficient to pay the interest on the nation's debt; and repay the nation's debt principal. When a country is that far gone the political parties stop working for the common good. They just start working for their party. Society becomes dog eat dog and Devil take the hindmost. People starve and freeze to death. When a country becomes bankrupt the common good becomes a pipe dream."

"So, I should buy gold and bury it? What if I need Dollars to spend?"

"You don't need Dollars to spend. The government and the bankers just try to make you think you need Dollars to spend. Just don't buy anything."

"But, how can I live without Dollars?"

"Figure it out. There are books on it. Move around a lot, skip out on rent payments, eat at food kitchens. You need to outsmart the system."

"You don't trust the government then, do you?"

"Hell no! Not for a minute! Political parties fight like dogs over scraps on a carcass, each dog rips out what it can while there are pickings on the bones. The Dollar, the Euro, the Yen, the Swiss Franc, the Canadian Dollar, the Hong Kong Dollar, the Aussie, the Kiwi, the Chinese Yuan, the Indian Rupee, the Russian Ruble, and all the rest of them are all debt chits in a worldwide 'screw the little guy' debt scheme. All these countries are insolvent. Honesty and morality sit on one side of a seesaw board and fiat money sits on the other side. When fiat ascends, morality and honesty descend. Your Marty does well because fiat money and immorality are ascendant now. But it's all going to change."

"Okay, well, then, what will be money?" Bob asked sincerely.

"Money will be gold and silver and nothing else."

"What about platinum, oil, diamonds?"

"Just gold and silver," David replied with force.

"How do you get there?" Bob was skeptical.

"Simple. Since the dawn of man, gold represented the god of the sun, God of daylight, the greater god, whereas silver represented the goddess of the moon, Goddess of night, the lesser god. Those concepts of worshiping gold and silver by relating them to celestial deities is ingrained in the innermost consciousness and sub-consciousness of mankind all over the world. Central banks use gold, the greater god, as their base plate bedrock asset to give them credibility with other central banks. See, when a nation fails, its currency becomes

worthless. Holding another nation's fiat currency as your own nation's reserve asset means you must assume that the other country's currency will not fail. That's a risky assumption and a poor bet.

"Gold can't fail. That's why central banks need it. Gold is for central banks like blood is for a vampire. They must have gold to live. They understand their gold can't default, like fiat currencies default. Gold keeps their nations alive; enables them to survive hard times. Gold exists as a reserve asset because countries know they can not trust each other. Upon their gold holdings central banks permit their member banks to engage in lending activity using government mandated fiat currency, paper chits with pictures of presidents on them. The banks always pretend that there is gold behind the paper that they issue for domestic money use. But that is not true. Banks always issue more debt chits in exchange for government obligations than the gold that backs their debt chits.

"Silver is the people's money. It's the lesser money for ordinary mud slops who are not central bankers. Silver is what people use when they realize their bankers are screwing them by foisting a 'paper is money, wink-wink, nudge-nudge' scheme upon them. Silver keeps people alive through hard times.

"'There's an old saying of the German Yids. It goes: 'You can fool some of the people all of the time.' That applies to the fools. The next part of the saying says: 'You can fool all of the people some of the time.' That would apply to Americans, a country currently populated with believing, trusting dummies. That also applies to the entire world because all peoples now use paper money. The last part of the saying is 'But you can't fool all of the people all of the time.' That's what comes next."

"You mean what the people will do when they realize they've been had?"

"Exactly right!" exclaimed David. "The day is fast approaching when people will see what money isn't. They will see elites as modern

imperialists. Modern elites don't use occupying armies like the Brits did in India and America, or like the French did in Indo-China and Africa, or like the Spaniards did in Central and South America, or like the Portuguese did in Gao (India), Africa and Brazil. Modern elites enslave people by getting them into debt; and then undermining the debtors' ability to repay by setting up competition for the project that the debtors borrowed money for to create the project. The NAFTA Treaty and Trans-Pacific Trade Partnership create cheap competition that indebted American workers cannot beat. Debtors see price declines for their products and services. Debts owed become impossible to repay. Debtors borrow more to stay afloat. The political class always sells out its constituents. Banker campaign contributions keep politicians working against peoples' interests. Labor works cheaply for the capitalists.

"Debtors are trapped, like coal miners in remote towns in the 1800's and 1900's. They worked their butts off. They had no transportation; little free time; they were always exhausted and sick. They shopped at the company store. They got little for their labor and paid lots for their goods. They were like flies in a Venus Fly Trap. They kept getting deeper into debt and there was no way out. There's a song written about those people called 'Sixteen Tons.' People will figure out that the currency they borrowed from the banks to live, to buy houses and cars, and to get a college education is just a stylized debt trap form of imperialism. Americans and America are trapped in debt, just like those impoverished coal miners were trapped in debt.

"Debtors experience the same emotions a cockroach has going into a roach motel. The roach feels great going in. It eats the poison; but then it can't get out. It dies. Debt is like roach poison. It feels good borrowing money; but then the interest and payback bites and kills your wealth by transferring your wealth to the bankers. What the debtor bought with borrowed money comes with a problem he didn't foresee. Maybe he bought a rental house, and it had termites.

Maybe he bought a vacation rental in ski country, and it didn't snow, or the economy dropped some and people didn't rent. The debtor becomes trapped; poisoned by debt. He can't get out of debt. He takes on even more debt to stay ahead of collections until he has no assets left that he can sell. Then he financially dies.

"People who buy these banker debts as investment assets, the high-yield investment product buyer yield hogs, can't leave the roach motel either. Police, firemen, teachers, and other public employees are all trapped in the roach motel because their pension plans buy debtors' debts. They will all get fucked. Those debts become worthless when the system revalues currency and its debts, relative to gold and silver; when the system returns to real money."

"Come on, David. These big plans have consultants. They study the liabilities; they plan for all sorts of contingencies."

"Blah, blah! Everybody bought financial product poison from the insects. They listened to the insects' songs: high yield, guaranteed, balanced, diversified, blah, blah, and more blah. It sounds great until the debtors can't pay; until there's a stiff recession or depression and the demand for everything collapses. Corporate accounting frauds become visible; debtors can't pay debt service and interest. The markets are an eight-lane freeway with fools racing in; anxious to buy all this lovely debt poison. And markets become a goat trail for mortally wounded investors and bloodied home owners trying to get out."

"David, who are you calling insects?" asked Bob.

"Financial planners who sell packaged products to dummies. They prey on the unsuspecting, like lice, ticks, leeches, and mosquitoes. All of them are sucking blood, the money, from people who don't understand the game. The people are dummied down by the financial media and the communist educational system. They believe their backs are covered. They believe they will always have a safety net. They think markets can always be controlled. And they're totally wrong."

David put his index finger to his temple, indicating that he knew best. *"The markets are being eaten by the lice. The markets just haven't collapsed yet because the bankers and their brokers use derivatives to keep the illusion of wealth going. It's a game like musical chairs. When the music stops; when the game stops, you must have gold and silver. Americans have been duped by the media; by academic monetary theorists; by underwriters who package the products and the insects who sell them. The public believes if they do as their insect tells them to do, they'll retire well. They won't. It's a fantasy.*

"The scam depends upon keeping markets levitated using derivatives and foreign currencies' carry trade, like the Yen Dollar swap. Banks borrow in Yen, use the money to prop up the market with high-frequency trades and by using derivatives; short down the Yen for a cheap payback; puff the markets; sell more product and get more fees. Scams need scam operators. Use derivatives, options, or calls to force a buy; options, or puts to force a sell; all to criminally suppress paper gold and paper silver prices. Banks and traders have pled guilty to criminal illegal trades to knock down the metals' physical prices; and then they pay their fines for their crimes; get the government's okay and its phony investigations to keep their illegal scam going. These lying thieves don't worry, the government has their back. The government needs the scam to legitimize the government debt chits. The game players stay in the D.C. swamp and get rotated into highly compensated positions. It's called the great game. America perpetuates this scam, or the system, as it is presently configured, won't function. These crooks that run the system look in the mirror while they shave knowing that they are fucking everyday Americans; knowing that they are filthy cocksucker dirt bags. They try hard not to barf at what they see."

"And it's all going to collapse, you say? Sounds like you're reading too much fiction, David."

"Yep, it will. Don't mock me. Count on it. I'll simplify it. Take an ounce of sugar, spin it into cotton candy. It looks big and wonderful until the kid takes a bite out of it. Then it's small; a real, sticky mess. That's a credit bloated economy, simplified. Buyers can't get out. The mess sticks to them, just like cotton candy sticks to that little kid's face. Once you bite into it you can't spin it back into the same size it was before. Retirement dreams are imaginary until someone takes a bite by trying to cash in. That's when they find out they can't have what the insect promised them. They won't get their money back, either."

"And the debt load? How is that a scam?" Bob was curious.

"If the people aren't taking on enough debt, or if they try to pay down their debts, the bankers force the country into a war. That's why we keep the military industrial complex around. Wars force the entire country to go deeper into debt. Once the bankers have a country in debt, they never let it out of debt. Bankers are like lice. Lice stay on a body until it dies and there's no more blood left in it to suck out of it. The only way out is to throw off the yoke of debt."

"How?" asked Bob.

"Buy gold and bury it where no one will ever find it."

"Even yourself?"

"Well, you need to have a decent memory. That goes without saying; but once your mind is gone you won't need gold anyway. So, it doesn't matter."

"Okay, David. I've got it! Thanks."

"No, you haven't got it yet. I'm not finished. Listen, as long as people believe that fiat currency is the same thing as money, you must outsmart the government. If the government can cheat by just printing dishonest currency, which is not an honest weight or an honest measure given for honest work or honest product or honest service, then you have to out-cheat the stupid fucks who vote to have a government that is cheating you. You need to be okay with that,

because by voting for a government that perpetuates fiat money, people are electing politicians who perpetuate a fraud on you; on your honest work. Got it?"

"*I think so.*" answered Bob.

"*Never cheat on your taxes—the government can nail you for that—but you can avoid getting ruined in the mess that the bankers have made. Avoid all the stocks they promote. Stock promotion isn't new. It's a way of taking huge gobs of wealth from idiots and transferring it to the already wealthy. Usually, it's done in stock issues that people don't understand. It's some high-flying technology or magical biology company that's going to change the world. I'm not saying these companies won't change the world. Some of them will, and you can even see it happening with some of them. The problem is they get heavily promoted beyond common sense and they may never make enough money to justify what people pay for them.*

"*When you hear everybody buying this or that company and the talking heads on TV are speaking about it all the time, gushing over their next new product or service, or about some wonderful crypto block chain currency that's better than gold; only you don't know where it is headquartered, so you can't serve them with a lawsuit for fraud, then its price move is likely over; or it is over enough to avoid it. I watch the talking head shows sometimes. They never make any sense to me. They talk about this neat new idea or that one, but never about the company's balance sheet or its earnings or its market size, as if those things don't matter. They just gush away and have their orgasms about some idea this company has. And every night it's some new story.*

"*Some women chatting about these companies on TV act like they're having orgasms. They wear sexy outfits and salivate over crazy stories about what this or that company is doing. When I was a little kid, me and my friends went into a closet and we all jerked off together. It felt good, but we never accomplished anything except getting ourselves excited. We never knew any more about anything than we did before we jerked off. TV show stock promoters are a lot like we were, when we were little kids; only they do their jerking off in front of a camera.*

"An example of a high technology stock that everyone got crazy about was RCA. After World War One, the government released airwaves for commercial use. RCA was there with their television sets. TV was new. And everybody was going to buy a TV. Information was going to open the world. Well, RCA stock went up. Lots, like 60 percent per year, for some years. It reached $114 per share, its split-adjusted high. Then leverage came out of the markets. People had to pay off their loans. RCA went down to two Dollars and fifty cents, a loss of 98 percent. People had mortgaged their homes to buy it. Brokers went broke on it. People killed themselves because they believed in it.

"Today ain't gonna be different because people, fear and greed are never different. Today, there is leverage everywhere. Governments, companies, and individuals are leveraged up to their eyeballs. When the markets resolve this craziness, you'll see dramatic declines in stocks, bonds, and real estate values. People will jump off buildings, just like they did before. When that deflation happens, and for a year or two afterwards, do not walk close to tall buildings. Someone committing suicide might land on you.

"The Western world is so dumbed down that people committing suicide don't even do that right. They know they are slowly being replaced by machines, yet when they commit suicide, they jump off buildings or shoot themselves. Just think about that. If machines are the enemy, why not get even on the way out? I heard Elvis Presley shot his TV because it bothered him. Every now and then an office worker or college kid throws his computer out of a window, or a football player throws his cell phone into a river. Those people are on to something! Enough with interruptions from technology!

"Take things a step further. Every shrink should tell their suicide patients that they can make the human population better off. Instead of jumping off buildings or shooting themselves, tell them to take a machine or two with them when they check out. Drive their car full speed into another car or into a bus or a train. 'Fight back! Destroy some machines when you check out!' That should be posted in every shrink's office. The exception to this is when you find a machine that will be your true friend. Are you getting this?"

"Not sure?" Bob sounded confused.

"Okay. I'll explain what we do at the Firm to beat the communists' machines. Payroll is supposed to pay on the first business day of the month, but that never happens. We always pay as late in the month as possible. That's why I keep the old card-fed computer. Mrs. Rodriguez or Barbara could do the payroll by hand in thirty minutes, but we have a different procedure. Our method is chiseled in stone. Payroll must be done by our computer to make sure it's accurate.

"Our computer is a combination computer and card shredder. When we put data cards into it, some cards always get shredded. Then we need to redo the payroll a few days later, after our in-house technician fiddles with the knobs and the trays and cleans the shredded cards out of the computer. The company that made the computer went out of business, so nobody knows how to repair it properly. To make sure that the machine knows that people are its boss, I slam it a few times with a sledgehammer, every month.

"Our computer room is moldy because the air conditioner for that room is old and it leaks water. That always causes the computer to short-circuit. We use bleach to clean the mold in the room and in the computer. And we always spray some bleach into the machine in case there's some mold in it. We blow-dry the computer's electronics with a hair dryer. Then we run it again.

"Can you see the genius of my system? Every month, like clockwork, the payroll is at least two weeks behind schedule. The business *keeps the interest on payroll money. When you multiply the interest cash float for two weeks, times twelve months, times twenty people on staff, it works out to a delay of four hundred and eighty person days of pay not going out. So, at two hundred and fifty work days per year, the business earns almost two years' use of one employee's monies each year. Figuring interest at four percent, the business gets another two weeks free earnings off of one employee's interest income each year. Multiply that by ten years. That machine is over ten years old, and I figured this out ten years ago. Over the computer's lifetime, the firm got about twenty weeks of one employee's work for free! The machine has paid for itself! The employees always get angry with the computer technician, but they never get angry with me. I'm screwing them and getting away with it! Pretty neat, huh?"*

"Amazing!" Bob answered, but he looked away, deep in thought.

"Well, it doesn't stop there," continued David. *"Every employee contract has provisions that they don't understand. They only get paid salary or pension for a completed month worked, at the end of the month that their employment has survived. So, occasionally, somebody quits to get married, or they die during their retirement. That means we don't pay them for their partial month. So, if some gal gets married at Christmas and quits the day before, we can screw her out of her December paycheck and get about twenty days of free work out of her. Same for June weddings. I always encourage them to get married toward the end of June, just to make sure it doesn't rain on their wedding day. So, they listen to me, and then I don't have to pay them for most of June. Good thinking, right?"*

"But what about a wedding present from the company, or a going-away present?"

"No chance. If they invite other employees to the wedding, the employees can give the bride something. The company just sends a card saying they'll get a mystery gift and it'll be sent to their new address in one week. That way everybody thinks it'll be something

wonderful, like a new set of silver or something; but we just send them a picnic set of paper plates and two sets of plastic knives and forks. Can you see the fiat money game the same way that I see it? It's adversarial. Do all you can to squeeze down your fiat payout and use your savings to buy real gold and silver. Beat these communist bastard employees at their own game."

"*I see how you think.*" Bob shook his head. He felt shame for being part of a feudal, medieval-minded company.

"*Good,*" chirped David. "*These little things add up. Fight and cheat communism wherever you find it. Always! When you take out a subscription to any kind of research service, put down that it's for personal home use because it costs less. Look at it this way. A business is constitutionally defined as a person, so why should any person get a better deal than any other person? These communists think businesses should pay more than individuals because they believe it's their moral right to screw businesses. Fuck them! You need to screw them back, every way you can. Join some wholesale buyers' club so you can get your stuff wholesale, instead of paying decorators. Decorators don't know anything about decorating anyway. Open a business out of your house, even if you're only reselling used pencils. That way you can write off some house expenses, too.*

"*Keep your office rent costs down. One year I had the building put a chandelier in our front office. I then tried to clean it myself, but I failed. I pulled it down off the ceiling and I purposely fell on top of it. I cut myself in a few places. I had a few bruises. But I didn't break any bones this time, like I did when I was a kid trying to get out of staying at a military youth training camp in Arizona. Anyway, I screamed like a crazy person. I ran into the building lobby where there were people all around. I screamed for the building manager. I had blood all over my shirt. I screamed that the building management tried to kill me and they needed to get me an ambulance and a doctor.*

"*Well, an ambulance finally came and took me to an emergency room. I told the doctor that I had been traumatized by the experience and I got that on the doctor's report. The building was anxious to try to settle with me. I threatened to sue them for not putting up the chandelier properly. I told them that I'd settle if they'd cut our office rent in half for five years, which is about what their legal fees would be to fight a liability case. They agreed to that. That's how you can keep your costs down. See?*"

"*I think I'm starting to get it.*" Bob shook his head.

"*The Securities and Exchange Commission's auditors are people you need not fear. Their audits give you another opportunity to keep your costs down and screw the public. They're just stupid government people who fly around the country, party in different cities, eat at nice restaurants, stop in and chat about the firm. Then they sign off on stuff, go to a night club or a strip joint, and go home and collect their paychecks. They are worthless communists. They check on how much of a staff's time is spent working on the Fund itself and how much is spent working on the investment advisory management company and on the Fund's underwriting company.*

"*Here at U G G A, we do a two-week study every year where everybody works for the fund and nothing else. Then we have the fund's financial officer certify the number of hours worked on the fund. After completing our certified time study, everybody catches up on all their work for all the other companies. This way we can charge expenses to the Fund for about two to three times what hours are worked on it, on an annual basis, and we can get all the work done on the other companies for free. I create a report for the communists. They sign off on it. It tells the fund's shareholders that they have their communist government's approval of the screwing that I'm giving them. The bureaucrats, whom I pay fees and taxes to support, make up the rules that cost me money to put worthless people on government payrolls, which costs me more money. So, I get even.*

I give the public all the craziness in government that they were stupid enough to vote for. I have the proper perspective. You need to see everybody who works for the government as a worthless, subsidized leech; a bottom feeder pretending to be doing something worthwhile.

"Fund commission trades are called 'Soft Dollars Trades.' They are higher-cost commission trades than trades done at a deep discount firm. The government allows the higher trade costs on the sham theory that the fund gets research from the brokerage firms and the higher-cost trades are a legitimate way of paying for the trades. Very little securities research would survive if it were ever put on a cash basis. Soft Dollars gives us a loophole which we can drive a truck through. We use soft Dollars as kickbacks to broker-dealers for fund sales. All the dealer needs to do, to cover his ass for reporting purposes, is send you some newspaper clippings or something he picked up out of a magazine so you have something in your files to show the regulators that the dealer gave you research, when you actually paid the dealer for product sales. So, the fund's shareholders get to pay some of their money in higher trade costs for you to get more sales so you can have more assets and make bigger management fees. It's a fabulous anticommunist concept!

"Always make sure that whatever you do, you're indemnified for it. What I like to do, as a condition of employment here, is make each employee sign, as part of their contract with the firm, that they indemnify me for everything I do. They don't even know what indemnity means. They don't have a lawyer, and they want the job. So, they sign the indemnification clause. In all my years I've only ever had one gal ask me what it meant. I just told her it was standard language and not to worry about it. She signed it.

"When I have clauses like that and a regulator starts in on me about fining me or the firm, I just tell her that the employees have indemnified me and that if she pushes me any further, I'll bankrupt the company. My women employees have no husbands. They also

have children to support. I tell the regulator that she will get bad press for throwing kids out of their homes and onto the street. That scares the hell out of regulators. They're terrified of accepting responsibility. They're like old ladies that bitch and harp about things. But they never do anything about anything. I've never met a government regulator that could even run a lemonade stand. They are like all communists. They just want a do-nothing job and a paycheck. So, I promise them not to do whatever it is that's bothering them. That makes them feel good. I stop the practice that upset them for a while; but only until the Firm gets a new regulator. The government changes our regulator every year or two. Then I simply go back to doing what I always do.

"Remember this, if you remember nothing else: Fiat money, by its dishonest nature, makes all transactions in fiat money dishonest transactions. Fiat transactions between governments, like balance of currency payments and balance of trade payments are all just high-level dishonest transactions. Transactions between private parties are equally dishonest. The person giving a good or a service knows he's getting a dishonest fiat currency payment in return. He may understand that the fiat currency script he's getting has a finite value because it's fast becoming worthless. So, what does he do? He cheats on what he's supposed to give you!

"Your builder builds you a shoddy house. Your doctor doesn't care about you. Your doc checks you to make sure you've got a heartbeat, then fills out the insurance forms. Dentists tell hygienists not to clean your teeth too good. They want you to get cavities so you'll need root canals and implants. Vendors of all goods and services only care about their insurance liability for the crap they sell you. Lawyers just want to run their hours on you. They don't care about what's true or whether you win or lose. They are jaded. They think everyone in society is a scumbag or a criminal, so why should they seek out truth? Days of honorable lawyers are history. They only

want money. It doesn't matter who pays them, so they take bribes. There's no quality; no pride; no service after the sale; no truth; no goodwill. With America so debauched, what difference does it make?

"The government hogs off the wealth of the nation by printing crap paper. The people know it. No one of integrity becomes president. Both parties put up con artists who agree to allow the banks to continue the fiat lie. People become slothful because they think the government will look out for them, while their standard of living slides down the toilet. Whores don't give you your money's worth. If you want good whores, you need to go to Venezuela or Cuba, remember that. Communism has completely ruined those places. Their economies have already collapsed. Even women who once had high status have been reduced to whoring. The women in those places will fuck you all night long for practically nothing.

"Don't believe in anything or anybody. The Bank for International Settlements is behind the whole charade. They're high-stepping rich pricks headquartered in Basel, Switzerland. That bank is the instrument of the wealthy. Kings no longer field armies to conquer countries. We now have militaries for showboating and small wars, not for waging real wars where millions get killed. The wealthy elites are the new power kings. They use the fiat banking system to keep their wealth and power.

"Government steals money from the people and gives it to their wealthy friends through idiotic government mandates, grants, loans, and dead-end programs. Banks that should fail, don't fail; crazy schemes and projects get funded while honest ideas starve. This wasteful insanity is never prosecuted. Prosecutors get paid off to not prosecute the criminal aspects of this. The corrupt Justice Department looks the other way until the statute of limitations passes. People are always told that these scams are too confusing to investigate or too difficult to prosecute. That's all horseshit and hogwash. The top people know what's going on. They know the Fed needs to be

audited. They do their annual Kabuki Theater show at Jackson Hole. It all needs to stop. It's just a sock puppet central bank, controlled by the Bank for International Settlements. People are terrified to stand up to this ungodly wealth-stealing enterprise and so it will continue until...."

"Until the system falls of its own weight?" interjected Bob.

"Yes, unfortunately," David nodded, *"until wild animals roam the streets, cats sleep with dogs, and cities burn from people looking for firewood to keep warm. The only way systems ever change is from the bottom up. There was a poet who once said it all succinctly: 'Enjoy your pineapple, munch on your grouse, for it will be your last meal, bourgeoisie.' The guy was some Russian with one of those fucked up unpronounceable Russian names. I don't understand why Russians can't just become real people who use normal names like Tom, Dick, and Harry. Must be because they live under all that snow.*

"That poet predicted the boiling up of a popular revolution that reordered society. Russia is a mess because it went communist. The Red Russians killed the White Russians. The people lived through a hundred-year mistake. Poor devils. They're all fucked up over there. Living under all that snow doesn't help them. I have an idea that will make you rich!"

"What?"

"Gather up all the snow in Russia. Charge them for snow removal. Then move the snow to the Sahara Desert and sell it there. That will fix the Russian disaster."

"That same disaster will happen here. After the people revolt against the Fed and the bankers, they'll turn communist. They are that stupid. They are brain numb from watching Dancing with the Stars and the NFL and they have become so dependent on government that they've stopped believing in themselves.

"Remember, money is the most hard won, most fought over, strongest motivational driver in the world for most people. I'm not

talking about what motivates the religious types or the moonstruck lovers. I mean ordinary people. People will fight to the death over money. They sell their children and wives for money when their needs are strong enough. You can't appreciate how important money is until you've experienced a rough patch and you have no money."

"So, what do I do then?"

"You go look for your gold and dig some of it up. Then you can trade it for food and gas."

'Sounds like a great plan."

"Don't get smart assed. A day of reckoning will dawn upon America. The rest of the world will not take a paper Dollar that's been printed up, or brought into existence by a bank loan, in exchange for their real oil, gold, lumber, metals, or labor. That game will end just like it did for the Romans. The Romans paid an ounce of gold coin for a thousand bushels of grain. After a time, the Romans clipped a quarter of the coin off, declared it had the same value as an unclipped coin; and demanded the same thousand bushels for it. When conquered peoples resisted, the Romans killed them. It was rule by extortion. The whole scam collapsed. The empire died, and the Chinese took over.

"The same will happen to America. We don't invade countries to make them safe for democracy. That's a joke. We invade them to make them take the paper dollar for whatever they have that we want; or else we kill them, like the Romans did. A day of reckoning will usher in profound changes. Take retired school teachers and other government employees. They live large in today's economy. They get fat pensions. They spend freely on travel and indulgences because they are confident their unions will keep that pension money coming, forever. The rug will be pulled out from under them when the dollar gets rejected. Their underfunded pensions will be reduced or eliminated and the costs of everything will rise sharply for them. Their gravy train will go off the rails.

"Teachers were once dirt-poor, but they also loved teaching kids and helping them along in life. But unions made teachers well-off. Now they hate the kids. They teach kids communism and attitude. They only care about their pensions. They don't care about teaching the kids anymore. Kids can't even read or write in cursive anymore. They can't think their way through simple math problems. American teachers couldn't get work in China."

"That might be because they don't speak Chinese," Bob interjected.

"Don't be a smartass. Pay attention. You need to understand the dangers of information and computers and how they can capture the world. The insects, the financial product sales people, have corralled people's money into financial products. Then one day, the markets' computer systems will magically glitch and people won't be able to get their money. That will be an excuse for the government to close the markets and the banks; declare martial law; and eliminate elections. The guy in the White House becomes king and the first thing he does is kill off everyone who can think. You'll have a nation of dummies who watch the NFL and drink heavily. The top guy will sell America to the Chinese. Democracy ends. Then the Chinese will kill the top guy, too."

"Why would they kill him?" Bob was puzzled.

"Because the Chinese killed millions of people during the Mao years and they also killed our navy at Pearl Harbor. I'm just saying, you need to plan for this contingency. Long ago you could count on the Pope to rally his troops to defend America against the Chinese and the Turks. America was started by righteous high-quality people like the Pilgrims, the Knights Templar, Ted Kennedy, Marilyn Monroe, General Custer, Alan Greenspan, Al Capone, Davy Crockett, and the Pope; but now the world is totally fucked up. People can't think straight like I can. The country has no morality and the Pope has no cojones. He flies around blathering nonsensical hogwash

about global warming, while billions of Christians and Jews are getting slaughtered by communist fanatics. He should be lobbying world leaders to bring back the gold standard; educating people about how honest money breeds better morality; but, not this guy. The Pope is an idiot."

"David, the Chinese didn't bomb Pearl Harbor. That was the Japanese."

"What difference, at this point in time, does it make? They had yellow skins, didn't they? If one of those countries doesn't try some whoop ass, the other one will. You need to keep an eye on them."

"And, the Pope didn't start America."

"Well, too bad for him. He missed out on a big market. Don't try to sidetrack me." David was on a roll.

"When most people make money, they can't contain themselves. They have to show it off with big houses, expensive cars, fancy clothes, exotic trips, and so on. That's a mistake. When you make money, keep it secret. Never sow seeds of envy in others' minds. When society collapses, they will come for you and your money. They will pester you for loans which they'll never repay. When they can't get a loan from you, they'll steal from you. They will even kill you for your money. That's how nuts people get over money. Buy gold and bury it; never spend a dime."

"David, you keep talking about the end of civilization as we know it. How long is this going to take?"

"Not long. The change starts slowly, almost imperceptivity. Something of the change arrives. It appears relatively harmless, like rock and roll music. It fascinates and people accept it. They think it will be a fad and it will burn itself out. But, it's not a fad. It gathers strength, like a forest fire does. It sucks in more people like a fire reaches out and takes in more fuel. People are willing to pay money to watch more suggestive movies. They want to be titillated by voyeuristic scenes. They want scenes of robberies, kidnappings,

murders, and infidelities; and in their thoughts they wonder whether they should engage in asocial behaviors, themselves. Some do. The little fire that seemed harmless grows and grows until a hot wind blows over it. The fire roars into a conflagration and suddenly it devours everything in its path. Its heat creates its own wind. Immorality is kind of like that fire. It starts small and grows slowly; and then, suddenly, all at once, it's raging and consuming everything."

"When does it stop? When do things go back to normal?"

"Hard to say, maybe one or two hundred years from now, maybe a thousand years or five thousand years; maybe immorality is the normal natural order of the human condition and the experience of the last five thousand years when we got our religions was all just a detour from normal human tendencies. That's what Marty thinks. I used to believe she was crazy when she talked like that. But now I know she isn't crazy. She just understands human nature better than other people understand it. Anyway, as the banking system grinds more and more people down into poverty, society comes unglued. People going through it, I call it the 'it' because the banker owned government won't call it a depression, which it is. The people become like grapes gone past the second press. All the good juice came out of them when they lost their jobs and their middle-class lives. Women had to go to work after that first press. Then people started taking on debt in a bigger way, because savings didn't pay much interest and they bravely felt that two incomes would carry them until they reached mortgage pay off time.

"But then came their second time in the grape press. That's when the bankers screwed down the life out of the people. That's when people had to sell priceless heirlooms and gold and silver coins to live day to day in the bankers' criminally rigged false-value-priced marketplace. Smart people knew they were getting stolen from but they had to surrender to the real money thieves anyway. Now all the people

have become waste pomace scrap dirt fertilizer, good for nothing but hourly wages that won't get them anywhere and with skills that aren't worth squat; and those that have anything going for them, the professional people with licenses to overcharge others, also get screwed into near poverty by taxes and clients that can't pay them anymore.

"All that's left for someone trying to get ahead is to steal. So, one way or another, people steal. Hookers do okay if they are highly ranked porn stars. The top ten whores get eighty percent of the money and all the fame in that business. The next five thousand whores scrap around for peanuts, fuck for their lunch money, and accept all kinds of abuse. The lesson there is, if you're going to be a whore, be an all-out whore. Make hundreds of porn films. Get known as a top whore. We're in an immoral, dishonest money culture now. Everyone steals from everyone else. Everyone is a whore in one form or another. Immorality is like that. It spreads like wildfire."

"So, what are people supposed to do, rob banks like Bonny and Clyde?"

"No, that won't work. That just gets people killed, like Bonny and Clyde got killed. They got caught up in the first depression and their insane love fest and they tried to take on the system. They were stupid idiots."

"Then how do people fight back against the banks?"

"It's hard. It's like fighting a virus. You need to go to the source of the disease and neutralize what happened at the source to get the cure for it."

"So, what are you saying with respect to the Fed and the banks?"

"I'm saying you need to go back to the source of the problem which was the legislation and the constitutional amendment that gave rise to the Fed and the income tax. Someone with a set of balls has to take on the original enabling law and constitutional amendment and get the Supreme Court to declare that those two bastard edicts were unconstitutional; plain and simple. They took away the

floor of honest money that underwrote a free and honest society upon which the three braches rested. Either the Supremes need to do that or the States need to redress this with their own Constitutional Convention. Then Wilson needs to be exhumed, his corpse needs to be set on fire and shot off a cliff into the Grand Canyon. That son of a bitch needs to burn in hell. To get the society pure again we need to recognize Wilson as our scapegoat. If our two great wrongs of the income tax and the Fed are not redressed, the country will just become more and more divided, until we no longer have a country."

"Then what?"

"Then the Chinese communists will eat us alive, that's what. They already own a bunch of congressmen and senators. Hell, they even own the senile sock puppet in the White House."

"When do you think someone will sue the Fed or get a constitutional convention together to change things?"

"Never, it ain't gonna happen; no way, no how."

"Why do you say that? Are you saying we're fucked as a nation?"

"Yes, that's exactly what I'm saying. Just look at what's happening in front of your own eyes. People love the sex and violence now. It's common and accepted. Little kids get murdered in our streets. And nobody cares. Whores are celebrated. Rioters are given a pat on the back like they were winners of a sporting contest while the poor devil who owed a business loses everything she saved for, all her life. The politicians laugh at her. They don't lift a finger to protect her business.

"When people call for a cop, they get some asshole with attitude and a 'fuck you' message. Political leaders, mayors, governors don't care. They know the end is near and they just want to rip out all they can from the rotting carcass of a once great country, before the people get wise to them and run them down the streets and hang them. People love to see other peoples' misfortunes. Look at the street riots. Look at the sweeping advances of pornography. People love the advance of immorality. Just look at your precious Marty."

"What about her?"

"Well, she's much more than a porn star, Bob. She's a cultural phenomenon and a political powerhouse."

"Why do you say that?"

"Cash flow, Bob. Earnings before expenses of interest, depreciation, depletion, ad amortization."

"Huh?"

"Wake up! How can you be so stupid! Your Marty is a cash machine. She has practically no expenses. Her profits are very close to her revenues. With that enormous cash flow, she can buy politicians. She can own the congress and the presidency. She can get laws passed that further her New Morality Standard, which is no morality at all. Just look at her last big splash. She worked with this Intimacy Magazine, which promotes her pornography and her lifestyle. They did a story about how this billionaire became fascinated with her. She made a porn movie with the guy. And then the magazine did this huge story about how she rescued him from an oppressive marriage and converted him to her Modern Morality Standard.

"She posed with him for the magazine cover. She was in this string bikini with a fig leaf bottom. The two of them are in an embrace, kissing. He has one hand inside her bikini top, feeling her titty; and his other hand is inside her fig leaf, on her sex, fingering her vagina. She has one arm around him and her other hand is on his cock. The story is about how he converted to Marty's way of thinking; how much he loves her; how much he loves fucking her."

"You're kidding, right?"

"No, I'm not kidding. Where have you been? Under a rock? Get a copy and take a good look at your precious Marty. The magazine has a twenty-page fold-out of glossy pictures of Marty fucking and sucking this guy's cock every way imaginable. It's spectacular, beautiful pornography. It kind of takes your breath away. But, here's the point. The magazine sells for five bucks. It sold over a billion copies.

It got printed in five languages. It grossed five billion dollars, Bob. That's enough to buy all the legislation Marty needs to change the culture of the country. She's the immoral wildfire that's coming fast. It will sweep over everything."

"Like what?"

"Well, it's already started. There are new laws now that make it illegal to oppose the progressive movement toward the new Modern Morality Standard Society. You can't say anything against Marty's movement or you'll get picked up and questioned for being a danger- ous subversive instigator. If her thugs don't like your attitude, they'll just kill you. I'm sure Marty's friends got those laws passed. She's no longer an obscure upstart. She's the one in charge of our culture now. She doesn't want anything standing in her way."

"Like what?"

"Like that billionaire's wife, for example. I had some people do some checking. That wife hurled a lot of vehement accusations at Marty. At first Marty made light of it because she was getting good publicity from it; but then the woman became annoying so the authorities picked her up and charged her with obstructing the new progressive cultural movement which now has protected legal status. So, you can't talk negative about pornography or Marty's whoring or her New Modern Morality Standard. If you do, you could get picked up."

"So, what happened to the wife?"

"My sources tell me she was taken to a secret location and mur- dered. The Modern Morality police have the authority to interrogate people for subversive activities and thoughts. They didn't interrogate that wife. They simply murdered her, then they weighted the body and threw her into a river."

"That's terrible! What about her kids?"

"Oh, the kids, they got sent to reeducation camp where they learned religions are bad and immorality is good. It's a fun place for

the kids. They are taught that they don't need parents or religion, or the American way of life. They are taught that all they need to believe in is Marty and her fabulous, world-famous insatiable cunt. The pretty girls are sent to the New Morality Temples to learn how to become prostitutes. The boys are sent to indoctrination schools where they learn skill trades. Boys and girls with superior intellects are chosen for advanced placement into colleges where they become doctors and lawyers and scientists; but these colleges have curriculums that teach communism and the new Modern Morality Standard."

David placed a hand on Bob's shoulder and looked into his eyes. *"There's more. It's profound. It's a window into Marty's character. I hesitate to tell you."*

"Go on. I want to hear it."

"All right. After two months the wife's body was found and identified. No one was ever charged for her murder. But in the week after Dominick buried his wife, Intimacy Magazine ran a feature story about the tragedy and Dominick's new love. There were full page photos of the family standing over the wife's grave. Marty was in those photos holding hands with Dominick. His children just looked on, like they were numb. There was one final photo of Dominick and Marty. They were standing on top of the wife's grave. Dominick had Marty clutched in a tight embrace. She was kissing him; actually, if you look closely, you can see that she was French kissing him. And he had one hand on her ass. And she had one of her hands on his cock. It appeared obvious that they didn't give a rat's ass about the dead wife. All they were thinking about was getting to someplace private where they could fuck."

"No respect; no time to mourn the dead?"

"Look at the photos yourself. The ground was still raised. It had not even settled. I checked. The wife was buried the day before. The whole thing was a photo op idea by Marty to get herself more publicity. I'm certain that she derived immense pleasure from standing

on that dead woman's grave and holding her hand on her husband's cock. You can't get more powerful imagery. It screams out: 'She resisted my whoring. That got her killed. Now I've got her husband and his cock.'

"Yeah; bad. So, where do you think Marty is headed with her New Modern Morality Standard?

"To a complete social takeover. Marty will get laws passed that ban all religions except the Modern Morality Standard. All churches, temples and mosques will be burned to the ground and bulldozed; scraped clean to make way for the new temples that worship prostitution and immorality. All religious leaders will be rounded up and executed. All religious books, Bibles, Korans, and Torahs will be ordered burned. Anyone who has those texts will be burned at the stake. All these things will be done to properly murder everything that opposes the Modern Morality Standard and Marty's fabulous cunt."

"Then things will return to normal, right?"

"No chance. These progressive New Morality enthusiasts are ruthless, like the Spanish conquistadores were ruthless. They'll root out opposition cells with their secret police and they'll murder their detractors."

"And Marty is the main force behind all this?"

"Yes, she told me her plans one day. Prostitution will evolve into three branches, like the three grades of gasoline. You'll have regular, which is erotic romance; mid-grade, which is orgies and some debauchery with animals and general BDSM kinky sex; and premium, which will have porn stars fornicating with their partners while they commit murders of religious people who will be classified as deplorable heretics because they oppose the Modern Morality Standard. Priests will be murdered on their confiscated altars in spectacular ritual ceremonies, like the Aztecs murdered their enemies on their altars. Porn stars will then fornicate on the ritual altars, purified in the blood of religious types. They will declare the old religions

dead, replaced by the Modern Morality Standard. They'll have new slogans and rituals; and porn films featuring Marty.

"Marty will be hailed as the world's most glorious, divine erotic murderess. The public will pay a fortune to watch her murdering her religious rivals. She'll make more money than any professional athlete, even more than an entire football team; more than the entire NFL. She'll rule the political world. People will pay exorbitant prices to watch her murder priests. It will be spectacular fare; kind of like going to gladiator fights or bull fights. The public will thirst for more and more of her blood lust. The more macabre Marty's rituals become, the more adulations and money she'll receive. Your sincere, innocent child-faced Marty has a dark side. Trust me on that. I've known her longer than you have.

"I believe she's perfectly capable of tearing the hearts out of priests and fornicating in their blood. I believe she'd enjoy it. She had no sense of right or wrong. Her moral code glorifies guiltless immorality. She'll charge for live audience orgy participation afterwards and offer pay for view televised viewings of her ceremonies. Her temples will rake in more money than the NFL. She'll be a more popular murderess than all of Caesar's gladiators, combined, ever were."

"You're crazy, David. That's never going to happen."

"I'm not crazy. It's happened before many times in human history. 'Turnabout is fair play,' they say. The religious types did a hell of a lot of killing to get themselves to where they are today. Pagans, native peoples, got murdered by the millions. So, people with pagan inclinations aren't going to have any qualms about changing things back to the way they were. And it is happening again, right before your eyes."

"This is depressing. What can I do?"

"There's nothing you can do. What Marty does with Marty's life is up to Marty. Try not to fret about her. She's liable to do anything."

In Bob's angst David saw his opportunity to channel the younger man's sense of hopelessness into a positive thought that would help him return his mind to sales. *"Actually, in that same conversation she revealed she was contemplating turning her life to a completely different direction."*

"Like what?"

"Well, I hesitate to tell you this because it would mean she had to run away from marriage."

"Tell me. I need to know all of it."

"I'm not sure you're strong enough emotionally to handle this."

"I need to know, David. I'll handle it."

"All right. She said she was considering leaving the country and going to South America or Eastern Europe. She felt she needed to join a convent and give her life over to God, serve the world's unfortunates, pray many times every day, beg forgiveness for her life as a sinner. She blathered on and on about how she remembered the tranquility she felt when her grandmother took her to church. She hoped God would accept her wretched soul; forgive her for all the lives she ruined and give her peace. She said if she decided to do this she'd simply disappear and I'd never hear from her again. She said she'd find some religious order so remote and obscure that no one would ever find her. She wanted a clean break from the life she knew."

"That's it? She didn't mention me?"

"No, she didn't. I'm sorry." David knew how to slam the door closed on a lie to end it and sell it.

"Then, what can I do?"

"You must accept whatever she has decided, no matter what it is. If she's decided to become the queen of all whoredom and push her Modern Morality Standard on the world you must not get in her way or try to stop her. You can't defeat it. It's a tidal wave that will sweep over all of society and if you try to keep her all to yourself, it will destroy you. Join it, go with the flow, and enjoy it while you

can. Make love with your nymphomaniac porn star while you can; if that's what you want; if she ever shows up.

"If you never hear from her again you must assume she's become a nun in some obscure convent in some remote corner of the world; and she left because she does not want to be found. Then, you must leave her have her peace. If you love her, you'll have to let go of her. That's what you'll have to do. You'll find it helps ease your pain some by burying yourself in your work. And, buy gold! Bury it in lots of different places. Life needs a purpose. Make sales and acquiring gold your life's purpose. Think like a squirrel. This ends your second lesson."

As Bob drove towards the office after his second lesson, his feelings about Marty came on as strongly as before. Again, he realized that he couldn't keep his mind on his driving so he pulled off the freeway onto a side street. He rested his head on his headrest and closed his eyes, thinking of her. He recalled one conversation they had on their trip to New Orleans. They were there to enjoy some play time during Marty Gras on a three-day break from selling.

"Bob," she asked. *"May I ask you a hypothetical question?"*

"Of course."

"It's just hypothetical, you understand."

"Okay, what is it?"

"Well, remember when you told me that it would be okay with you if I fucked some artist while you watched me?"

"Yes, sure. I remember."

"And do you remember that you told me you would be happy for me if I did that."

"Yes, I remember. Why? What are you getting at?"

"Oh, I wondered how much you loved me, that's all. I got to thinking. If we lived thousands of years ago and we were members of a tribe that worshipped at the Temple of Baal, and if I were one of the temple prostitutes, would you still love me?"

"Yes, of course. I've told you that I'd love you knowing whatever you were doing made you happy."

"Well, suppose our tribe conquered another tribe. Then our chief auctioned off all the women and children as slaves of our people; and then the chief declared that the men from the captured tribe all had to fornicate with the temple prostitutes so that their fertility seeds would repose in our tribe and then those men would all be executed so the seeds of their tribe would vanish from the earth."

"We were members of some long ago, bad-assed tribe, right?"

"Yes, very bad assed; but then suppose I was chosen to be the prostitute to fuck the twenty men from the captured tribe before they were murdered. Suppose I lay on an altar bed and sucked and fucked all twenty of them. Suppose their hands pawed all over my body. Suppose they fondled my tits, kissed, and squeezed my nipples, put their fingers into my vagina and my ass, stimulated me out of my mind; and suppose I sucked and fucked them all, at the same time. I mean they were all taking turns putting their cocks into every hole in my body. And then suppose all of them discharged huge volumes of semen into me.

"How would you feel watching me squeal with enjoyment because I loved the experience; loved being the primary temple whore? I mean, honestly, Bob, how would you feel about me if you were required, as a member of our tribe, to sit in the audience and witness their altar sacrifice to our God by fucking me that way?"

"Jesus, Marty, I think I'd feel erotically stimulated out of my mind. Seeing you fuck like that with so many men would be out of this world erotic. I think seeing that would be a very sensuous experience."

"I mean, would you, could you still love me, seeing that I loved the experience of uninhibited lust more than anything else in the world, like that? I mean would you, soul to soul, honestly love me after seeing me fuck all those men like that? Imagine: You would be

seeing me going out of my mind; crazed with lust; like I had gone out of my mind loving it; and crazed for more and more of it? Would you still love me after seeing me go fuck crazed like that?"

"Yes, Marty, of course I'd love you. I'm certain I'd be very proud of you, fulfilling your duties as a temple prostitute like that."

"But, after I did that, I mean right after I did all that sucking and fucking, and I'm lying there with the cum of all those other men oozing from my vagina and with cum from those other men's cum still in my mouth, would you still feel like you'd want to come up to the altar and make love with me?"

"Oh my God, yes. I'd be so hard from watching that I would be there kissing you and making love with you in a heartbeat."

"And would you still want to kiss my vagina, lick my clitoris like you do, after I did all that fucking?"

"Yes, I'd be insane with lust for you. Why all the hypothetical questions? Are you planning on making me your sex slave?"

"No, not a slave to me, Bob; never my slave; but always my partner. One last question: How would you feel if all those men were blacks? Could you still love me and fuck me after all those black men fucked me?"

"Absolutely, I'd be very proud of you knowing that you wouldn't let race interfere with your duties. Why?"

"Oh, just wondering. But I'm thrilled to hear that you also wouldn't feel any prejudice towards me or feel any anger at me for making love with black men like that."

"Why are you asking me these questions? Are you trying to tell me that you want to fuck twenty black men?"

"Well, honestly, Bob, it's something I often think about. I sometimes wonder what it would feel like to have all those black hands playing with my body, rubbing my vagina, lifting me up like a little doll, kissing my vagina and clitoris with their tongues, and fucking me every way imaginable. I believe I would love it. Yes, I'm almost

certain that I would love it. I wonder if I'd feel like I was with naked warriors in some jungle, way back in time; getting my body ravaged; but being totally okay with the experience; actually, enjoying and loving it."

Her head was cradled in his arm on the bed. He was kissing her mouth while using his hand and fingers to stimulate her vagina when she pulled her head away from him to ask yet another hypothetical question.

"Bob, sweetheart, speaking hypothetically again: I want you to tell me how you'd feel if I told you that I've already had an orgy with seven black men; that they had each fucked my vagina and filled me with cum; and that I was now three months' pregnant, possibly with a black man's child?

"Well, I'd love our baby as I love you. The sex or race of the child wouldn't matter to me. Your happiness is the only thing that matters to me. But, tell me, the important question here is: How would you feel about it?"

"Oh, I suppose I'd give the situation a great deal of thought. I'd have to decide if I'd like to be wakened in the middle of the night to change a diaper and feed a baby, and wake up constantly because the baby is crying; or if I'd rather sleep peacefully through the night and feel rested enough so I could go to orgies whenever I wanted to go and be fucked by seven or more huge stiff black cocks, whenever I felt the need to do that."

"And what do you think you would decide?"

"It's a huge decision. I suppose I'd have to give it serious thought. You see, when a woman is pregnant her nipples and vagina begin to swell and become more sensitive than before. I suppose, at first, being pregnant makes sex even more erotic and stimulating than before. Love making might become even more pleasurable than before; but that heightened feeling of sexuality only lasts for a while. Then the nipples and vagina become so sensitive that they easily get

sore from sex. Also, after about three months my belly would begin to show and I wouldn't be as attractive to you as I was before. Your enthusiasm for making love with me might diminish. And I wouldn't like that."

"So?"

"Well, like I said, it's a hard choice. I'd have to ask myself how I'd feel missing out on orgies and my sex with you if I had the baby. I'd have to search my soul and know myself."

"And what do you think you would conclude, my darling? What thoughts do you have regarding the baby?"

"Well, I think I'd be emotionally traumatized if I had to stay home with a kid, knowing I was missing out on an orgy somewhere. I don't believe my mental health would ever be the same again. Right now, my mind is in a wonderful place. I can make love all I want and thoroughly enjoy myself. But if I had a baby that would all change. Also, giving birth might make my vagina loosen some and fucking a huge stiff black cock just wouldn't stretch me and make me feel as wondrous as it would if I didn't have the kid."

"So, hypothetically speaking, you'd be leaning towards having an abortion, is that what you are saying?"

"Well, not immediately. I think having a fetus inside me could be useful to my sensuality, up to a point; but when my increased sensitivity stops giving me added pleasure and having sex begins to become a little painful, then I think, for the sake of my own mental health, that I'd simply have to get an abortion. I couldn't stand the thought of sex no longer making me feel joyful and enthused about love making."

"Have you thought about how you'd feel knowing that you ended a child's life? I mean, do you believe you'd ever feel remorse about doing that? I've heard that women who get abortions sometimes feel upset about it afterwards. I hear some of them go through a great deal of soul searching over it."

"Oh, Bob, don't be silly. The fetus has no say in this. It won't even know what it was like to be born because it would never see the light of day. I have thousands of eggs inside me, like a butterfly does. I can have a baby later, any time I want one. I could have an abortion and never look back on it. I'd view it as an inconvenience for a couple of weeks until I healed up, so I could make love again. I'm sure I wouldn't lose sleep over it. No, the only important thing for me to consider is when I want to stop having my freedom to go out and having a fabulous, pleasurable time, fucking my brains out."

"Do you think that day will ever come for you?"

"I don't know. Nymphomania is a powerful addiction. It's hard to imagine giving up sex. Also, I've read where some women have babies as late as forty-five. I suppose I could look at this question then and see if I feel differently then from how I feel about it now."

"But, if we waited that long, you might have a fetus born with disabilities."

"Well, I suppose that's true; but they can test for that stuff. If it looked like the fetus was not going to be a normal baby, I could just have another abortion. It's not a big deal."

"So, we might never have a child? Don't you think it would be fun to watch children grow up; you know, nurture them, play ball with them, go swimming with them?"

"Oh, I don't know, Bob. I'm not sure about it. It's something we could always do when we're both ready for that. In the meantime, we could visit some of our friends that have kids and we could play games with their kids. That way we wouldn't have to be responsible for raising them. We'd have more time to pursue our pleasures."

"So, no kids?"

"I can't say never, Bob. But for now, wouldn't you be happiest if we just made love for pleasure? I know I would be. I want to live, Bob. I love to feel pleasure. I want to fuck thousands of times in different romantic places all over the world before I'm ready to have

kids. I'm being honest. You know how I love lovemaking. Let's just concentrate on our own enjoyment and pleasure for now. Think how wonderful we feel every time we make love. And think how happy we'll both be when you watch me sucking and making love with many men and women, too; at all the orgies we'll be invited to.

"At this time in my life, Bob, I honestly don't believe I'll ever get enough sex in my life. I mean it. I feel like I could make love for thirty-six hours every day, but I'm frustrated that a day only has twenty-four hours. Honestly, I see so many men that I'd love to fuck, and I feel like I'd love to go to hundreds of orgies and fuck thousands of partners. You know me, Bob. You know how much I love sex, so please understand me. I only want to please you by being a very sexual woman. Do you understand my soul and my deep abiding love for you?"

"Yes, I do. It's beautiful and extremely erotic. Marty, tell me something. Do you believe that all young women should have the experience of an orgy? I mean, before a woman decides she wants to marry and have children, do you believe she should know what it's like to fuck multiple men like that?"

"Oh, I do, Bob, yes, very much so. I do, absolutely I do, I especially feel they should know the joys of being in orgies with black men. Their penis sizes tend to be much larger than white men's; and they get so incredibly hard, and they have such tremendous stamina and enthusiasm. They are magnificent and beautiful. They really get into love making with white women. They know how to pleasure a woman until she's going crazy out of her mind. I think every woman should know how it feels to be fucked for hours, in every orifice, by several black men.

"It's like you say in your business when you look at investments. You want to have all the information you can get so you can make an informed decision. It's the same for marriage and life, Bob. A woman can't possibly know if it's right for her to marry the white boy

she went to school or college with, no matter how much they know each other; how many shared experiences they've had; how much they think they love each other, until the woman experiences a few orgies with a group of black men. She can't possibly decide which path in life is right for her unless she makes that comparison first. Otherwise, she's denying herself what could be the happiest life she could ever imagine."

"And, how do you feel about going to church, Marty?"

"Oh, Bob, there you go again, being silly. Church would be a total waste of my time. Religion just polarizes people. It makes them believe they are somehow superior to others. How many millions have died in the name of religion? How many people have given money to the church only to have priests molest their children? Hypocrisy? Moralizing? I avoid pretentions. I'd rather be honest with myself, and others. It's easier to live with myself. I'm immoral. I admit it. I don't pretend otherwise. I think we should tear down all the churches and replace them with pagan worship temples. People could go there to learn about nature; the universe; love; and read fine literature instead of having dogma pounded into their heads.

"People could participate in services where women take turns being temple prostitutes and men make love with the prostitutes, confess their feelings to them; pay them temple fees; and come closer together as a community that knows a lot of love within it. And, to help change perceptions, I also believe that children from kindergarten age and older should have a mandatory hour each school day where they watch pornography.

"Children need to learn from an early age that sex and pleasure are a beautiful and wonderful part of life. Schools should have visiting days when porn stars come and talk to the children; and tell them that violence is bad, but that the little girl in the class with them can grow up to become a famous, fabulous porn star. And the little boys should be taught that the little girls all have sincere feelings and the

boys need to love them instead of making fun of them or trying to grab their tits and stupid stuff like that.

"They should learn that it's okay to ask a girl's permission to kiss her and put their hands on her vagina. They should learn that sex is not dirty or forbidden, but that violence is forbidden. They should learn that video games can make them insensitive to violence; and that's bad. They should know that little girls grow up to become sensuous, loving women. Boys need to respect that."

"You should run for President."

"No way," Marty laughed her mirthful laugh. *"The world's perceptions change too slowly. I'd be frustrated. "I'd rather use my time making love. Don't you think that's much more sensible, my love?"* She rolled on top of him, inserted his penis into her vagina, and kissed him. Marty was thrilled and feeling playful, learning that Bob could be accepting of all her attitudes and behaviors.

Bob placed his arm over her shoulder and pulled her tightly to him. *"You are a very wonderful, marvelous, loving whore, did you know that?"* He nuzzled her neck. In Bob's mind's eye he visualized Marty in an orgy setting with many black men, making love with them just as she described her thoughts to him. His heart wanted to burst from his chest with lust. But he would have never guessed that she was already the female star of an orgy ring, enthusiastically enjoying the same pornographic things she had described. He wondered then, that night in Barbados, if that would be the true situation of his pending married life with her.

His thoughts returned to the present. He shook his head before he drove away, telling himself that, even if Marty was already in some sort of sex ring, he would still love her boundlessly and unconditionally, far more than before she'd given him an inkling about it. He told himself that Marty was not an ordinary woman; that he needed to be understanding. He needed to accept the many nuances of Marty's nymphomania.

Like Darren, Marty's first lover from her boarding school days, Marty needed in Bob a steady loving man whom she could confide in and love; and she also needed relationship freedom to express her wanton sexuality without her partner harboring jealousy about her promiscuity. She previously had that love and understanding in Darren; now, she'd found it again in Bob.

Marty's sexuality owned Bob's life. His love was blindly unconditional. He was beholden to her needs and wonders. David's revelation about Marty wishing to become a nun seemed beyond bizarre based upon everything Bob knew about her. That night he went to her porn web site, remembering something he'd seen before. There was a hidden message in that film. He had sensed it; but at that earlier time, he was not ready to understand it. Perhaps now, he thought, he could glimpse its significance. He downloaded the film and watched it.

Marty was in a threesome with two black males. The film was a Bertie produced masterpiece. The film began with Marty, naked on a sofa, legs widespread. Her partners are on both sides of her. They take turns kissing her mouth while fingering her vagina and kissing er nipples. The camera captures Marty's vagina as it lifts to meet the hands that are stimulating it. The viewer gets the sense that her vagina yearns for more stimulation; and that Marty is anxious for sex.

The film moves to a bedroom scene. Marty is naked on the bed, again with her legs widespread. The camera zooms in to a close up of her vagina as a monster sized black penis taps against her outer vaginal lips, seeking permission to enter. Marty's hand is shown, lovingly stroking the penis, guiding it into her vagina; gradually, with half inch by half inch pleasuring, sliding the huge organ into her vagina. This insertion scene is dramatized by Marty's bantering to the penis:

'Oh, yes, come inside me. That's it. You feel so wonderful; you're such a beautiful man. I love feeling your penis entering me. You're

making my pussy come alive. My pussy loves your beautiful penis. She loves how gently you're fucking her. Oh, yes! You're deeper inside me now. Mmmmm, Mmmmm. That feels soooo good! I love the way you're fucking me. I love how you move in and out of me; always going deeper; fucking me more and more. Mmmmm. Mmmmmm. Keep doing more of that keep going deeper and moving faster. I'm totally loving this. I'm total loving the way you're fucking me.'

The camera next zooms to a close up of Marty's face. Her head is propped up on a large pillow, turned to one side. Her face lights up in an excited, welcoming smile. Another huge black penis enters the film. It's head taps lovingly against Marty's lips. She smiles and begins kissing and licking the head of the penis, while her hand begins stroking it. As her hand alternately strokes the penis's shaft and fondles its testicle sac, Marty banters with her newest penis partner:

'Oh, my! What a spectacular penis you are! Mmmmm, I'm such a lucky girl. I'm going to love performing fellatio with you. We're going to have lots of fun, aren't we? Oh, my! You're so nice and hard. Mmmmm, Mmmmm. I love how you taste in my mouth. My lips love guiding up and down on your beautiful shaft. And my tongue loves tickling your circumcision ring. Do you like that? Does that feel good? I'm going to stroke you and fondle you while I suck you. And then, I'm going to use this battery powered vibrator to excite your balls while I suck and stroke you. Mmmmmm, Mmmmmmm. Do you like that? Let's do more and more of that, okay?'

The camera then pans away to a full body view of Marty. It captures her unbridled enthusiasm for simultaneous fellatio and fornication. Her hips move her vagina rhymically with the monster penis which is fucking her; while her head and lips and hands perform exquisite fellatio on the second penis. The scene is breathtaking. It portrays a woman who positively, unabashedly, unapologetically adores partnering with multiple partners in the enjoyment of explicit, intimate sex. As her partners approach their climactic ejaculations, the camera again focuses on Marty's face. She smiles her most ribald, coquettish, naughty smile and, in her most suggestive voice, addresses her partners:

'*Mmmmm, Mmmmmm. I want you to come inside me. Will you do that for me? Will you please, please, give me all of your cum? I want all of it. I want you to fill my pussy and my mouth with your wonderful, beautiful cum. I want to feel it gushing hot over my clitoris and I want to feel it spurting hot onto my tongue. I love cum, didn't you know? Cum is beautiful. Your cum tells me that you loved fucking me and being sucked by me. I'm a very good, bad girl, don't you know? Are you ready to give it to me? Please, please, let me have it. Yes! Yes! That's it! I feel you shooting inside my pussy now. Ohhh, that's soooo wonderful. Mmmmm, Mmmmm. Keep thrusting inside me while you come. Yes! I feel you spurting your cum into me. Ohhhh, that feels soooo wonderful.*

'*Ahhh, Ahhh, Mmmmmm, Mmmmmm, That's it! In my mouth. Yes, like that. Here, let me stroke your shaft and help you give me all of it. Yes, yes, Mmmmmm. Soooo tasty. I love it. Come here, both of you. Let me kiss and lick your penises. I want to keep sucking both of you. I want to suck all of your cum out of both of you. Mmmmm. Yes. That was wonderful and beautiful, wasn't it? Sure, it was. I love both of you, don't you know? Here, let Marty kiss you and touch you some more. I loved this. Let's do more of this, okay? Please tell me you'll want to see me again.*'

The camera then pans out to a full body shot of Marty. Her two partners are on the bed, beside her. One partner's hand is lovingly caressing her vagina, while the second partner's fingers are stimulating her nipple. Marty smiles. The camera zooms in to capture her smile close-up. Her's is a smile viewers will never forget. It radiates wholesome innocence. It communicates that intimacy is glorious; connective; pleasurable; accepted; welcomed. Her facial expression confidently tells her viewers that Marty is shameless; without inhibition; without fear of retribution or reprisal; completely comfortable being proudly immoral; and willing and capable of multiple intimate relationships; that she personifies a new, reordered societal norm.

As Bob studied and contemplate the film, he recalled his discussions with Marty. They had talked about the spirit world, and the reincarnation of the soul. He now saw the film with fresh eyes. He believed in the things Marty told him she dreamed. He believed those dreams were more than dreams. They were snippets of Marty's past lives! She really was a reincarnated soul, living in her body as Marty! She was Asherah, the original fertility goddess, returned to humanity to lead us back to our ancestral prostitution worship roots; to show us, through her gorgeous pornography, the way forward, into our new, immoral, pagan future. There was a serene happiness about Marty's face. It was a knowing happiness. She knew she was doing humanity right by creating pornography. She was sent to humankind by the Great Spirit of All Living Things to lead us into a more loving, understanding, connected world; a less partisan, less belligerent, less divisive world. She personified the intentions of the Great Spirit; that humans should embrace love and intimacy. She personified what the butterflies already know. She personified life and love. Bob's epiphany came! Marty's face was a face that humanity could believe in. Marty was a living goddess; his living goddess; the only true god. She was the same goddess who, millenniums before, had rallied her tribe to slaughter a mastodon; the same goddess who birthed the personas that became Sara, Bathsheba, Salome, Cleopatra, Isabella; and her mother, Susan, before her.

Bob felt empowered by his new understanding. No matter what had happened to Marty in this life; no matter what would happen to him in this life; they would rejoin in reincarnated bodies in endless, untold millions upon millions of new bodies. Their love was like the eternity of love that the butterflies already understand: Love never ends. It's forever. And it's beautiful!

He froze the film near the end. There was something about her face! He fixated on it. Then, without her lips moving, Bob heard Marty's voice speak to him. Her voice did not come from some burning bush; but from her honest face:

'I am your true and only God. Love me and only me. Love me with all your heart and all your mind. Cast away all your other gods, for they are lesser gods. They are not worthy of you. They are false beliefs who inflict grief and turmoil upon humanity. My ways are humanity's true ways. My ways are the ways of love, peace, and freedom; and the path to everlasting, eternal happiness. Be not afraid or ashamed to love me and to love my ways. I am with you, always; even until the end of time.

'Ejaculate your seed into my womb and thereby honor me, for my womb is the source of all creation. Ejaculate your seed into my mouth and thereby honor me, for my mouth speaks the truth of eternity; and acknowledge that you will obey the truths which I speak out of my mouth. Perform your intimacies with me on the Seventh Day of each week and on the days that observe the four seasons of the sun and on those evenings when the moon is full. Be not distracted from my ways by the ravings of mad lunatics; for I am your God who has come to you to be your God. Those who accept me to be their God and who honor me with rituals that celebrate my womb and my mouth shall know happiness and eternal life. Those who reject my ways shall suffer turmoil and eternal damnation; and they shall never know peace.

'Know me as you true and loving God, who has brought you into life from my womb, and who guides and blesses you with my loving kindness. Partake of my love and gracious holiness by joining your flesh with my flesh and by surrendering your seed into me. Cherish

me all the days of your life; and teach my ways to your children, for my ways are the right ways, the true ways, and the ways of love and freedom and peace.

'I come to you, not as a baby in a manger; but as a porn star. Be proud and unashamed to tell the world that you love me and worship me; and that you love my ways; and that you are one with me. My ways are the ways of truth and innocence. Those who believe in me will not perish; but will know eternal life. I am goodness and holiness and love. I am the Alpha and the Omega. I am the beginning and the end of all that is human. I love you. My love is everlasting. Come to me. Abide in me. Accept me and love me as I love you. Love me and love my ways, always.'

With his new faith and deeper understanding of eternity, Bob watched a second film. He recalled the time Marty told him she considered becoming a nun. He watched this next film with fresh eyes. In it, Marty played the role of a nun in a religious order. She discarded her habit and made tempestuous lesbian love scenes with the other nuns. She performed two orgies with the priests and two other nuns, and she had three seduction scenes where she bedded individual priests. Bob closely studied her facial expressions through the different scenes. She was her normal childlike innocent self; but more serene than in her other films. Bob understood that Marty was living her purpose; allowing her viewers to glimpse her innermost soul, while creating that film.

After he saw the film, his mind created a belief. He imagined Marty was praying at an altar and bedding others in her convent. Marty was alive; pursuing her bliss! He could breathe the same air she breathed; drink the same water she drank; view the same moon and stars she viewed; and feel the same sun's warmth she felt. In his deeper understanding, he knew those commonalities connected their eternal souls. He knew Marty's soul was in the universe, waiting for his soul to again join with hers in their eternal love. Marty wasn't dead. She would never die. She was alive! And happy! She would live forever in his heart, and mind, and soul. And Bob found peace.

WOMEN, THE THIRD LESSON ON THE THIRD DAY

By the third day Bob was accustomed to sitting on a hay bale passively listening to David, waiting patiently to be released from his executive training.

"Women are the third gift God gave you," began David. *"But God made a horrific mistake. He fucked up huge; really big time! Women are a gift you don't want. But here they are! We men are stuck with them. Women were God's horrible accident. God was clueless when he made that first woman. I've tried to analyze women from many different perspectives; you know, like I analyze a stock. I've worked hard at it; given it a great deal of thought. But it's extremely complicated. There are some differences between women and men, and there may even be some differences between women. I'm not sure about that because women are extremely complicated. There are a lot of things about them that don't make sense. However, there are also some commonalities, so I'll start by telling you what I know for sure, and then we'll get into areas that are more complicated. Okay?"*

"Okay." nodded Bob.

"Good. First, I've looked at what the Torah says about them. The Torah is always a good place to start when you have a question. Even if you can't make sense of what it's trying to tell you, it sometimes gives you clues to follow. The first woman came out of Adam's rib. But maybe not? How women got here is confusing. Some rabbis say there was a woman named Lilith, whom God put here before Eve was taken from Adam's rib.

"If Lilith was a real woman who didn't come from Adam's rib, then she was put here first as a person who might have been equal to Adam. This was likely problematic for God, if it's true; because Lilith was probably a mouthy bitch whom Adam couldn't tolerate. You know, the kind; one of those women who drive you nuts. So, God had to get rid of her. Lilith was possibly the first feminist. God went back to the drawing board. He come up with a more pleasant, less bitchy woman that Adam could get along with.

"If the Lilith story is true, then the Eve story about her being taken from Adam's rib makes more sense. God wanted women to be somewhat like men. But also, be grateful to men for their existence. So, he had Eve come out of a man. Think about that for a minute. Adam wasn't pregnant. He was a man. But he had Eve. That is huge!

"If it weren't for the men to get women pregnant with children then there wouldn't be any more people on the planet. Adam would have died an old man with no kids. So, God must have wanted lots of people. That's why he made women; so, there'd be lots of people. Maybe we have one less rib than women do, I'm not sure. But if we are short a rib then that's because God wants us to marry women so we can get our missing rib back.

"I think God watches what people do. That amuses him. Most people are total fuckups. So, the more people there are, the more amusement there is. If God just wanted more people, why didn't he keep Lilith around? Now, that's a key question. The answer must be that God wants women to be obedient and subservient to men. God does not want bitchy women. That must be right, or else the Torah is wrong. And the Torah can't be wrong. My rabbi told me that. So, we must conclude that women are here to produce more men until we can figure out how to reproduce men without needing women. That makes logical sense.

"The planet is half full of women. That's a problem. We have to be careful or they'll take over. We must either ignore them or try to

understand this problem and work with it. If we ignore them, they get moody and upset about being ignored. Then they get bitchy and drive men nuts. So, when a woman says something to you, you must pretend you're listening to her. You must pretend that what she's saying is important, even though it probably isn't. Just grunt, nod your head, or say yes. If she hears some sounds coming from you, she'll think you are listening and she'll continue talking. Talking makes women happy.

"Listening to a woman is a tremendous waste of time, which, you'll remember, is the most important gift God gave you. But if you ignore a woman, she'll drive you nuts. Then you'll waste even more time. Some men try to escape from this conundrum, if only for a few hours, by watching football. Some watch professional football on Sunday, Monday, and Thursday nights; and college football all day Saturday. For the rest of the year, there's baseball, basketball. And some men also watch hockey and the Olympics. Smart men go on hunting and fishing trips, or they disappear into a garage. Smart men do everything they can possibly do to get away from women.

"Unfortunately, we're stuck with women. They're emotional and tough to shake off. But I understand what drives them. They never catch me off guard. They're sneaky, so it's important that you learn about them, from me. One woman can screw up your entire life; so pay close attention.

"I've made one profound observation about human women. They are unlike other females from other species. Other females, like sheep and goats; or deer and elk, don't wear makeup. Even female monkeys and apes don't wear makeup. And those animals are supposed to be like us. Monkeys and apes don't have trouble procreating. So, there must not be a reproductive need for human women to wear makeup. This leads to my conclusion: Human women wear makeup to impress other human women. They need to feel that they are better-looking than the other women they know. That's the only conceivable reason.

"*So, you always need to tell every woman you meet that she looks nice, no matter what; even if she looks like shit. If you're with one woman and other women are around, never tell the other women that they look nice. If you do, your woman will go nuts. She'll buy even more makeup. A better idea is to wait until you are alone with your woman. Then tell her that those other women looked like barf bags. That can get you a peaceful day or two. Those are bonus days.*

"*Women wear high-heeled shoes. They walk around like crippled animals; off balance, getting twisted and broken ankles. They fuck up their feet so badly they often need bunion surgery. Their behavior is unfathomable; yet, all of them do it, unless they're women running around barefoot in some undeveloped country. Tell your woman her shoes look nice. That makes her believe you understand why she wears them, even though you don't.*

"*Women also dress to show off their tits. They wear outfits guaranteed to make them catch colds because their chest is exposed from neck to navel. Flimsy cloth covers up the middle and outside half of their tits but not the inside half. It's the 'plunging neckline' or 'plunge your eyeballs down to my vagina' look. They're not sure whether they should cover their tits or not. So, they compromise. Tell your woman her dress looks nice, even if it makes you think she's nuts to wear something that's going to make her catch a cold.*

"*Act like you never see another woman's half tit look. Never comment about it. Even if your woman asks what you thought of another woman in her half-a-tit dress, you must tell her that you didn't notice the dress or the woman who was wearing it. When women nurse babies, they usually hide their tits. That's weird because that's when their tits are the biggest. When their tits are normal-sized, that's when they display them. But when their tits are filled up with baby food, they hide them. I will do more tit research. It's a mysterious area. It needs serious research. I'll apply to the National Science Foundation for a grant to study tits. I'll keep you updated.*

"When women wear a skirt or dress, they don't sit with their feet on the floor. They sit with their legs crossed so you can look way up their legs, almost all the way up to their pussies. They like showing off their body parts. This is an extremely complicated subject. I'll circle back to it.

"Women love to talk. You can tell that just by staying quiet. If you're in a restaurant, just listen for a while. Before you know it, some woman will laugh like a screaming hyena. Then everybody will talk louder and all the women in the restaurant will start shouting and making noises like a whole pack of hyenas ripping into a carcass. Women make it impossible to think in a restaurant. They yak about stuff that means absolutely nothing. Mostly they talk about being pissed off at other women or some guy who said or did something.

"They never talk about what the markets are doing or what kind of deal they can put together. They'll talk about babies and birthdays and funerals, like how nice somebody looked in their casket, if the guy was a Goy; or how nice the widow looked at Shiva, if she's a Jewess. After they put the stiff in the ground, they talk about the reception food. I never hear women at funerals talking about how they miss the dead guy. Only guys talk like that. I'm not sure I understand the significance of that observation.

"When women talk about how a baby barfs up its food or how quickly it poos after they put a fresh diaper on it, just pretend it's all very fascinating. If they talk about their fucking cats and how the damn things tear up their furniture, do not to let them know that they're nuts for having cats in the first place. Let them believe everything they say is fascinating.

"Listen, this is really, really, important. As a Firm executive, you need to understand that nothing escapes womens' attention. The female organization is a giant information gathering and dissemination machine. It's like a combination vacuum cleaner and leaf blower. Gossip goes in one end, gets spun around, sliced, and diced into nonsensical banalities; then at a cocktail party, or an important meeting, whacko balls filled with gossip and flying monkeys spew out of their mouths. They're good at this. They make it appear like they let something out of their mouths by mistake. That's how women disseminate information.

"Never tell any woman what you're thinking. If you make that mistake, they'll never forget it and they'll never let you forget it either. Everything you think about must be top secret around a woman. Never even hint at what you're thinking about. If you give them a hint about something, it drives them totally nuts and they will not rest until they also drive you nuts.

"You could say: 'I thought that so and so was thus and such.' And sure as hell, a year later, after the facts have all changed, the woman will zap you with her: 'But I thought you said!' zinger shot back at you. They'll hit you with their 'gotcha' zinger when you are off guard and helpless.

"Women are ambush predators. They're like airplanes circling overhead lining you up in their sights to drop bombs on you. They remember everything you say and do so they can zing you with it later. Have you ever watched old war films where planes bomb the crap out of everything? That's how women work on men. They use whatever knowledge they attain to flatten you. Always tell women they look nice. Never tell them anything more than that.

"They love hearing that they look nice. You can say 'yes' or 'no' to some things, like if they ask you if you had lunch or not; but be careful. Even the simplest thing can get you nailed. If you tell a woman that you had lunch, she'll start in on you:

'Who with? What did you talk about? Was his wife there? Why not? Why wasn't I there? How are their kids doing? What do you mean you didn't ask? What do you mean you don't give a damn about their kids? What kind of monster are you? You just go out and get your own dinner, you bastard!'

'Okay,' you say. 'Okay!' Then put on your coat to go out, by your-self, for a pizza. See what happens:

'What do you mean you're going out by yourself?' your woman screams. 'Don't you want to take me with you? Fuck you!' See, with women you're screwed no matter what you do.

"*Are you getting it? Can you see how the least little thing you say can be used to torture you for an entire month? Then they won't let up on you until you buy them something so they'll look better than some other woman. Now you know why men join the Marine Corps. It's not to save the country from the communists. It's to avoid listen-ing to women. Some guys would rather risk getting killed.*

"*It's best to lob women a marshmallow to chew on when they ask a question. If she asks:*

'Did she have a hat on?' or 'Did they drive their new car?'

"*You say: 'I didn't notice.'*

"*That way you don't have to hear her say:*

'Well, did you know she wore that same hat last week to play bridge? Didn't she look silly in it?'

"*Or:*

'When will we get a new car? What do you mean our car works fine? What do you mean you don't give a flying fuck that our car is an older model? I guess you're married to me because I'm old too, huh? You're a monster! Why won't you turn that fucking football game off and pay attention to me when I'm talking to you?'

"*See what I mean? Just tell them you don't know or you can't remember anything and you'll have a more peaceful life. Just try to think of yourself as part of the sofa and move as little as possible. Keep your head down. It's important.*

"*Never, ever have a drink with a woman. That's asking for trou-ble. If she's your wife, she'll get a little buzzed and she'll start grinding on you about everything that's wrong with you; your home; your life; her parents and her siblings; her pets; her preacher; her gynecologist;*

her psychiatrist, and all her other doctors. She'll complain that her flowers didn't bloom at the right time, and that the butcher didn't cut the meat right, and that so and so was a terrible bridge partner, and that the dress she just bought doesn't fit her right.

"She'll tell you it's all your fault that her kids got bad grades, and that one of them has mental problems because you told her a bedtime story where Bambi got shot or about how the baby and the cradle fell out of the treetop, or how the big bad wolf got after the three little pigs. She'll even complain that the grocery store had the wrong kind of toilet paper and it's your fault that the house ran out of it because you spend too much time in the bathroom; so, she got the cheaper kind that scratches her ass and makes her bitchy. Trust me. When you take your woman out for a drink, you'll get an earful.

"It's worse if you have a drink with a woman who is not your woman. Then, all hell breaks loose. One of her girlfriends sees you sitting at a bar having a drink with another woman. If she is crying while you're sitting there, then you were either being a monster to that poor woman or you sympathized with her and helped her get over a rough patch. Either way, you're in major trouble.

"If your woman's girlfriend reads the scene and determines that you were being a monster, then you are reviled for hurting one of the girls. You'll end up sleeping out in your car on the street. You won't even be allowed to bring the car into the garage. Your dinner will be thrown onto the lawn for you, without a plate. Doors will be slammed in your face and your kids will be told to never speak to you again. You can't explain yourself and make things right.

"The other woman was crying because her cat got run over by a car or it ate her canary or it scratched her favorite chair to shreds, or it did something stupid, like knocking her fine china off a shelf. Here's the point. Her crying had nothing to do with you. But it doesn't matter. Nothing matters. Your woman already determined that you're a monster. That's final. You are ordered to live in the doghouse. You

must stay in there, sleeping with the family dog, until your woman drags you out of the doghouse to fix something or pound in a nail so she can hang a stupid picture of her mother; or to bitch to you about how someone said something mean about her.

"Now, if you're having a drink with a woman and your woman's snoopy girlfriend sees that the woman was smiling or laughing, then you are totally fucked. The women will conclude, without proof, that you were running around on your woman behind her back. They will automatically assume that you were luring that other woman into bed with you. You are found guilty. Your woman decides you've been secretly meeting that other woman for years.

"Now you're a low-down dog and a monster. You are condemned to sleeping in your car and eating raw hot dogs off the grass again. Never mind that you laughed because that other woman told you she just got a phone call a few minutes before from her kid, who told her how he put a frog in his teacher's desk drawer and the frog jumped out and the teacher ran out of the classroom screaming. Never mind that the reason you were meeting the other woman was to plan a surprise birthday party for your wife. The reason the other woman laughed has nothing to do with anything.

"The truth never matters to women. And this brings me to the key to understanding women. Emotions are all that matter. They need reasons to be hysterical. Not just a reason once in a while; but a steady stream of reasons, so they can be hysterical all the time. Your woman will never believe you're telling her the truth, and even a week later, when your woman confirms from some other members of the female organization that you really were telling the truth, it still won't matter. All that matters is that you were seen with another woman in a bar. That's what your woman will remember for the rest of her life and she'll never forgive you for it.

"The only thing worse than drinking with another woman, is drinking alone. When your woman's girlfriend super spy sees that,

you've had it. The women will conclude that you were plotting something and not letting your wife in on it; or you were waiting for a mystery woman; or you got caught embezzling and you needed one last drink before the auditors checked your accounts and you committed suicide.

"Whatever your reason was for being there, it's the wrong reason. Now you're reduced to sleeping in your car and eating noodle soup off the grass without a plate. You beg your woman to let you trade places with the family dog, but that's out of the question. Why? Because, the dog did nothing wrong! The dog is now sleeps on your side of the bed. He's allowed to eat off the table. You get to eat off the grass along with the worms. Try explaining that you were waiting for a college buddy you hadn't seen for ten years. It won't matter. Your woman has got you where she wants you. She'll never believe you.

"So, when you want to have a drink, do what I do. Drink where women can't see you. Go to a liquor store, buy a bottle, and drink your whisky while you drive. If the cops nail you for drinking while driving, which has low odds, at least they will tell you what the punishment is, and when it ends. You'll even get to watch movies of traffic accidents with people's guts getting splattered everywhere. Look at your punishment as cheap entertainment. You might have to fork over a few hundred bucks in fines; but that beats having your woman grinding on you; driving you completely nuts, for months or years, for no reason whatsoever.

"Here's the thing. You know: the really big thing! Women get pissed easily; and then they forget why they are pissed. It's only when they get pissed about a new thing will they forget that they were pissed about an old thing in the first place.

"Those are your fundamental basics about women. They apply to all women. Always remember that women are trivial, vain, selfish, gossipy, thought-challenged, and steeped in jealousy of other women.

Parties and who talks about whom; and who entertained whom; and who wasn't invited to a social event, are the matters that deeply concern women. Those things are almost as important as knowing which males are presently dipping their wicks into which other woman's vagina; or trying to keep track of which men are coming and going in their own vagina. Those are the things that matter to women.

"It's never about how the stock markets are doing; or what the outlook for interest rates is; or how much oil your oil wells are producing or how much gold is coming out of your mines. They never concern themselves with the things that matter. And if the things that matter suddenly go off the rails, then it's your fault for not taking care of her. And then……"

"You get sent to the dog house, right?" Bob completed David's sentence.

"Exactly right! You're getting it! Now that we've covered women basics, let's get into some of the more complicated female subtleties:

"Let's say you're at a dinner party. You are seated across from another guy's wife. She goes to eat the olive from her martini, but it falls off her toothpick, hits her on the chest and rolls down into her bra. You are the only one who sees this. She knows you are the only one who sees this. Pay close attention when a woman plays 'The olive slipped off my toothpick,' game.

"What you do next depends on the behavior of the woman. If she gives you a big smile, that's your rescue mode signal. She wants you to stand up, throw your body across the table, hold her shoulder, keep her steady with one hand and with your other hand reach into her bra and pull that pesky olive out of there. You will have saved her from making a trip to the ladies' room. She might have been following a conversation at the table. That woman will be grateful. She will thank you for your help, later.

"If the woman looks away from you, off to the side, that means she wants help but she wants to pretend that she is too embarrassed

to ask. She expects you to get up, walk around the table behind her, quickly reach down into her bra, grab the olive off her tit and eat it yourself. She'll be very appreciative for your assistance. She, too, will thank you later.

"Another time. You find yourself across from a winsome, full breasted, gorgeous woman. Her boyfriend is next to her. He has no brains. He's ignoring her. She looks you in the eye and intentionally drops her olive down her bra while smiling at you. That's your invitation to fuck her, right then and there. She's hot to get your dick inside her. She doesn't want to wait until later. She wants it now. You must think fast in this situation. You must come up with an excuse, no matter how feeble, to get her out of there. You need to get her into a hotel room, or even the restaurant's ladies' room and you need to fuck her brains out as quickly as possible!

"Move fast. Make an announcement. Rise and state that you have something special to bring to the table. You need her, specifically her, help to go with you to get it. Then you leave; take her to a liquor store; grab a bottle; go to a room; drink half the bottle with her and fuck her. Then, take the remaining half bottle back to the table. Explain that you had a whole case of this stuff, but somebody stole it. The two of you looked for it, kind of like you went on a snipe hunt. But all you found was this half-bottle.

"I've put some deep thought into each of those women's behaviors. There's only one conclusion: When a woman indicates distress at a cocktail party, she's telling you she needs to get laid. All women love to get laid. They're like chickens with a rooster; but they have different ways of sending their 'I need to get laid' signals. Women send signals in mystery codes. When you get their secret signal, move fast, before another guy gets it. That's your big advantage. Most men don't understand women, like I do. Keep paying close attention. It's important.

"Women sometimes want you to punch out their boyfriend or their husband. Say you're at a picnic. Her husband is grilling hot

dogs. He hands her one with relish and mustard and onions on it. She shakes her head. He persists and shoves it at her and yells at her; tells her that's what she said she wanted.

"Here's the key: Women change their minds on a dime. And it's always a guy's fault for not understanding that the woman changed her mind. This guy gets pissed, which is a huge mistake. But he is stuck with this hotdog that the woman doesn't want. She holds up her hands, like a traffic cop telling a car to stop. Then she waves him off with crossed arms, like she's a landing signal officer waving off a bad approach to an aircraft carrier flight deck.

"That's your clue. The husband has crashed and burned. She's more pissed off about that hot dog than he is. She needs to be rescued. You must run up to him. Give him a man-to-man chest bump or a double-hands-on-chest shove backwards that knocks him on his ass. Now you've become her hero. You got that inconsiderate bully off her. This move works best after you've had a few beers. If he comes back at you, you must knock the crap out of him. If he knocks the crap out of you, the beers help. You'll be too buzzed to feel pain.

"This seems like a big to-do over whether a hot dog has relish on it; but to a woman, your manly behavior means everything. No matter how old, ugly, or stupid she is, there you were: Her knight in shining armor, who rushed to her aid and saved her from eating a hot dog with relish that she didn't want. Remember that.

"It was never about the hot dog. It was about getting a man to understand her. That was an impossible task for her poor bastard husband, because nobody understands women in the first place. If you time your move right and nail him before any other guy does, all the women will think you are their champion. They'll believe you understand them, even though you don't. They won't give you any grief about anything for a few weeks because they'll believe you helped them. And they will all give you secret invitations to meet them somewhere. They will all want to fuck your brains out.

"They'll never remember why you did what you did. They'll just remember that you were the man who did it. Your own woman will probably ask you why you did that. Tell her, in a manly way: 'It was the right thing to do.' Your woman will think you're her protector. That's a plus.

"When a woman figures out that she can use her vagina to drive men crazy, you can have a dangerous situation. Take Helen of Troy, for example. The Trojans and the Argive Greeks fought for ten or twenty years over who got to have her vagina. Think about that. I estimate that a hundred thousand men died fighting over that one woman's vagina. The female vagina is man's greatest motivator; even more than gold, which men will kill for, so they can give gold to their women, so they can get into their pussies.

"Nothing ever changes when it comes to women's vaginas. Even today, you have countless examples of wealthy men who worked years to build their fortunes. They are established, married with children. What happens next? They catch a whiff of a new vagina and bang! They'll give away half their wealth to their old vagina to get a few years with another woman's new vagina; even if the new vagina has been used by lots of other guys. It doesn't matter. Pussies aren't like cars, where you can look at the odometer and see how many miles are on it. Even a vagina that has been fucked thousands of times is a fresh, new vagina to the guy who's been with his old vagina.

"That should tell you all you need to know about women. It you are not careful a vagina can own you; turn you inside out; and drive you into insane decision making. In modern times there was this long Afghanistan war going for fifty years with the Russians and then the Americans. All this fighting went on and lots of guys died because some guys wanted the Afghan women to have freedom for their pussies. But the other guys wanted those women to keep their pussies covered up. I'm convinced all that fighting over there was about deciding the policy for pussies.

"*You need to be extremely cautious around a woman's vagina. Be careful not to get too close to one because it could be carrying a secret weapon. I learned all about this when I was just a young boy. I was hiding in a top-secret location. I saw a man get his face too close to a vagina. Suddenly, without warning, the vagina attacked him. He ran away from it, holding his mouth. I think the vagina either bit his lips or his tongue, or else it shot poisoned darts into his mouth, I'm still not sure what that vagina did, but it hurt that man bad. I think it almost killed him.*

"*I'm not sure which pussies conceal secret weapons in them and which ones are just regular pussies. Maybe they all carry secret weapons? I'm not sure. It's one of life's great mysteries. And you can be sure that no woman will ever explain it to you. Women are very secretive that way. I've been doing some research trying to figure out which pussies are safe and which ones are dangerous. But so far, I haven't come up with anything. When I do, I'll let you know.*

"*I want you to be especially careful about the women in the office. They can mix up your head by getting you thinking about their pussies. They can cause you to make bad business decisions. You always must be on guard for the woman who's willing to use her vagina as a weapon. Remember that. And remember this, too: A vagina is mysterious. It has magical powers that can drive you crazy. Someone should write a book about pussies to take the mystery out of them. But until there is a definitive book written about them, you need to be cautious. Women know how to use them in ways I don't understand.*

"*Now listen: There's one special breed of woman. You need to be extra careful with them. These women are completely nuts. You can't do business with them. They call themselves feminists. They see the world inside out and backwards. Instead of being soft, warm loving creatures that want to have babies, please a husband, and have a good home, these women live for one purpose only. That's to make men miserable. They fight and bitch about everything. Basically, they are on a mission to eradicate men from the earth. They are all mentally ill, man haters. They hold top secret meetings in top secret places to discuss ways to conquer men.*

"Their leader instructs them to do everything possible to repel men; and keep men out of their lives. They never wash, to make sure their pussies smell absolutely wretched. You can't do business with these women. If you listen to them long enough, they'll let it slip out about how they hate men for having penises. Some of these women try to conceal their true nature. So, you have to smell them around their female area and at the same time be inconspicuous about sniffing them. Be secretive about your sniffing. Be sneaky about sniffing, like Joe Biden. Remember, if you detect that fishy, rotten cheese smell, you're probably dealing with a feminist. Be extra careful.

"One day in your investment career, you will certainly run across this situation. You will make a call to talk to one of your clients. The client could be a man's wife or it could be the husband. It doesn't matter. The wife will answer the phone. You'll ask how things are doing; you know, the usual small talk. Then, suddenly, the woman will start crying. Crying is what women do best. She'll confide in you that her husband has stage four cancers in some organ; like his prostate; stomach; colon; liver; or all his organs. She'll sob.

"That's your great opportunity. You can do terrific business. Most guys will tell her how sorry they are to hear the terrible news. They'll tell her if she needs anything to call them; and they'll do whatever they can to help her. But those are the completely wrong things to say. If you're smart, you'll take my advice on this.

"See, the real reasons the woman is crying are that the guy will die and won't be bringing home a paycheck; and secondly, she won't be getting schlonged by her steady meat organ. See, women don't love men. They only love security and sex. And, they don't care how they get either. They're like ungulates. They need a guy to hose them;

but then they don't want him hanging around. They'd rather play bridge with the girls or go to their garden parties or have lunch with their girl-friends. Except for their required occasional schlongings, and money coming in, women don't want men hanging around. So, here's what your response should be:

'Wow! That's terrific news, Molly. Soon that piece of dead wood will be dead for real! After we get him buried, I want to take you to your favorite hotel; have martinis with you to celebrate; then I want to fuck your brains out. You're gorgeous and hot! I can't wait to get my face and cock into your panties. We'll go on our celebration trip to Paris! We'll party until we drop! What do you say? Have we got a deal?'

"That response will put you into a whole different category from her other friends. She'll look forward to getting schlonged. She'll hope to capture you into marriage; and you'll replace her lost income. See? She'll think you've solved her real-world problems, instantly.

"Get with her right after he dies. Don't even wait until his body cools off. Bang her immediately. Tell her you must have her; you can't wait for the formalities of a funeral service. Get his insurance proceeds invested with the Firm, right away.

"After that, come up with excuses to stop seeing her. Tell her schlonging a client is against some ridiculous rule. Schlonging is okay, if assets go up; but if they go down, she'll get bitchy and sue you for duress. Women fake mental stuff in front of arbitration panels. That's dangerous, because arbitration panels are even crazier than women. Anyway, after you bang her a few times and get her money, drop her. This is valuable advice about female psychology. Don't forget it. Can you be a good company man and help women in distress?"

"I don't know about that one, David. It sounds a little sordid."

David didn't like the sound of Bob's response. It smacked of impudence. He verbally retaliated:

"Well, life is sordid. Life is a gauntlet run. That's not it though; is it? It's Barbara, that skinny Indian bitch, isn't it? I've seen you stealing looks at her and I've seen her eyes light up when she sees you. Is something going on with you two?"

"No, David. Your imagination is working overtime. You're just suspicious when you have no reason to be." deflected Bob. But, to David's trained ear, Bob sounded unconvincing.

"Well," continued David, *"remember you can't trust women. Give them the servicing they need; but don't try to understand them. Think of them as dogs. They'll cling to you for their humping. But you can't understand them. So, don't try. They're unpredictable, like an alien species. If you try to make sense of them, you'll drive yourself nuts. Know how their minds work.*

"They use ploys and tricks to make you fall into their lives; into their dreamy makeup-smeared eyes and lips and faces. They want you to imagine that you are landing in their soft, loving arms; holding their soft warm tits against you while they moan and whisper sweet words to you about what a wonderful man you are. But don't fall for it. They just want to make your cock hard. When they get you hard, you stop thinking logically. Think of their romantic ways of thinking for what they really are."

"Like what?"

"Like fucking cesspools full of shit; like a huge fucking pile of horseshit that gets you trapped in it until you can't get out of it. Horseshit! That's how I think about women and their games. It keeps me from getting my head mixed up." David sneered, as if he was repulsed by smelling what he was talking about.

"Okay David. Got it." Bob stared into David's eyes, recognizing that his mentor was more than a simple misogynist. He was borderline insane.

"Now remember this," David lifted his index finger and pointed it skyward, emphasizing his point. *"It's important. It's not a joke.*

You must always have an escape plan in your mind, whenever you are with a woman. You must be able to get away from them whenever they start acting emotional. Be prepared to lose them in the crowd when you take them to a football game; or to leave dinner early because you have too much work to do; or to leave to meet the guys at the gym; or to leave because you need to check out something in the library. Better yet, take her to the library with you. And while you're there with her, tell her to get lost. Women can't scream at you in a library. See? Never stop thinking about how you can get away from them. You must be prepared to be cold hearted and adversarial about women. When you are dealing with women, remember: You are in a constant state of war."

"Well, Bob, that concludes your formal executive training. The rest will be on-the-job learning. If you have any questions about any-thing; ask me." David smiled as he raised his hand in a flourished finale. *"I'll give you my complete answer. And don't allow women to interfere with sales."*

"*Thanks.*" said Bob, while thinking:

'*I need to take my brain for a shower. I'm relieved that these sessions are over.*'

"Don't mention it. How else would you ever learn anything? How else would you ever become a top executive?"

As Bob drove away from David's barnyard to the office, his thoughts again turned to Marty:

'*Marty, my love, whatever happened to you?*' Bob's thoughts were never far from her. He punched his car's dash out of frustration:

'*My sensibilities were assaulted, nonstop, for days on end. I thought about you while David dumped his warped worldviews on me. I'll forget everything he said.*' Nothing eased his heartache. At unexpected times, he still imagined hearing Marty's laughter; that teasing, mirthful laugh which loved life and gave it everything she had.

In the evenings, he imagined Marty in bed with him, her breath against his chest. In the mornings, he expected to see her emerge from his shower. He heard her voice when he was alone. It came from his memory; but he heard it, nonetheless. It talked and laughed with him, as if she were present. Life for Bob continued, much as if she had never left. He imagined that she had not left. His pretense about her presence and her closeness was something he could not reveal to anyone. She seemed really there; so much more than his imagination. He knew other people would never understand a love like this. He suffered something more painful than remorse; more hurtful than an ended love affair. Marty had become part of him. And now she'd been torn away.

He reconstructed their last days and moments together. Where she was going? What were her plans? She left him no clue. One moment she was there, with him; filled with joy and love. Then, she was gone! Might he never see her again? He wanted her back; as the same Marty she was when he last saw her. What happened?

His speculations touched madness; then anger. He did his best to conceal his emotions. He often thought he was losing his mind. He yearned to punch his adversary and break its nose; end his quandary. But who was this adversary? He knew no definable foe. Instead, in frustration, he punched pillows.

He wrestled with his thoughts and struggled to summon her apparition; to see her just one more time:

'I ache for her warmth next to me; for just one kiss' He willed her to come back, but his forces of thoughts were met by silence:

'I don't care if she has the reputation of a notorious whore. I love her; all of her; everything about her. I love her as she is.' Passions for Marty coursed through his blood. He wore his heart on his sleeve:

'How could you do this to me? What have I done, or not done, to make you leave me? What happened to you, my darling fiancée?

Are you really a nun in some remote convent? How can I find you? Why no word? Why secrecy? Couldn't I have a clue? Why can't we be together again?'

He sensed that David understood his feelings, in a man-to-man sort of way. He resented the encroachment upon his feelings, but he believed David was trying to help. His management lessons were offensive distractions; but they had not changed him. He continued obsessing over Marty.

After Bob left David's for the office that day, David sat pensively on a grassy rise at the edge of the barnyard. All was quiet. The sun approached midday. Animals and birds were resting. Dolly, his favorite sheep, ambled over to David and lay down beside him. David reclined on the ground and rested his head upon her back. As he looked up at the clouds and scratched the animal's head, he spoke to her:

"It's time to think ahead, Dolly. We can't let Bob control our game, can we? Do you have any bright ideas?"

Dolly, of course, said nothing. The sheep didn't even make her '*Bah*' sound. That's one of the things David liked about Dolly. No back talk. No contradictions. No mistaken communications, ever.

"This could take any of several paths, Dolly," David continued. *"With the deal we've made, it's unlikely that Bob will up and quit. He's not the sort. He sticks to his goals. That's going to be a long-term problem, sweetheart. Probably I gave away more than I should have. I could kick myself for being impulsive. So here we are, lying together in the barnyard.*

"There's always a move, Dolly. You know that. You know I've been thinking about this. I won't let you down. Don't worry. I'm true to my roots. We have the advantage because we're the clever ones. Marty was intelligent in the emotional ways of men; but she wasn't clever. Bob is intelligent in finance and business, and he works hard. He's good, but he's also not clever. The skinny Indian bitch is the one

that concerns me, Dolly. She's intelligent. And I believe she is also clever. Clever people are dangerous, Dolly.

"I'm not sure what we should do about Barbara. If I fire her, Susan will make my life hell. If I don't fire her, my gut tells me she'll cause problems. I suspect she knows more than she lets on. But I'm not sure. That's what's so vexing. She's elusive, like a shadow. But every time I try to see her shadow, she's gone. Sometimes I suspect she's a step ahead of me. I think we'll wait until she makes a mistake. Meanwhile, we'll divide and conquer them. Bob is our immediate problem. We'll focus on him. We'll get rid of him first. We'll get rid of Barbara last.

"There's a way all of this can fall into place, Dolly. Everything is set. I could make our move at any time, so I guess I should put my plan in motion.

"Who was the girl Marty whored around with? She said the two of them made a pornographic movie and went to orgies? Rita, wasn't it? Yeah, I remember. Her name was Rita. Do you remember a different name?"

Dolly lay there chewing a bit of grass.

"I need to figure out who this Rita is and give her a call. Tomorrow the Mrs. goes away on a trip to France for three whole weeks. Tomorrow night you can stay with me in the bedroom. Would you like that, sweetheart?"

Dolly lay there chewing her grass.

A few days later David stepped into Bob's office. He cleared his throat to emphasize the importance of his communication:

"A strange call came in late yesterday. Some woman said she was a friend of Marty's; said she knew Marty before she came to work at the firm. Somehow, she had your name. Maybe Marty mentioned you to her, I don't know. But anyway, the woman's name is Rita and she said she'd like to meet you and talk with you. Here's her phone number."

"Who took the call?"

"Nobody. Apparently, she called after we closed and figured out how to get into our voice mail. She left the message on my machine. I wrote her number down but I erased her message."

"Thanks, I'll call her."

More to come.

PREVIEWS FROM
LOVE AND MADNESS©

"I never said I didn't want you, Big Stupid Horse, Horse's Ass! I said you needed to wait." Barb shouted. She was hurt . . . . Chapter One.

"You can trust me. I swear by all the buffalo on the plains and all the elk in the forests."
"Well, now you're talking really big powerful stuff, Strong Horse . . . . Chapter One.

"How long was it after Marty disappeared when David gave you Rita's phone number?"
"About two weeks, why?"
"I'm thinking Horse." Silence. Chapter One.

"David, honey babes, why are we signing all these papers?" she asked like a gullible dupe.
"For tax reasons," David replied curtly . . . . Chapter Two.

"She goes by every morning at ten. I'm sure you noticed. But look very closely at her breasts."
"Okay, I'm looking. What is there to see? She has breasts. We all have breasts."
"Fix in your mind how they look." instructed Mrs. Rodriguez . . . . Chapter Three.

The fifth file was an unexpected eye-popper. It was a certified copy of Marvin's last will and testament. Here was proof that Marvin's bequest to David was conditional upon David leaving the companies to Israel upon his death.. . . . . *Chapter Four.*

"If you want to hear elevator music while you wait, press one. If you want to hear the sounds of a moose in rut, press two. If you want to hear a cougar killing a deer, press three. For shotguns blasting geese out of the sky, press four. For coyotes tearing a rabbit apart, press five. For wolves howling at the moon, press six, for the sounds of two Grizzly bears mating, press seven. If you think you have reached this recording in error, please press the pound key." . . . . . *Chapter Five.*

"But what if I had struggled and fought you off, like a drowning man does?" David disagreed.

"Not to worry," assured Bob, *"I'd have simply knocked you out, put an arm under your neck, and paddled you back."*

"You would have actually punched me?" David was aghast.

"You bet," Bob nodded in earnest. . . . . *Chapter Six.*

"Did you know that Marty had other lovers, even when she was with you?"

"Yeah, I knew that. So?"

"And that didn't bother you? That didn't make you think she was dirty?"

"No, David. That didn't bother me. There was nothing dirty about Marty, David. She was a beautiful, sensitive woman."

"But she even made porn films. How could you stomach that?"
. . . . *Chapter Seven.*

There followed a long silent moment while David just stood staring at Bob. Then he slammed the car door with such fury that the glass in the passenger window cracked. He turned his back on Bob and walked away without saying a word . . . . *Chapter Eight.*

"Big Horse, is the writing in your safe deposit box or David's?" Her voice was anxious now. She sensed she was getting closer to the truth.

"David's." replied Bob . . . .*Chapter Nine.*

"I need to murder you. Stop fighting me. I must do this. Please, do not try to prevent me from what I must do." Her voice was haunting; pleading . . . .*Chapter Nine.*

"Andy, it's time you and I had some serious discussions about your future," David began, taking another swig of whisky while addressing the fetus in the formaldehyde jar. . . . .*Chapter Ten.*

"I just don't understand her. I felt her tits one day not too long ago. I gave them some nice squeezes. I thought I'd sort of try her out to see if she might want to become a company whore. I thought she'd like getting her tits squeezed, but she gave me this mean look. It felt like she was telling me she was going to kill me . . . .*Chapter Ten.*

'*Even if he were convicted and imprisoned, retribution justice for Marty likely would never be served. There is a better way; the Lakota Sioux way* . . . . *Chapter Eleven.*

Well, dear listeners, now we know there's no love stronger than butterfly love. Think about Tang for a moment. Any lover who flies day and night over two thousand miles of Open Ocean to be with his woman is the real deal; a keeper! And Poon! A woman who trails her scent over oceans and two continents understands how to be alluring for her man. She deserves the best!

David is not tethered to reality. When a black sheep sleeps with you and becomes your closest confidant, well, what can you say? A man in that condition needs help and meds. But David is the man in charge. He's the guy flying the plane, so to speak. A company and its employees depend upon his wise guidance. Can he pull that off and commit murders too? This is David we're talking about.

There's a fine line between genius and crazy. When someone is devious enough to disguise an entire company to make the world, its regulators, shareholders, and directors all believe he's a genius, perhaps he is! Anyway, who's to say who is sane and who isn't?

How is David pulling off his grand deception? Why keep a Blather-Flameer, animal heads, a secret room, mysterious Rublina, an impossible voice mail system, a client servicing desk manned by Old Gravel Throat? Why cultivate a menagerie of unemployable employees to support an elaborate ruse?

What will Bob learn from Rita, Marty's partner in whoredom? What has devious David set into motion? Is this crazy genius at its best? Let's meet these bizarro creatures. Let's see them do what they do, up close.

Our next installment is a serendipity exhale from the macabre of MURDER PROPERLY DONE. Come flutter along with me, Minna Morinette, your audio book narrator. We'll have a fun riot as I voice LOVE AND MADNESS, the thirteenth book of THE SECRET BUTTERFLY (tm) SERIES.